Love Me As I Am

SYNITHIA WILLIAMS

DEDICATION

To my readers. Thank you for all your support.

CHAPTER 1

Woman of the Year.

Renee Caldwell glanced at the stark white nomination letter sticking out of her handbag in the passenger seat. Just like a know-it-all back seat driver, the letter annoyed her. She wanted to win. Had worked her tail off at Caldwell Development to be one of the most respected businesswomen in the state of South Carolina.

Still, the nomination felt…mocking. The Woman of the Year should be a woman who had it all. Renee had confidence, wealth, and respect. She did not have it all.

She eased her cocoa-bronze Cadillac ATS coupe around the circular fountain of the Westin Poinsett in Greenville, SC, and stopped before the valet attendant. As he came around to open her door, she shoved the envelope deeper inside her handbag before slipping her arm through the black leather straps.

What appeared on the surface to be an award was actually cleverly disguised pressure for perfection. If she had the option, she'd tear the letter into little pieces and toss it in the trash. That choice was not available.

She opened the door and nodded to the attendant. She glanced at his nametag, then met his eye. "Thank you, Gary."

He gave her a welcoming smile and she slipped the keys into his hand. Another hotel attendant had already pulled the overnight bag from her popped trunk.

The cool fall air and soothing sounds of the fountain outside the hotel did nothing to relax the knots in her shoulders, ease the dull ache in her legs from walking all day in new heels, or relieve the tension in her lower back after driving from Columbia to Greenville at the end of a long workday. Her mother said she worked too hard and would end up with unnecessary wrinkles. As if working less was acceptable for a member of the Caldwell family.

Pain shot through her toes as she crossed the cobbled drive to the hotel's front door. Despite the muscle-seizing cramps of her feet, her practiced stride did not waiver. Beauty was pain, and a woman never showed the discomforts of beauty. Still, this was the absolute last time she

1

would buy shoes a half-size too small. No matter how fabulous they were, or whether they were the last ones in the store.

The roar of a motorcycle pulled her attention away from her pinched feet and aching calves. She slowed and glanced back at the driver who pulled up behind her car. The rider revved the motor of the black and chrome bike then popped out the kickstand and cut the engine.

She wasn't into bikers. Never had been. Silly fantasies about jumping on the back of some bad boy's bike and riding into the sunset were a waste of time. Still, curiosity kept her gaze on the man.

She may not have been into bad boys, but she could appreciate a nice looking one. He pulled off his helmet and ran long fingers through thick, dark hair in need of a haircut. Renee stopped completely. He was gorgeous. His curly dark hair and sun-kissed skin made her think of a sun soaked beach. A straight nose and a dimple in the middle of a strong jaw, dusted with a five o'clock shadow, framed sinfully delicious lips.

When another valet attendant strolled over, the guy shook his head. "I'm just here to drop something off for someone. I don't need valet."

The warmth of his smooth, Southern drawl spread through her. Her stomach clenched. For a second, she allowed the indulgence of imagining what it would be like to not have a Woman of the Year nomination letter in her handbag. To climb onto the back of that bike, wrap her arms around his slim waist, and ride off for a night of fun and passion.

Not any kind of passion, but the hot, sweaty passion she saw in movies. Passion that made her forget about ruining her hair or getting her designer clothes wrinkled. The kind that would make her forget everything but the feel of his hard body pressed on top of hers, driving hard and deep all night long.

He caught her staring. Her body froze. Her mind froze. Light eyes, lined with the darkest lashes she'd ever seen, zeroed in on her. Heat shot across her cheeks. Her heart stuttered. The corner of his mouth tilted up in a *this-bad-boy-is-all-kinds-of-fun* smile.

The urge to smile back ran deep. Renee pushed the idea aside. Not for her. Biker boys, even those with sexy Southern drawls and muscular thighs in worn jeans, were not for her. She had a plan for her life. An image to uphold.

She raised her chin and gave the guy the icy look that normally made other men look away. He held her gaze. The spark of challenge flashed in his eyes.

She spun toward the hotel and hurried to the door, all too mindful that he watched. She could feel his gaze in the center of her back. Five steps in and the heel of her shoe caught on one of the cobbles and snapped.

Renee stumbled. *Frick! Not my new shoes!*

Her friend Mikayla would laugh at her for not cursing. Cursing was

2

vulgar. Renee avoided doing so, even in her thoughts.

"Are you okay, ma'am?" The attendant carrying her bag asked.

She cringed. *Ma'am.* A horrible word. A reminder that two months ago she'd turned thirty and was, as her mother reminded her, still single.

"I'm fine. Thank you," she said with an easy smile. "My shoe broke." She pulled off the shoes, preferring to walk barefoot into the hotel instead of hobbling.

Don't look over your shoulder. The order was a drumbeat in her head. She couldn't help herself and slowly looked back for a quick peek. Biker guy's full lips were spread in a knowing smile. Her stomach tightened and heat spread through her midsection. Embarrassed that she'd been caught gawking, again, she turned away and strode purposefully inside.

She was only there for one night, so the process was quick. She sent the attendant ahead to take her bag to the room while she searched in her purse for the pair of folding flats she always carried for end-of-day, high-heel pain. She refused to walk barefoot all the way to her room.

Her cell phone vibrated just as she got her hands on the flats. She pulled the phone out and the word "Mom" flashed on the screen. Renee took a deep breath. She didn't want to hear the latest round of how-to-ensure-Renee-won-Woman-of-the-Year plans, so she pressed the ignore button.

Biker guy walked in and distracted her from the guilt of sending her mother to voice mail. He strode confidently across the spacious marble lobby. Off the bike, he was taller than she'd guessed. Well over six feet of muscle draped in butt-enhancing denim and shoulder-hugging leather. Her long-held belief that too much bulk on a man was off-putting wobbled at the sight of his broad shoulders, powerful arms, and strong, slightly bowed legs. The guy had to have muscles on top of muscles to be so big. He probably sweated pure testosterone.

Her phone vibrated again. For Victoria Caldwell to call right back, it must be important.

Renee answered.

"Renee, I left a message." Her mom's cultured voice came through the phone.

"You know I never listen to messages. I made it safely and just checked into the hotel. Please tell Dad and Ryan I'll call them as soon as my meeting with Joanne Wright-Miller is over. I don't think it'll take much to convince her we'll preserve as much of the land as possible during the development."

When Joanne informed Renee that the family was ready to finally let go of their property, Renee had agreed to the deal instantly. The hundred acres near the heart of Greenville would be the perfect location for a new subdivision. A subdivision Renee wanted to ensure Caldwell Development orchestrated. Joanne wanted to maintain some of the development rights. They'd finalized those details and Renee was here to deliver the signed contract and discuss the next steps.

"That's nice, dear. Though it isn't why I called. I don't know why your dad sent you to meet with her. You're going to miss the LeFranc's dinner party. Weren't you and Daniel getting close earlier this year?"

Renee crossed to one of the unoccupied plush beige sofas to put on the flats before going to her room. "I'm here because she doesn't respond well to pushy. Anyone else, including Ryan, would make any development plans stall." Her twin brother was the polar opposite of patient. "I make the most sense. And as far as Daniel LeFranc, nothing is going to happen there."

You're too cold, Renee. A man wants a passionate woman, not an ice tray. Daniel's voice rang through her head. No way would Renee let her mother know why she and Daniel hadn't worked out.

"I don't see why not," Victoria said. "He's primed for a national run next year. I wouldn't be surprised if that man becomes president one day."

One of the reasons Renee had considered Daniel a suitable boyfriend. Her parents expected her to pick boyfriends that were suitable and benefited Caldwell Development. Daniel was well connected, rich in land that Caldwell Development could build on, handsome, and upwardly mobile. She'd thought they'd make a perfect power couple. He'd wanted to sleep with her and make a profit selling land to Caldwell Development. Daniel had gotten what he wanted. She'd been told she was an ice tray in bed.

Score zero for her ego.

"We're not compatible." Renee slipped on the flats.

"Renee, you really are too picky."

"When I was less picky you accused me of lowering my standards."

Victoria's sigh held no regrets, just exasperation. "If I'd thought you would have really been happy with that customer service guy, then I would have approved. But I knew he wasn't good enough. He knew that, too. That's why he broke things off. Now Daniel, on the other hand, would not be so easily intimidated."

Hard not to be intimidated when everyone Renee knew kept telling her she deserved better, but Renee was done making that point. She'd done so numerous times with no change in her mother's opinion.

"Just take my word on this. Daniel and I are better as friends."

"How so?"

"We don't suit."

"That's nonsense. Give me a *good* reason why."

Renee pressed a hand to her temple. "Mom, will you just let it go? Daniel and I are not happening. Don't bring it up tonight, okay."

"But—"

"I'll call you tomorrow. I love you, good-bye."

She ended the call, then prayed her mom kept her nose out of her brief and embarrassing history with Daniel. Avoiding Daniel and the LeFranc family dinner party was the reason she'd readily agreed to rush off to Greenville today and insisted on spending the night when she could have easily driven up the next day.

She turned as the biker settled on the other end of her couch. He got comfortable, stretching one arm across the back. He bent one of his legs onto the seat and faced her. He wore a blue and white plaid shirt beneath the jacket. Weird for a biker. Weren't they supposed to live in black?

Then his eyes distracted her. Far away, they were nice; up close, they were beautiful. They were blue, not a deep sapphire but lighter with hints of gray. She could imagine the number of women he'd seduced with those eyes alone. He smelled good, too. Like leather, obviously, but there was something else. A masculine cologne or aftershave that made her want to curl up next to him and snuggle in his arms.

You're staring, Renee. Biker guys are not for you.

She raised her chin and glared. Didn't he know the unwritten rule that when a stranger occupied a seat, you didn't sit beside them without asking permission? She opened her mouth to ask if she could help him when he gave her a smile so tempting and delicious the words to Marvin Gaye's famous song "Let's Get It On" slid through her mind. Flutters filled her chest and she stuttered for words.

Son-of-a-beast this guy is sexy! Renee took a deep breath and channeled her thoughts. Sexy or not, a Caldwell didn't stutter.

She tilted her head to one side. "May I help you?"

His sexy grin didn't falter at her frosty words. Nor did the lyrics stop playing in her mind.

"For what it's worth," he said in a smoky bourbon accent that spread fire through her better than the Grand Marnier her father kept in his office. "My mom tries to hook me up with unsuitable people all the time."

The flirtation in his eyes brought back the fantasy of jumping on the back of his bike. She could almost feel the trembling of the engine between her thighs, or maybe she was trembling for other silly reasons.

"Eavesdropping."

"Sorry." He shrugged, but didn't look a bit remorseful. "You weren't exactly whispering."

"Not whispering isn't the same thing as inviting you to comment on my conversation." She reached down, picked up her shoes, and scooted forward on the couch. "Good-bye."

His hand brushed her arm as she rose to stand. A jolt of electricity shot across her skin. Something she hadn't felt in years. His hand was warm, rough. A working man's hands. The men she dealt with had smooth, manicured hands. She liked the roughness of Biker Guy's.

Her gaze rose to his. He watched her with desire, yes, but he didn't gawk or make her think he was imagining her naked. He steadfastly maintained eye contact. The focused attention made her struggle for words, where leering would have had her jumping from the couch and marching to her room.

He dropped his hand, but the spark remained in his eye. "Can I buy you a drink?"

"I don't drink."

"How about I buy you a meal?"

She narrowed her eyes and crossed her arms. He didn't follow the movement and lower his gaze to her cleavage. Impressive, but not surprising. Her breasts weren't much to drool over. Not for the first time, she wished her breasts were bigger. A man his size must love big breasts. She gave herself a mental shake. This guy's breast preference didn't matter.

"Look, sir, I realize you overheard a rather awkward conversation, but I'm not looking for company. I'm not going to fall in bed with you."

He crossed his arms and mirrored her. "Good thing I'm not trying to sleep with you."

"Oh, really? Then what are you trying to do?"

"I saw a beautiful woman checking me out. Don't bother denying it," he said before she could open her mouth to argue. "And I thought I'd take a chance and see if she'd have dinner with me."

She'd been called beautiful most of her life. She spent enough money on clothes, makeup and personal training to keep looking good. She knew men found her attractive, but after working so hard to live up to being the beautiful, perfect daughter of Philip and Victoria Caldwell, the compliment had lost its luster. Yet, something about the way the word rolled off his tongue in that damned sexy drawl made her want to flip the bangs of her short cropped hair and giggle like a school girl.

"I was not checking you out. Your bike was loud. It caught my attention."

His smile said he thought she was lying, and he rubbed his hand across his chin. "Is that a no?"

It really should be. "I don't know you."

"We can get to know each other over dinner."

"You could be a serial killer."

"I promise I'm not."

"What serial killer would admit it?"

His head tilted forward as if to acknowledge her point. "Follow me." He stood and strolled away. Renee blinked to make sure she wasn't hallucinating. He stopped at the sign in desk and motioned her over. With a raised brow, Renee followed him across the room.

"This woman is going to dinner with me. Please take a good look at her, and me, and if she turns up missing you can identify the person she was with."

The hotel clerk looked between the two with a raised eyebrow. Renee shook her head and smiled. Okay, he was slightly amusing.

"My shoes are broken." She held up the shoes in her hand.

He chuckled then pointed to her feet. "Forget the shoes. You've already changed into something else."

"I haven't even been to my room yet. I'll go upstairs to change and put away my shoes." She turned to leave, but he stopped her with another light touch on her arm. Attraction sizzled across her skin. She sucked in a breath and tried to hide her reaction by smoothing the back of her pixie cut.

He didn't appear phased by the touch. "If you go upstairs, you'll talk yourself out of it."

"You don't know that." Though that was exactly what she would have done. Two minutes away from him and she would second guess her decision, remember that she was crazy to go out with a strange man, and spend the night forcing all thoughts of him from her head.

"I won't take you far. A place right around the corner. The wings are hot, the jazz seductive, and I promise I'll dance with you all night. Come on, have dinner with me."

His sexy eyes, killer smile, and seductive drawl combined to bring to mind heat-filled stares and whispered promises in the middle of mind-blowing sex.

Would she have to pretend if she slept with him? Something about this man made her think he would pull a very real response out of her. For a man this sexy to be no good in bed would be a terrible disappointment.

She wanted to know. Badly. Wanted to ignore the voice in her head that said bad boys were off limits, forget Daniel's ice tray insult and melt in Biker Guy's arms. She glanced down at her purse. The Woman of the Year nomination letter was in there. The perfection required to achieve that goal didn't involve fantasies with unsuitable men.

Renee took a step back from temptation. "Thank you for the offer, seriously, but I've got a long day ahead of me. I'm going to call it a night."

"Are you sure?"

She was sure, but she was also surprisingly displeased with her decision. Turning away a man had never seemed like a missed opportunity before. "I am."

Disappointment clouded his gaze but his smile didn't waver. "I can't say I'm not sad to hear you say no, but maybe I'll run into you another day."

"I'll give you a rain check. Just in case we meet again."

"Be careful with a promise like that," he said. "You may actually need to keep it one day."

For the first time that she could remember, Renee actually hoped for the opportunity to fulfill a promise to a stranger.

CHAPTER 2

Thoughts of the beauty from the hotel still filled Jonathan's thoughts the next day as he drove his Harley down the long, tree-lined drive toward his grandparents' house. He'd been at the hotel to meet with his aunt, who'd not surprisingly *forgotten* Jonathan was coming into town to see her. Getting to flirt with the beauty, even though she'd rejected him, had put a small bright spot on the failed visit.

Typically, he easily moved on after a turn down. His ex-girlfriend cheating on him had quickly toughened up his male ego, but the woman from last night lingered in his thoughts. Not being able to get her out of his mind surprised him. She had none of the qualities he typically went for. She'd been polished, poised and beauty-queen perfect. He preferred a passionate, exciting, down for whatever vibe. He'd half expected the dismissal, but he'd been attracted enough to approach her. The interest in her eyes and hint of doubt when she'd turned him down had led to long hours of erotic dreams and a morning hard on.

His grandparents' home, the Big House as the family called it, appeared in all its antebellum glory at the end of the drive. The two-story mansion built in the Greek Revival style with white pillars framing the large wraparound porch had been in the Wright family since right after the Civil War. His family may have been Yankee upstarts back then, but they'd quickly entrenched themselves in Southern culture until that part of the family tree was dismissed.

The war had ended over a hundred years ago, but Jonathan had the misfortune of being born into a family that still missed the blessed good old days. His grandfather, card-carrying member of the Sons of Confederate Heroes and filthy rich good ole boy, hadn't taken it well when his oldest son, Jonathan's father, married a black woman. Which was why Jonathan had prepared himself for a fight when he'd gone to the hotel yesterday and tracked his aunt down here today.

The Big House was his. It had been passed down to the oldest son for generations. A tradition that stopped after Jonathan's parents were married and his grandfather removed his son from his will. After his grandfather died, Gigi, his grandmother, had left the house to Jonathan. Gigi lost her battle with breast cancer a month before, taking away the only person in his dad's family that Jonathan believed actually loved him and his sister. He'd let his aunt have time to mourn, but now was the time to settle the estate and give Jonathan his inheritance.

Jonathan parked next to his aunt's silver Lexus. Bitter childhood memories flooded his mind when he got off of the bike. His parents had only visited the Big House a few times during their marriage. Mostly at his grandmother's insistence. His grandfather typically caused any visit to end badly.

Jonathan raised his hand to knock on the door, but stopped. Grandfather was dead. The house was his. He didn't have to fear the repercussions of entering. He twisted the knob and swung open the door, pushing aside old feelings of fear and inadequacy that typically wrapped around him at this place.

"Aunt Joanne," he called out. "You in here?"

There was what sounded like an outraged gasp before the click-clack of heels approached from the back of the house. Jonathan left the entryway to go down the hall to meet her. Halfway down, he stopped. The walls were bare, the furniture in the front parlor was gone and covered in the study.

"What in the hell?" he muttered to himself.

The footsteps stopped at the end of the hall. "Don't you know how to knock?"

Jonathan turned away from the empty walls to his aunt. Two years younger than his dad, Joanne would still be considered by many as the epitome of southern beauty and charm. Her brunette hair framed her face in a stylish cut. She wore a tan Chanel suit, modest heels and pearls.

"I'm family, Auntie. I don't need to knock." He grinned and filled his voice with sweet charm. Calling her auntie would piss her off.

Joanne's blue eyes turned ice cold and she frowned. "I should be used to your bad manners by now. What do you want, Jonathan? I've got a lot of things to do today and not a lot of time to waste."

"If you would have met me yesterday like we planned to, I wouldn't have to take up so much of your precious time today." He pointed to the walls. "What's going on in here? Where's all the stuff?"

She snorted then turned and strolled down the hall into the living room. "If you came here to scavenge, then you're too late. I sold the house."

Jonathan stood there dumfounded while the words crept into his brain. Sold the house? She couldn't have. Anger tightened his shoulders. He followed her into the room with long purposeful strides. "The house is mine, Joanne."

She walked behind one of the couches before turning to face him with cool, mocking eyes. "No. It is not." Her tone was light, callous even, and she dismissed his words with a little flick of her wrist.

"Not only did Gigi let me know that she was leaving the Big House to me," Jonathan kept his voice low and even. Holding back the angry frustration clawing inside him to lash out at his aunt. "She showed me the provision in her will. Now I've let the matter lie long enough. It's time to settle the estate."

"I am settling the estate. Momma gave me power of attorney right before she died. Which gave me the ability to handle her affairs. I signed the contract to sell the house."

Jonathan's hands clenched into fists. Love for his father and the microscopic bit of respect his dad had for his sister kept him from calling her every vile word that ran through his brain. "When?"

"It doesn't matter when. I had the right to do it."

That was his answer. He'd bet his farm it was after Gigi had passed. "You took advantage of her sickness."

Joanne raised her chin. "I handled things the way Daddy wanted them handled. He didn't want my traitorous brother getting the house, and he certainly didn't want someone like you having it."

He felt the insult like a slap in the face. Funny how after thirty-two years of knowing one side of your family hated you the pain never lessened.

Years of having insults flung at him like knives had taught him to hide his feelings. Which he did now by giving his aunt a smile he doubted hid his frustration. "Gigi's will clearly states that the house belongs to me. I don't care if she did give you power of attorney. You can't do this. Especially after she died."

"I can." She smiled gleefully. "I have."

She didn't deny the timeframe. Anger stiffened his spine. Any attempt at a smile dissipated. "I'll fight you over this. I'm no stranger to being denied the privileges of being a Wright, but I won't stand for this."

"This isn't about denying you anything. This is about doing what's right. Daddy made it very clear that my brother and his offspring were no longer part of this family. If anyone deserves this place, it's me," she said. "This is for the best anyway."

"Best for you." Jonathan shook his head and let out a humorless laugh. "I never understood how anyone so pretty can be so petty and evil."

"Call me petty and evil all you want. It changes nothing. My lawyers have said I was well within my right to sell this house. I don't know why you would even waste your time fighting me. Why do you even want this place? You were never welcome here." She cocked a brow. "Still not."

Which is exactly why he wanted it. He felt a strong sense of satisfaction knowing he'd own the place his grandfather loved to kick him, his mother, and sister out of. He couldn't erase the hurt of his grandfather's hate, but he could do something to ensure that his niece, one day his kids, and any other future generations weren't denied access to their family history. No matter how painful that history may be.

"Because it's mine."

Joanne sniffed disdainfully. "Spoken like a greedy—" She bit her lip. Eyes much like his father's darted away.

Jonathan glared and he took a step in her direction. "Greedy what, Auntie?"

Her lips pressed together in a thin line. Joanne met his gaze but didn't answer. No need, the disgust in her eyes told him exactly what she wanted to say. Jonathan's heart beat heavily with anger, pain.

The doorbell rang. Joanne frowned and glanced at her watch then glared at him.

Jonathan lifted a brow. "Expecting someone?"

"Only the new owner of this place. You're welcome to stay. We're discussing the plans to build a neighborhood on the grounds."

She crossed the room to the door but kept plenty of distance between herself and him. Jonathan almost laughed at her caution. His aunt was an evil witch, but he wouldn't hurt her. He couldn't say the same for his sister Nadine. Nadine would love to take a whack at her.

"I'll be happy to inform your buyer that they've got a legal battle on their hands."

"One you'll lose," Joanne tossed over her shoulder.

Jonathan clenched his teeth as she left the room. Did he really have a case? Sure, Gigi had shown him in black and white that the house was coming to him, but if Joanne had power of attorney before Gigi died, did her move trump the will?

The sound of two sets of heels coming down the hall pulled him out of his thoughts. "My brother's son was just leaving," Joanne said. "Then we can discuss business."

"That's fine." A smooth, seductive feminine voice. "I'm happy to discuss the plans with any other members of your family."

Jonathan froze. They'd only spoken for a few minutes but he instantly recognized that voice. The same voice had whispered in his dreams all night long. A heartbeat later Joanne came back into the living room with the beauty from the hotel right behind her. She looked even better today. Smooth, golden brown skin, stylish haircut, and all slim curves and sophistication in a pair of cream pants and a dark green top.

She jerked to a stop at the door. Her rich brown eyes widened and her full lips parted when she saw him. What the hell was she doing here? With *Joanne* of all people?

"Renee Caldwell, this is my nephew," Joanne said, practically spitting out the word nephew and oblivious to the fact that Renee stood frozen at the door. "As I said, he was just leaving." Joanne emphasized the last words.

Her name burned through the fog that had taken over his brain when he'd seen her. Renee Caldwell. Caldwell!

"Andre's cousin?" he asked.

The stunned look on Renee's face gave way to confusion before the calm mask of perfection took over her face. "You know Andre?"

Jonathan had met Andre Caldwell in college. After they'd broken each other's noses in a fight, they'd somehow become friends. Andre wasn't on the side of the family that ran Caldwell Development. Though Andre's side of the family were far from being considered saints, he'd heard enough of the stories about the lies, double crossing, and shady dealings of Renee's side of the family to reach their goals.

"I'm Jonathan."

Her brows drew together for a second before recognition dawned. "Andre's friend." She gave him a cool, practiced smile. "It's nice to finally meet you. I've heard so much about you."

Jonathan was perfectly fine with forgetting that they'd met, flirted, the night before. His assumption that she was about as different from the type of woman he typically went for as a grape was from a grizzly bear was correct. Beautiful, rich, and spoiled. He'd heard enough about Renee from Andre to know they wouldn't be good together. Andre's fiancé, Mikayla, who once worked with Renee and considered her a friend, was eager to hook up Jonathan and Renee. Jonathan had purposefully avoided Mikayla's efforts. Renee was the type of woman he staunchly avoided.

"I've heard *a lot* about you, too."

***

It took everything in Renee not to cringe at Jonathan's words. She could imagine the types of things Andre had said about her. For most of their lives, Andre's relationship with her side of the family involved a bitter feud with her twin brother Ryan.

"I'm sure," she said, thankful that her voice came out practiced and professional even though her heart raced.

She'd avoided meeting Jonathan mainly because Mikayla had insisted they'd be great together. While there was a definite attraction, Renee knew enough to know they definitely would not be great together. According to Mikayla, Jonathan worked for the conservation district, something to do with farms and conservation planning. He also made extra money raising and selling beef cows. She was no farmer's wife and had no desire to ever want to be one.

His winter-sky eyes turned to Joanne. "So you're trying to sell this place to Caldwell Development?"

Renee frowned and glanced between the two. "Trying to? This deal is done."

Joanne nodded. "Of course it is. Jonathan, you can leave now."

"Now why would I do that, Auntie?" His voice took on that bourbon-smooth drawl that had made her hot the day before. Stiff shoulders and a straight back diluted his easy tone. "You said I could stick around and hear your plans for the Big House. I think I may, just for kicks and giggles. Seeing as how none of your plans are going to come to fruition."

"What do you mean?" Renee asked.

His sharp gaze flew back to her. "Didn't she tell you? Her mother left the house and the land to me in her will."

"That's not possible. We signed the contract this week."

Jonathan's laugh was bitter. "She didn't have the right to sign that contract. I plan to fight this in court."

Renee felt a very lucrative deal slip through her fingers. Handling this development smoothly would not only benefit Caldwell Development; it would also go a long way toward demonstrating her ability to spot a good deal and get her the needed Woman of the Year votes. Out of her newfound respect for her cousin, Andre, she didn't want to get into a bitter land dispute with his best friend, but out of respect and pride for her professional goals, this wasn't a fight she would walk away from.

"Then we'll see each other in court. Caldwell Development has already agreed to share the development rights to the land. We're going to make this one of the premier subdivisions in the area and we've offered your aunt a very generous portion of the profits." She looked to Joanne. "If it's money, then I suggest you work out internally how you'll split the profits among the family."

"There's nothing to work out internally," Jonathan said before Joanne could respond. "The house is mine." He glared at Joanne. "You may have taken advantage of Gigi's trust in you, but you won't take advantage of me. I'm going to fight to make sure you don't get a dime out of this house."

His cold gaze shifted to Renee before he marched out of the living room. A few seconds later, the front door opened and slammed. Joanne flinched then pressed a hand to her forehead. "I'm sorry about him. My nephew isn't one you'd consider to be civil."

"I've got my own history with uncivil relatives," Renee said. "Is what he said true? Did you sign this contract knowing the terms of your mother's will?"

"I did what my daddy wished." Joanne's tone was defensive. "He wanted me to have the house. Momma always had a soft spot for Jonathan. He knew that and played upon her heartstrings. She only changed the will after he coerced her when she was diagnosed with breast cancer."

"But you defied her will."

"I had power of attorney and I could sign whatever papers I wanted in her name. Jonathan can try to take us to court, but he'll lose." Joanne's eyes filled with worry. "Will this make you back out of the deal?"

Renee shook her head. "This complicates things, but I want to build here. You're right, you had power of attorney, but signing after her death will make it harder to defend. I'll get with our legal team when I get back." They'd tell her what type of a headache they were in for.

Joanne's smile was relieved and she pressed a hand to her chest. "Good."

When they'd entered this deal, Joanne had displayed the attitude of someone looking for a new business venture. The relief on her face now, when Renee said they'd be okay, was the look of someone who needed this project to go through. Renee wondered about the woman's financial situation. Joanne's husband had died a few years ago, and she had no children. She didn't appear to be in need of extra cash, but looks could be deceiving.

"Shall we go through the house now?" Renee asked. Joanne had invited her up to tour the house. Joanne had suggested they use the house as a central clubhouse and rental venue for the new subdivision instead of going through the expense of tearing it down.

"Of course," Joanne said.

They toured the house and Joanne gave her some of the history. According to Joanne, the place had been the heart of a small plantation before the war and then the heart of the Wright family after. She smiled and nodded politely at the nostalgia for the good ole days in Joanne's voice. Interesting how some people talked about life before the Civil War as if it were perfect for everyone.

"Daddy always said if we would have won the war we could have turned this into a much bigger plantation."

"If you would have won the war it's not likely I would have been able to offer you such a great deal to develop this property."

Joanne blushed and pushed her hair behind her ear. "Of course, I didn't think about—that was Daddy's saying. Not mine."

Renee smiled and nodded before holding out her hand for Joanne to continue the tour. She didn't believe for one second that it was just Joanne's father's saying. Fortunately, everyone's money, or land, was green. She didn't have to agree with Joanne's politics to make money off her.

Joanne finished their tour. Saving the house for residents in the subdivision to use was a superb idea. The place would make a great location for birthday parties, weddings, and anniversary celebrations. With a pool out back, it would be perfect.

After telling Joanne good-bye, Renee left and headed to her car. To her surprise, Jonathan's motorcycle was still in the drive. She'd expected him to be long gone. Movement beneath one of the trees to the left of the house caught her attention. Jonathan paced back and forth while talking on his cell phone.

She hadn't known about their family situation when Joanne made the offer. She couldn't afford to feel bad for making the deal with his aunt. That was business, but she didn't want this deal to cause friction in her personal life. Mikayla and Andre were getting married in a few weeks. Mikayla had a crazy notion that Renee and Jonathan would hit it off. They wouldn't be hooking up, but she could at least try to prevent an all-out fight.

She walked away from her car and strode in his direction. He stopped pacing to watch her approach. The steel in his gaze put her on guard and thrilled her. Maybe, in another life, she and Jonathan would have been good together. A life where every personal decision—boyfriends included—wasn't driven by the need to make Caldwell Development better.

"Let me call you back," he said to whoever he was on the phone with. "Are you finished divvying up my inheritance?" His voice was lazy, humorous, but she was under no impression that his feelings mirrored his tone.

"I hope this won't make things awkward at the wedding in a few weeks."

"You and my aunt conspiring together to completely ignore my grandmother's wishes. What's awkward about that?"

"The fight is between you and your aunt. I didn't make her sign the paperwork, nor did I approach her about purchasing the land. She brought this deal to me. I'm not the type of person to turn away a potentially lucrative deal."

"Look, I get that this isn't all on you, but that doesn't make me like the situation any more. I also get that we have to play nice at Mikayla and Andre's wedding, but I'm not going to back down on this. Especially knowing your family isn't trustworthy."

Renee jerked back. He knew nothing about her. "You have no reason to make assumptions about my family."

"They're not assumptions. I've heard enough about the Caldwell family to know that you're capable of anything."

She spread her legs and placed her hands on her hips. All thoughts of keeping things from getting awkward disappeared after he insulted her family. "You know nothing about my family."

"Really. I think Andre would disagree."

"Andre's fight was always with my brother. Not me. Despite what you think of my family, we're not the ones to play on the illegal side of the fence."

His jaw clenched, but he didn't respond. He couldn't. Her family was shrewd in business, but despite what Andre assumed, they were honest. Brutally honest at times. She'd never broken the law to secure a deal. Andre may have gotten better when he got with Mikayla, but Jonathan couldn't say the same about Andre's family.

Renee took a step closer to him. "All I'm asking is that you don't take what is ultimately your family's fight to Mikayla's wedding. She and Andre are happy. I won't let you ruin their day just because you're mad about this. We'll have our time to fight things out in court."

His blue-gray gaze homed in on hers. The heat from his body brushed against her like velvet. Sinful, soft, and seductive. She'd gotten too close when she'd stepped forward. Close enough to see the stubble on his chin and smell the slightest hint of masculine cologne. Her body sizzled with awareness. Only her pride kept her from backing away.

"Then we'll save the fight for court," he said in a low, determined voice.

A tremble went down her spine. She wanted to blame it on the threat of court instead of his intoxicating drawl. She wanted to pretend her hands clenched in anger, not because she wanted to run them over the solid strength of his chest. The need to flee before she said, or did, something ridiculous gripped her. "Good-bye, Jonathan." She took the step back she needed.

He tipped his head in acknowledgement. "Until next time, Renee."

CHAPTER 3

"Thanks again for all your help, Jonathan," George Hanover said as he and Jonathan walked back to his home after inspecting George's cow pasture.

"That's what I'm here for." Jonathan gave his usual response when thanked for doing his job. Even though his response was the same, he was far from blasé about his work as a district conservationist. The local conservation office had helped his dad start his own small cattle operation after he'd been kicked out of the family. Now Jonathan got to return the favor and spend most of his days outdoors working with farmers on ways to preserve their land for future generations.

"Us new guys don't always get a lot of help," George said. "Those big commercial farms were the ones who get the most say so." He lifted his John Deere ball cap and scratched his forehead. George was about ten years older than Jonathan and worked full time as a high school biology teacher. A year ago, he'd decided to try his hand at raising cows and had come to the Conservation Department for help.

"That's why I suggested you join the Cattle Farmers' Association."

"I did," George said. "But I'm not only new, I'm small. I don't get a lot of say so in the organization."

Jonathan couldn't really dispute that. He'd been a member for years and served on the board in various ways including president one year. He did speak up for the newer and smaller guys in his position. Knowing first-hand the obstacles they faced after putting time and effort into their operations.

"Stay in long enough and they'll start listening."

"They listen to you." They'd made it to George's driveway and stopped next to Jonathan's silver Conservation District truck. "You should really consider running for president."

Jonathan leaned an arm on the bed of the truck. "I've already served as regional president."

"No, on the state level. You've already made a name for yourself locally. Why not go higher and make sure the issues of us little guys are heard."

"I'm not good at the politics of it," Jonathan said.

"You may not think you are, but believe me there are a ton of us around here that know you are."

George held out his hand and Jonathan shook it. On the ride back to the district office, he considered George's statement. He'd gotten encouragement to be more active on a state level before. His grandfather may have disowned his son and his son's family, but that didn't mean people weren't aware of who Jonathan was. His grandfather had been a strong member of the State Senate and lost by a slim margin when he'd run for governor. The Wright name was respected. Not talking to his son due to what was publicly considered a small personal dispute didn't lessen that.

Jonathan could do a lot for the organization at the state house. But the thought of lobbying politicians and granting favors in order to get legislation passed made his stomach heave. He'd rather leave that to the guys with their own political aims and agendas. He had his own fight to contend with.

He arrived back at the small brick building that held the conservation district offices. He pushed through the glass double doors into the small lobby. Laura, the cute blonde receptionist, perked up from behind her desk. Her smile was as bright as the fresh daisies she kept in a vase on the edge of her desk, and her blue eyes friendly as ever.

"Hey, Jonathan, you have a visitor."

Jonathan checked his watch. It was nearly noon. "My dad?" They were supposed to meet for lunch.

"Yep. I told him he could wait in your office." She pulled her lower lip between her teeth. "I hope that's okay."

"It's fine." He smiled and winked at her.

Laura leaned forward onto her desk. "Oh good. I'd hate for you to be mad at me," she said in a rush. Her bright eyes filled with hopeful adoration.

"I could never be mad at you, Laura." He said sincerely. Pink dusted Laura's cheeks and she fiddled with the neckline of her shirt.

Jonathan gave her one last parting smile and walked down the hall toward his office. Jacob Wright sat in one of the wooden chairs across from Jonathan's messy desk, flipping through the pages of the latest agricultural digest.

"Sorry I'm late," Jonathan said, coming into the room and putting his clipboard and the papers with the conservation plan for the Hanover farm on a shelf.

"I just got here," Jacob dropped the magazine on one of the many piles of paper on Jonathan's desk and stood.

Jacob wore his standard denim shirt and jeans with a brown Cattle Farmers' Association hat over his graying blonde hair. Jacob's ice blue eyes were the same as his sister's, but unlike Joanne's, they were always filled with pride when he looked at Jonathan. Everyone said Jonathan favored his dad more than his mom. He got his wide shoulders and height from his dad, but also his straight nose, eye color, and cleft chin. Jacob's nose was crooked from where it had been broken several times when he was younger. At least once in fights defending his family against his cousins.

They embraced briefly and Jonathan sat on the edge of the desk when they broke apart. "Nadine tell you what Joanne did?"

Jacob scowled and jerked his hand back and forth over his chin. "My sister never ceases to surprise me."

"How could she do that to Gigi? Do you think…" Jonathan didn't want to believe that his grandmother had lied to him. Not when she'd been the only champion they'd had against his grandfather's ignorance. She'd shown him the will and had made him a copy on her small printer the last time he'd seen her. An unsigned copy. She could have changed the will.

Jacob shook his head. "I don't think so. When I spoke to Momma in her last days she said that she was making things right and leaving the house to you."

"I still think you deserve it more. You grew up there."

"She asked me if I wanted it when she drafted her will. When my dad kicked me and your mom out of the house, that place was no longer my home." Jacob's flat tone hid the mountain of disappointment Jonathan knew his father carried. Once, when Jonathan was in his early teens, Jacob confided how much he'd looked up to his father. How he'd wanted to be just like him until he'd been rejected for falling in love with the "wrong" woman. "I told Momma to leave the place to you."

"Why?"

"Because it's your legacy. Take it and make it a place your kids will be proud of."

Jonathan sighed. He pulled off the district hat he wore and ran his hands through his hair. "This is going to be an ugly fight. She sold it to Caldwell Development."

"Andre's family?"

Jonathan nodded. He didn't want to think about Renee. Didn't want to think about the way her dark eyes had sparked with interest that night they'd first met. Didn't want to consider how he couldn't shake the curiosity that nagged him to find out how much would her eyes spark if he kissed her perfect mouth.

"Yeah."

"Maybe she hasn't sold it yet. Otherwise, they wouldn't have met at the house when you were there. Maybe there's some kind of deal on the table. Which means the land may still be in Joanne's hands."

Jonathan wished it were that easy. "The contract was signed last week. Renee let that slip. Which means the fight won't be pretty. I've already called my lawyer."

"I'll have your back in this fight. You wouldn't even be in this situation if my dad hadn't turned out to be a bigot." Bitterness edged Jacob's tone. "We'll make things right." The simple statement sounded like a vow.

Jonathan hoped they could fix this. "Come on. Let's grab something to eat. I've got to visit another farm at two."

They left Jonathan's office and strolled back to the front. "I'll be back in about an hour, Laura."

Laura nodded and tilted her head to the side prettily. "All right, Jonathan. Hurry back."

Jacob looked at the two of them before turning an expectant glace in his son's direction. Jonathan ignored his dad and pushed out the door.

"When are you going to ask that girl out?" Jacob asked.

"Who, Laura? She's not my type."

"What could possibly be wrong with her?"

"I didn't say anything was wrong with her." Jonathan stopped at the hood of his work truck. He'd driven his motorcycle to work. "I just said she's not my type. She's a sweet girl. Looking for marriage and stuff. I'm not ready for that."

The smile on Jacob's face gave way to a concerned frown. "Don't let that situation with Karen keep you from getting out there again."

"This has nothing to do with Karen." He turned away and jerked open the door of the truck.

"You want to be pigheaded," Jacob said after he opened the passenger door. "Fine."

"Until I feel that I could be with someone forever, I'm not stringing anyone along. That's one of the reasons Karen said she…" He blew out a breath. He had strung Karen along, and she'd retaliated by bringing another man into her bed. He wasn't about to put himself in that situation again. "I want what you and mom have. Something worth fighting for."

Jacob sighed. "Fighting and thriving are two different things." A trace of sadness filled his voice.

Jonathan turned away from the wheel and stared at his dad. "What's that supposed to mean?"

Jacob shook his head. The concerned look on his face clearing up. "Nothing."

Jonathan wanted to argue, but Jacob grinned and tapped his arm. "I won't bother you about Laura, anymore. I forgot, you like your ladies thick."

Heat spread up Jonathan's face, but he laughed. "Yes, I do."

He turned on the car and backed out of the parking space. He did prefer his women curvy, but the image of a slim and sexy developer plagued him as he drove to lunch.

***

"Renee, do you have any idea where Ryan could be?" Philip Caldwell interrupted Renee's wandering thoughts.

Renee jerked out of her woolgathering and dropped the pencil she'd been using to doodle circles on her notebook. One glance around the conference room table revealed every eye was on her. Every Tuesday morning the key Caldwell Development staff met in her father's office. Typically, she was focused and eager to report. Today her mind wandered back to earlier that weekend and her encounters with Jonathan.

"I'm sorry, Daddy, I was thinking about another project. What did you say?"

The glare on Philip's face would scare most people. But most people weren't his beloved daughter. He might glare, and wasn't afraid to share his disappointment if she screwed something up, but her father was never mean to her.

"Your brother," he said slowly. "Do you know where he is?"

Renee did another sweep of the occupants at the table. Her father, Alicia, the new hire that Renee was training to take over the acquisition of property, Rory from finance—also a new hire after their previous finance manager helped embezzle funds, and Dennis, Ryan's second in command over the construction department.

"I have no idea." Renee pulled up her cell phone and checked her text messages. "He's supposed to be here."

"That boy. I don't know what's wrong with him," Philip said, clearly exasperated.

Her dad went on to complain while Renee sat there reeling. She'd been in the meeting for at least five minutes, completely oblivious to who was in the room. This was not like her. Why in the world couldn't she get the situation with Jonathan out of her mind?

Is it really the situation, or the man?

Renee pushed the thought aside. The man was intriguing, sexy, and not the type of guy she should be infatuated by. He was too big, too blunt, too rough. She needed someone polished, refined, connected. Someone who would help further the reach of Caldwell Development.

Even if they were compatible, he wouldn't get over that fact that Joanne sold the land to Caldwell Development and Renee wouldn't let go of a deal. When she succeeded in taking control of the development of his family's property, he was going to hate her. No matter that his aunt was the one who'd betrayed him. In her experience, when there was a family dispute for property the wounded party tended to hate the buyer as much as the family member selling.

Philip's voice rose with agitation. Renee pushed away thoughts of Jonathan to focus on her dad who thankfully was not focused on her. Dennis received the brunt of his frustration.

Dennis pulled out his cell phone and stood. "I'll call him now. Maybe he headed to Holly Hill early. We have a meeting with the school board later."

Doubtful, but a good try. Renee was pretty sure Ryan wouldn't head to any meeting early. In the past year, her brother had taken a trip from casual party boy and ladies' man to downright debauched libertine. Men were dumb that way when it came to broken hearts.

The two of them were often sought out because of who they were and what they could offer. Renee had resigned herself to using this to her family's advantage. Ryan, on the other hand, still thought he'd be able to find the perfect woman who wouldn't see Caldwell Development dollar signs when they looked at him. The year before he'd broken Mikayla's heart for a woman who'd later broken his. To make matters worse Mikayla and Andre had fallen in love and were happy. After those two blows, he'd given up on trying to find "the one."

Dennis shook his head and slid his phone back in his pocket. "No answer."

Philip swore and pulled out his own cell. The door to his office opened. Ryan strolled in, a loose grin on his face. His tan suit was impeccable, haircut perfect, and hands manicured. Only bloodshot eyes gave away he'd spent another night drinking and partying.

"Sorry I'm late," he said, his smile not wavering. "I was a little tied up this morning."

He plopped down into the chair next to Renee and pushed the seat back so that he could stretch his legs out in front of him. "What did I miss?"

Renee shook her head. "Ryan, really?"

He swung his head her way and shrugged. "Really what?"

"Are you drunk?"

He shook his head. "No, and as soon as the ibuprofen I took earlier kicks in, there won't be any reminders of my hangover."

Renee rolled her eyes and groaned. "You're too old for this."

"And you're too young to act like a stuck up prude."

Renee's hands clenched into fists in her lap. "Excuse me."

Philip cleared his throat and glared at the other staff members in the room. "If you'll give me and my children a moment."

The rest of the staff quickly filed out of the office without a backward glance. The door closed with a hasty snap and Philip whipped his angry glare on Ryan.

"Ryan, what in the hell is wrong with you?"

Ryan spread out his arms and shrugged. "Who says anything is wrong with me?"

"You're partying too much, drinking too much, shirking your duties, and leaving the development of our new project in the low country to Dennis. I get that Angelica handed you your balls in her manicured hands, but that's no reason to act like a bitch."

Ryan and Renee both flinched. She agreed with her dad, but that was harsh.

Ryan jerked forward in his chair. "I'm nobody's bitch."

Philip glared back. "Then stop acting like one. We all told you that woman was no good, but you didn't want to listen. I get it, you thought you were getting married and she didn't want you. You got played. It happens. Move on. But you won't, will you? Because that's your problem. Wear your emotions on your sleeve instead of thinking things through like your sister."

Ryan glared at Renee. She looked away. This wasn't the first time Philip compared her calculated approach to things to Ryan's hot and reckless approach.

"That's Renee's problem," Ryan said. "She thinks things through too much. Picks guys on principles and pedigrees. That can backfire, huh, sis?"

Renee's eyes snapped to Ryan's. "Don't try to turn this on me."

Not for the first time she thought Ryan was itching to tell their dad about how Daniel had only been with her to get more money for his land. Even though she hated that she'd seen more in Daniel than there really was, she didn't hate that she chose not to jump into relationships just because of a fluttery feeling. Fluttery feelings tended to backfire too.

"This isn't about Renee, it's about you, Ryan," Philip said bringing the conversation back on track. "If you would have thought things out a year ago, instead of thinking with your balls, you could have made things work with Mikayla. Then maybe she would be marrying you instead of your cousin Andre."

Ryan's tan skin paled. Renee wanted to curse. She definitely hadn't wanted anyone to tell Ryan about the wedding before it happened. The way his moods were going, she couldn't say for sure he wouldn't pop up and make a scene. Ryan had broken Mikayla's heart, and though he said he'd accepted that Mikayla was with Andre, sometimes she felt that Ryan still harbored resentment.

Ryan turned accusing eyes her way. "She's marrying him?"

Renee nodded. "Next week."

"And you didn't tell me?" An accusatory tone.

"She doesn't want it to be a big deal."

Ryan placed a hand on his chest. "I was her friend long before she met him."

"But you're also the guy who cheated on her. The wedding will be small. Just her father, me, Isaac, and his friend Jonathan. They're having it at their house."

"You should have told me."

"Why? She's over you, and you're over her." The second half of the statement was more of a question. The pained look on his face made her second guess that assumption.

Ryan gave a stiff nod and rubbed a hand across his nose. "If she's happy then I'm happy. The marriage didn't have to be a secret."

Philip sighed heavily. "Forget about the wedding and focus on the fact that your reckless behavior is the reason Mikayla ended up with Andre in the first place. Instead of making things work with a good woman you threw it all away for trash. Now you're throwing away your chance to prove you can run this company one day."

"How?"

Philip looked at Ryan as if he'd sprouted a second head. "How?" He leaned forward. "How can I trust you to help your sister take over? One woman hurts your feelings you start skipping meetings, staying out late partying, drinking and sleeping with anything in a skirt. You need to get your life in order."

"My life is in order," Ryan said in a low, angry tone.

Philip leaned forward and pointed at Ryan. "Then prove it instead of behaving like a heartbroken thirteen year old. You're embarrassing yourself."

Ryan stood so quickly the chair tilted and almost hit to the floor. He jerked on the front of his suit jacket. "Forget this. I've got to be in Holly Hill by lunch."

He glared at Philip then Renee before storming out of the office. Philip cursed and pushed up from his seat. He crossed to the wet bar in the corner of his office and poured his favorite bourbon out of the crystal decanter into a highball glass.

"Dad, it's not even ten," Renee said.

Philip took a long sip then pointed to the door. "That boy…"

Renee sighed and rubbed her eyes with her fingers. "Is confused. He'll come around."

Philip grunted his disagreement. Renee's head hurt. She hated seeing Ryan spiraling out of control, but a part of her envied his passion. That was his biggest flaw. She'd never yearned for anything more than the success of her family's business. Marriage and relationships all served a purpose. Her parents were proof of that. Her mother had been wealthy in land but not money. Her dad was starting a new development company and needed to acquire land. Their marriage started as one of convenience, and luckily, they'd grown to love each other. A part of her wondered what having the type of passion that Ryan had had for Angelica, or the love Mikayla had with Andre, felt like.

"Tell me something good, Renee," Philip said from the bar.

Renee shook her head, clearing the useless yearning away. Time to get back to business. "Unfortunately, my update may upset you."

Philip strolled over, and took another sip of his drink. "Can't be worse than your brother. How are things going with the Wright property?"

Renee briefed her dad on what happened with Jonathan and Joanne. "I've alerted our legal team. They seem to think that although the will left the house to Jonathan, we can argue that Joanne's power of attorney gave her the ability to sign it over."

"Damned family disputes," Philip grumbled. "Keep me updated as things play out."

"Absolutely."

Philip moved to turn away, but stopped and swiveled to face Renee. "Her nephew, he's Andre's friend, right?"

"You knew that?"

"I did some digging into the family after Joanne approached you with this deal. I knew the old man Wright had a son he pretty much disowned some years back. A little more digging led me to his grandson's connection to Andre."

No need to ask how her dad knew all that. His sources could tell him the exact start date of her cycle if he cared to know. What she didn't like was him checking up behind her. "Are you doubting my ability to handle this situation?"

"Not at all. You've proven yourself a number of times. I still can't believe you convinced Daniel to let go of that land they'd owned for years down in Charleston. When you closed the LeFranc deal, you proved yourself. Too bad you two didn't work out. He's a good man."

She barely stopped herself from snorting. Daniel was a selfish man. Too bad she'd discovered that too late. "Then why look into the Wright family?"

"Joanne was once on the Woman of the Year committee. I didn't want her to use the connection as a way to draw us into a bad deal. The situation with the family shows I didn't dig far enough."

"Jonathan will be a problem."

"Change his mind?" Philip said with a confidence that she could do so as easily as she started her car engine.

"I don't think I can change his mind. I've suggested that we both remain civilized during the wedding for Mikayla's sake."

Philip's eyes brightened with calculation. "You have the perfect opportunity to get to know him and convince him that this deal could benefit him as well. We can amend the contract to include him in any profits. Use your connection with him to see what his ultimate asking price is. Everyone has a price."

He glanced at his watch and cursed. "No need to call everyone back in here for the meeting now. Will you get with each of them and get any updates? I've got to go downtown for a meeting."

Renee nodded. "Of course." She stood and gathered her stuff.

"Thanks, sweetie," Philip said. He walked back toward the bar then stopped and turned to her. "At least I know I can always count on one of my kids."

Her smile was weak, but Philip turned back to the bar to put down his glass. Renee left and went to her office next to his. Inside she closed the door and leaned heavily against it. Barely ten and she was already tired. Renee pushed away from the door and paced toward her desk. She ran a hand across the back of her head.

Maybe she could use her connection to Jonathan to help win the fight. They'd be together for a weekend, for a happy occasion. Mikayla would be determined to push them together because she thought they'd make a good couple. As the saying goes, you catch more flies with honey than vinegar. If she was nice to him, engaged him in conversation and he happened to mention his thoughts on what would make him more agreeable to the deal, that wasn't necessarily a bad thing.

Something whispered that she was making excuses, and weak ones at that, to indulge her interest in an unsuitable guy. She pushed the voice to the very back of her brain. This was business. She was only going to be pleasant to him. Flirt a little. Bury the proverbial hatchet. All avenues toward victory were fair when it came to business.

CHAPTER 4

Renee sat in the front row of metal chairs set out in one of the meeting rooms at the Still Hopes Family Shelter and listened as Destiny Knight, one of the girls in her mentoring group, practiced her presentation for her civics class the next day. Thursday night mentoring session at the shelter had become one of Renee's favorite nights of the week. Though Tuesday night book club was just as fun.

A little over a year ago when she'd casually read an article about the challenges Still Hopes faced raising funds to provide shelter for homeless mothers and their kids, challenges that meant the women and children would have to move into a larger shelter that housed men some considered violent and possibly dangerous, she hadn't been able to get the place out of her mind. A week after reading the article, she'd walked through the door and asked how she could help. A board position and volunteering had been the first thing offered. She'd accepted without hesitation.

"And that's why I think the Supreme Court shouldn't ban abortion," Destiny finished. She twisted the papers in her hand and gave Renee a questioning look. She still wore the khaki skirt and dark blue shirt that was her high school's uniform. Her thick braids were pulled up into a ponytail on top of her head.

Renee shook her head. "Don't say 'I think.' This is an opinion piece. Therefore, we know this is what you think." Renee stood and took the few steps to stand beside Destiny then she turned to the four other girls in the room. "Remember that the key to most debates is exhibiting confidence in what you're saying. Saying 'that's why the Supreme Court shouldn't ban abortion' is more direct than saying 'I *think* they shouldn't.' Hear the difference?"

The girls all nodded. Renee turned back to Destiny. "Your presentation was well thought out. I can tell you did your research and that you feel strongly about your side in this argument. Remember, no matter what the other person says, don't lose your temper during your response."

"I won't, Renee," Destiny said. Renee had insisted the girls use her first name instead of Ms. Caldwell, or worse, ma'am. "I'll channel my inner Renee, Power Business Woman, while I'm up there tomorrow."

Renee smiled and wrapped an arm around Destiny's shoulders in a half hug. "Then I know you'll do great." She looked up at the clock. It was eight twenty-five. They were supposed to finish at eight. "All right, girls, that's it for tonight. I've got to get home and finish up some work and you all have school tomorrow."

The girls grumbled a little bit about the school reminder, but they all got up and started gathering their things. Renee checked her watch as she collected her purse and sighed. Her shoes fit today, but that didn't make the heels any more comfortable after eight hours. She had a stack of contracts to review that night along with going over the latest design plans from their engineer for a new project. There was no way she would get in bed before midnight and she couldn't go into the office late because of an eight a.m. meeting with their lawyers. She'd stop for the largest, strongest coffee she could find on the way home.

After she got her purse, she turned to find Destiny huddled up with Patricia Gomez by the door. The two were having a hushed argument. Patricia turned to come toward Renee, but Destiny grabbed her arm and pulled her back.

"Go ask Renee," Patricia hissed.

"Ask me what?" Renee walked toward the front of the room to face the two girls.

Destiny shook her head. "Nothing. Patricia is just overreacting."

Patricia rolled large brown eyes and shoved her thick, dark hair away from her forehead. "I'm not overreacting. You just don't want to face reality."

"I do want to face reality," Destiny replied, but didn't sound nearly as confident as she had while doing her presentation earlier.

Renee shifted her weight to one side and crossed her arms. "What's going on?"

Destiny didn't crack her lips. Patricia blew out a breath. "Destiny likes this boy but he won't go with her to homecoming if she won't have sex."

Renee cut her eyes toward Destiny. "Is that what he said?"

Destiny shook her head, but didn't meet Renee's eyes. "No. He said he'll go. Then he mentioned going to a party on the lake."

"The same party that everyone knows you go to because the kid's parents aren't there and everyone has sex," Patricia said.

Renee lowered her head until she could meet Destiny's eyes. "Do you want to go?"

"To homecoming yes. To have sex." She shrugged. "I don't know."

"I told her to talk to you, Renee," Patricia said. "You'll know how to handle this guy."

A little bit of panic waivered inside Renee. She was so not the right person to give advice on boys. "Isn't this the type of stuff you should talk to your mom about?"

Both Destiny and Patricia rolled their eyes and shuddered. Destiny held up a hand. "No. Momma wouldn't let me get past the word sex before she freaked out."

"And she wouldn't be real," Patricia said. "You're always real with us, Renee."

Renee couldn't be real with Destiny. Real was telling Destiny how she'd lost her virginity at eighteen because she'd been in love with a guy. Only to have him break up with her because *he* wasn't good enough shortly after meeting her family. His words, not hers. Since then she'd only dated men who had similar backgrounds as her. Men like Daniel who considered her cold as an ice tray. Renee was thirty and knew nothing of *handling* men.

She could at least give Destiny run of the mill good advice.

"Before you do anything," Renee said carefully. "Make sure he's worthy of you. Sex is powerful and special. If you're not sure, tell him. See how he reacts."

Destiny twisted one of her braids between her fingers. "What if he doesn't want to go to homecoming with me?"

"Do you think he'll change his mind about going?"

"I have no idea. I mean, we've been flirting and stuff. He acts like he likes me. He even knows my family is staying here." She glanced around the room. "He doesn't seem to care."

Renee didn't have the heart to say he would act like her family situation didn't matter while trying to have sex with her. That bit of cynicism was best left for another day. "If he really doesn't care then he'll be fine if you say you don't want to go to the party. He'll understand that you're not ready for sex."

"And if he does care?"

Renee ran a hand up and down Destiny's arm. "Then you've got your answer."

Destiny wrung her fingers together and looked at Patricia. Renee could empathize with the girl. When you were a teen every decision felt like it was a life or death one. The decision to possibly end things with a guy you really liked probably seemed tantamount to pressing the button that started nuclear war.

"I'll tell him tomorrow at the football game."

"Good," Renee said. "You never want a man that doesn't really want you. You only want someone who will love and care for you just as you are."

Words she didn't believe, but sometimes wished she could. Her future husband, if she ever got married, would be someone like Daniel LeFranc. A man who benefitted from marrying a Caldwell just as she would benefit from marrying him.

Destiny grabbed Renee's hand and held tight. "Come to the game."

Patricia nodded and turned eager eyes on Renee. "Yes, come."

"What for?"

"So you can check him out. You don't pull any punches, Renee. You'll tell me if he's full of shit or not."

Renee shook her hand. "Cursing is vulgar."

Destiny covered her mouth with her free hand. "Sorry. Please, Renee, say you'll come."

There were dozens of things Renee would rather do on a Friday night besides go to a high school football game. Organizing her desk, catching up on laundry, taking her car to the car wash. But she couldn't say no to the two big, pleading pairs of eyes staring up at her.

"Fine. I'll come to the game."

***

Jonathan hadn't signed up to coach high school football this year, but that didn't stop him from traveling with the team to away games. He still went down to the sidelines and cheered on the boys, and delivered any advice on holes in the opposing team's offense or defense that he could see from the stands. Sometimes he missed coaching, but honestly, the time commitment had made it hard for him to monitor things at his property with the small herd of cows he cared for.

Not being coach did allow him to enjoy the game as a spectator. Including the ability to wander around during half-time as he did now. Each high school stadium had its own feel. A vibe brought to the place by the fans. It was kind of fun to tap into that instead of being stuck on the sidelines.

He made his way to the home side and found a seat near the top center. He scanned the crowd and spotted Renee a few rows down. He blinked, rubbed his eyes, and looked again. No illusion, it was definitely her. She was sitting alone, clutching a Styrofoam cup in her hands, and sitting bone straight in the bleachers. She shifted in the seat and tugged on the lapels of her tan leather jacket, pulling them closer. She stared at a group of kids standing at the bottom of the bleachers.

Before he knew what he was doing, he was crossing the bleachers in her direction. He told himself it was because they'd be with each other the following weekend for Andre and Mikayla's wedding. He agreed with her suggestion that they act civil toward each other for the occasion. He was going over to be friendly. Not because she looked lonely sitting by herself.

"Having fun?" he asked when he reached her.

She jumped then twisted in the seat and looked up at him. For a second he was lost in the warm cocoa centers of her eyes, then she blinked. "Oh, hello, Jonathan," she said, just as calm and collected as she pleased.

She took a sip from the cup then raised a brow. "I'd be having more fun if I could feel my toes." She looked at her booted feet and lifted her toes.

Jonathan smiled. "It's not that cold. This is perfect football weather."

She glanced at him again. "Do I look like a football girl?" Her voice was dry, but the corner of her lips lifted in a sexy half-smile.

"Nah, not really."

"The cocoa is great though." She raised the cup with one hand.

"Great? Really?"

"I stood in line for twenty minutes for it. Of course it's great."

He wanted to laugh. Surprising. When they'd first met, she'd tried to be aloof, even though the attraction had hummed between them. He'd expected the same when he walked over. Not for her to be...cool.

"What brings you here if you're not a football girl?"

She used her head to indicate the group of kids she'd been watching before he came over. "My girls asked me to come."

"Your girls?"

"They're not really my girls. I mentor them as part of my volunteer work at Still Hopes. It's a shelter for families with nowhere else to go. Destiny, the tall one, asked me to come and check out the guy she's asked to homecoming."

Renee volunteering at a family shelter didn't surprise him. Renee coming to a high school football game just to check out a boy at the request of one of the teenagers at the shelter did. If he didn't know any better he'd think his enemy had a heart.

He put one of his feet up on the bleacher beside her and rested his arm on his bent leg. "And the verdict?"

She tilted her head to the side and studied the kids. "Still out. She hasn't told him the important news yet. His reaction will be my ultimate call."

"What's the important news?"

"Not my business to tell," she said.

He nodded, respecting the fact that she wouldn't betray the girl's secrets.

"What are you doing here?" she asked.

"I used to coach for the other team. I don't anymore, but I still make the away games when I can."

"I've never met a biker football coach before."

Jonathan shook his head. "I'm not a biker. I ride a motorcycle."

Her head lifted and lowered in agreement and she took another sip of her hot chocolate. "I'm surprised you came over to speak. I am the enemy."

"You are," he said without any heat. "But you were right about next weekend. We can be civilized for Mikayla and Andre's day."

Determined brown eyes met his. "Then pick up the fight again afterward."

"I'm more than ready to tangle with you, Renee," he said, grinning. The sudden flare of awareness in her eyes made him want to sit, slide close and brush his lips over hers.

She sucked in a breath and looked away. "Did you come to the game by yourself?"

He let her change the subject. Flirting with Renee would only muddy the already murky waters. "I did. You?" He dropped his leg and sat next to her. She scooted away. He wished she hadn't. He had to stop himself from closing the space between them.

"Just me," she said.

"When I first saw you I thought you might be here with a date."

"I'm not seeing anyone." She glanced at him out of the corner of her eye.

Good. The thought was unexpected and unwanted. He broke eye contact and pretended as if he were tugging on his pants leg but really the movement allowed him to shift and put a little more distance between them. Renee's relationship status meant nothing to him.

Yeah, tell yourself that.

"I guess you'd rather be somewhere else than here?"

"I wouldn't have minded seeing Carmen tonight," she said. "The Arts Foundation is doing a performance of it. But I made a promise to Destiny."

"Carmen? That's an opera, right?"

"It is. Have you been to the opera before?"

"Do I look like an opera guy?"

She eyed his brown Carhartt jacket, red plaid shirt, and jeans. Her full lips twitched before she shook her head. "No. You don't."

Footsteps pounded on the bleachers as the two girls ran toward him and Renee. They both glanced at him with bright, curious eyes before they looked at Renee.

"I told him, Renee," the one Renee identified as Destiny said.

Renee raised a brow and leaned forward to rest her forearms on her legs. "And what did he say?"

The girl grinned. "He still wants to go. We're going to go out to eat before homecoming and then hang out at the fun park afterward."

"No pressure to attend the lake party. Or for anything else?" Renee put emphasis on her last sentence.

"No pressure," Destiny said, shaking her head.

The other girl waved. "You should still meet him, Renee."

Renee looked between the two. "If Destiny wants me to."

"I do," Destiny said. "Please?"

"Sure," Renee said. "Bring him up here."

The girls grinned before they turned and hurried down the bleachers to the boys. "They call you Renee?" Jonathan asked.

"I prefer that to Ms. Caldwell. And it makes it easier for them to talk to me."

"About boys?"

She nodded. "And other things."

The girls were on their way back with the boys behind them. After they joined them, the girls introduced the two boys. When the girls gave him another curious look, Renee introduced him as a business colleague. They weren't in business, but neither were they really friends. Still, the introduction rubbed him wrong. Almost like they should be more. He was crazy.

Destiny watched Renee's reaction to the boy she liked with extreme interest. While Renee talked to them about their plans for the upcoming homecoming dance, Jonathan noticed how she interacted with the teens. She was still prim sophistication and grace, but an edge of steel lined her voice when she told the boy that she hoped nothing put a damper on Destiny's night. She obviously cared about the girls and wanted the young man in question to realize that too.

"We're going to go walk around for the third quarter of the game," Destiny said. "Are you sticking around for the second half?"

Renee shook her head. "Probably not. I feel good about leaving now." She gave Destiny an approving look.

Destiny grinned. "Thanks, Renee." The girl looked at Jonathan. "You and your *colleague* have a good night."

Destiny and the other girl, Patricia, both giggled before they hurried away with the boys. Renee had gone stiff beside him and narrowed her eyes at the retreating teens.

"I think they think we're dating." Jonathan said, humor in his tone.

"Kids," Renee said, shifting next to him. She glanced at her watch. "I don't think I'll stay for the rest of the game. I guess I'll see you next weekend for the wedding, where we'll keep the cease fire going."

"I won't shoot if you don't."

"Then it's settled." She picked up her purse from where it sat between her feet and stood.

Jonathan stood with her. "Are you parked nearby?"

"There wasn't anything close when I got here, but I'm not too far."

It was dark and while he liked to think there wouldn't be a problem, he didn't feel comfortable letting her walk alone. There wasn't always trouble at football games, yet the occasional fights did break out during and after the games.

"I'll walk with you."

"There's no need for that. You're here for the other team and look," she pointed to the field where the teams were running back out. "The next quarter is about to start. No need for you to miss it because of me."

"I have my ticket stub, they'll let me back in. Besides, I just don't feel right letting you walk alone in the dark."

She appeared surprised by his statement. Her mouth formed a cute little O and her cocoa eyes widened a fraction. A second later, she composed herself, but the corners of her lips were tilted in the barest of smiles. Her pleasure created a reciprocating flutter of pleasure in his chest.

"If you insist."

They were silent as they walked out of the stadium and through the gate. Renee's not far turned out to be a few blocks away from the school. He was glad he walked with her. Though security inside the stadium was tight, there wasn't much outside the stadium. Several groups of rough looking kids, and adults, hung out in the parking lot and in between the cars along the streets. Rough looking didn't always mean trouble. He made a point to nod in acknowledgement when he passed each group.

"This is my car," she said, stopping by the Cadillac she'd driven to the Big House. She turned and faced him. "Thank you for the escort."

"No problem."

They stared at each other. The moment suddenly had the awkward feeling of the end of a first date. The urge to hug her overcame him. His gaze dropped to her lips. There were urges to do other things too. Like taste her lips.

Jonathan looked away and took a step back. No way in hell should he be thinking of kissing Renee Caldwell. "Well, I'd better get back."

"Yes, thanks again f..."

Jonathan focused on her but her gaze was over his shoulder. Her brows drew together before her eyes shot to wide circles. Jonathan swung around, automatically pushing Renee behind him. A young man ran in their direction and another man chased him. Jonathan stepped back, pushing Renee into the side of her car as the first guy passed.

The other man stopped and reached into his pocket. A second later, he pointed a handgun in the direction of the man running. "Fuck you, punk!"

Jonathan spun, grabbed Renee, and hauled her into a crouch next to the car. Two seconds later gunfire blasted. Renee screamed and clutched the front of his jacket. He wrapped his arms around her shoulders and squeezed her close to his chest. Fear and anger pumped through him with every frantic beat of his heart. Car alarms went off, people shouted, and then there was the sound of footsteps running away.

Jonathan glanced over his shoulder. He could see the gunman running across the street. Away from the scene. Renee pushed against his chest. His arms tightened around her. He slipped back just enough to look into her eyes. They were wide, full of fear and some of the same fury that ran through him.

"Are you okay?" She was trembling. He ran his fingertips across her cheek.

Her nod was jerky. She opened her mouth but no words came out. Jonathan brushed her cheek with his thumb. Her skin was smooth, warm, perfect. Her eyes met his. He lost connection with their surroundings, and was completely fixed by the pull of her gaze.

Her fingers still gripped his jacket; they tightened. The slightest of pulls brought him closer. His body went taught, his senses heightened by the heat of her body, the silky call of her perfume, the enticement of full lips. Heat spread through him like liquid fire. Her lips parted in the barest of invitations. Her long lashes lowered over eyes filled with hot, forbidden promises. His head lowered toward hers.

"What happened?" a man called out.

Jonathan blinked, jerked his head back. Renee's hands sprang from his jacket. *What the hell, I almost kissed her.*

They jumped to their feet. Renee ran her hands over her face. They were shaking. He fought the need to pull her back into his arms. He turned to face a man heading in their direction.

"Two guys were running," Jonathan said. "One pulled a gun and started firing."

The man scowled. "Idiots. There are kids out here."

The blue lights of a police car came down the street. The man flagged down the car. Jonathan turned to Renee. "We'll have to tell them what we saw."

She nodded. "Of course."

"Are you okay?" A dumb question. They'd been shot at. The bullets may not have been for them, but the gunman hadn't cared that he fired in their direction. Then there was the almost kiss. That shook him more than the bullets flying in their direction.

"I'm fine."

He didn't believe her, but he wasn't going to push. The cop got out of the car. The officer took in the scene before getting Jonathan and Renee's statement. More cops arrived and a manhunt for the gunman started. By the time the police finished with them, and Renee said a hasty good-bye, Jonathan had pushed aside the brief moment and hoped the memory didn't resurface later in his dreams.

CHAPTER 5

Jonathan sat on the wooden deck on the back of the lake house Andre shared with Mikayla. It was a cool day, with a few clouds blocking the rays of the early autumn sun. A small fire in the fire pit provided extra warmth. Jonathan had just finished bringing his friend up to speed on meeting Renee two weeks before, her deal with Joanne, and what happened at the football game.

"Damn," Andre said, shaking his head and taking a sip of the beer in his hand.

Every time Jonathan saw Andre in the year since he and Mikayla got together, his friend seemed more and more relaxed. And not just because he'd traded in tailored power suits for slacks or jeans like he wore today. There weren't any more lines around his dark eyes, or scowls on his face. The love of a good woman tended to do that for a man.

"Did the police catch the guy?" Andre asked.

Jonathan shook his head. "Nope. They said they would call us if they rounded up any suspects. I'm just thankful no one was hurt."

"Good thing you were with Renee." Andre lifted the beer bottle to his mouth. His hand stopped and he chuckled. "Mikayla is going to eat this shit up."

"Eat what up?"

"You shielding Renee from gunfire with your body," Andre said, humor still coating his deep baritone. "This wedding was her opportunity to finally hook you two up. She knows you both have been dodging her attempts to introduce you to each other."

He had been dodging Mikayla's matchmaker attempts. After Karen cheated, he wasn't ready to get back in a relationship. He'd spent the last year rebuilding his wounded ego with quick hook ups and non-committals. He liked Mikayla too much to play with one of her friends like that.

"Well, she's going to be disappointed. There's no way I would hook up with Renee. Not after the stories you told me. Not to mention the dirty trick she and Joanne played after Gigi died."

He had to keep reminding himself. The memory of holding her in his arms had haunted him in the week since the shooting. More details arose every time it popped into his mind. The way her body had curved perfectly in his arms. How her perfume smelled a little like the cherry blossoms that bloomed at his parents' house. Then there were his damned dreams. In those, he'd kissed her and she'd kissed him back. The dreams were the worst.

"My beef wasn't with Renee," Andre said. "It was mostly with Ryan. Renee just took her brother's side in our petty fights. She was always there with that cold ass smirk that she's perfected whenever he got one up on me."

"Are you saying she's not as bad?"

"Ryan is a hot head. Impulsive and in your face. Renee has more of a laid back type of cold. She's more like Uncle Philip. Methodical and calculated. They'll both cut you. You just won't realize it's done until you've bleed out on the floor."

"How did she and Mikayla become friends?" Mikayla was the warmest, realest woman Jonathan had met. Always ready with an open smile and infectious laughter. Mikayla's personality was nothing like Renee's cool, practiced perfection.

"Mikayla says Renee has a heart of gold." Andre shook his head. "I think it was just a little bit of hero worship on Mikayla's part. Renee helped her when she first started at Caldwell Development and kind of took her under her wing. I've said that, but she swears Renee is a sweetheart underneath it all."

"Maybe so," Jonathan said. He brought his beer to his mouth and took a sip then thought about Renee and those girls at the game. She definitely had a soft spot where they were concerned.

"Just watch out for her." Andre gave Jonathan a searching look. "You know what I mean?"

Jonathan shifted forward in the wicker chair to better face Andre. "No. I don't know what you mean."

"Mikayla's going to try to push you two together. Renee's going to be nice because Mikayla is pushing it. Even though she said you two shouldn't get into a fight over the Big House up here, don't be surprised if she brings it up casually. She'll try to squeeze information out of you. I wouldn't be surprised if she asks for your ultimate asking price to prevent a lawsuit."

"She won't change my mind."

"She may try every trick she has."

The warning slithered down Jonathan's spine. "What do you mean?"

"Isaac heard a rumor," Andre said, referring to his brother. "It came from my dad, and you know how unreliable anything Curtis says can be."

Jonathan did. Curtis Caldwell was a cruel and vindictive man. Part of the reason Renee and Andre's sides of the family were at each other's throats was due to the feud between Curtis and his brother Philip. That didn't mean Jonathan's curiosity wasn't piqued.

"What rumor?"

"Just something about her and Daniel LeFranc. That guy is just as crooked as my dad."

"Daniel LeFranc?" Jonathan said slowly. "I don't know him."

"He's a big shot attorney and former state house representative. The family is rumored to be rich, but Isaac thinks the money ran out. They do own lots of land. Land the family held onto for years and said they never would get rid of. About six months ago they sold a chunk of it to Caldwell Development."

Jonathan shrugged and sipped his beer. "So?"

"According to Curtis, that deal was sealed in the bedroom."

"How would he know that?"

"How the hell does my dad know anything? The man has eyes everywhere just to find a way to blackmail people later." The cold anger that always used to accompany Andre before he finally left his father's successful waste management firm to strike out on his own frosted his voice. "If she did, I'm not knocking her. I've done a hell of a lot worse to secure a business deal before. All I'm saying is just be aware that with my family, nothing is what it seems. Especially when it comes to blurring the lines between their business and personal life."

Jonathan didn't respond. He sat back in his chair and considered Andre's words. Coming from anyone else, he wouldn't take rumors seriously, but Andre had fought and played backstabbing games with Renee's family for years. Curtis Caldwell was a Grade A dick, but his information on people was usually good. He too couldn't judge Renee if she'd slept with Daniel to seal a deal. He'd slept with plenty of women for immoral reasons.

Andre's warning did make him re-think her reaction after the shooting. He'd driven himself nearly to blue balls thinking about what kissing her would have been like. Believing she wanted to kiss him back. He'd have to remember that with Renee Caldwell, a kiss may just be a tool to distract him from the fight to regain the Big House.

***

Renee took a deep breath and shook her hands to calm her nerves as she stood at the front door of Mikayla and Andre's home. She was here to support her friend at her wedding. There was no reason for her stomach to flutter or her palms to get sweaty just because Jonathan was also here. She was going to be nice to him, maybe try to figure out a way to get him to drop the lawsuit. She'd played nice with opposing business rivals before. It made no sense to be so wound up over seeing him.

Because you almost kissed him. And it wouldn't have been a planned, premeditated kiss, but an honest to God, passion fueled kiss.

Passion hadn't ruled her life in years. She'd never had gunshots fired in her direction before either. Strange emotions pop up when adrenaline starts pumping. Everyone knew that.

She pushed aside thoughts of what had almost happened with Jonathan, straightened her shoulders, and rang the doorbell. A few seconds later Mikayla answered. A big grin split Mikayla's face. Her dark hair was longer than the last time Renee had seen her and hung in a sleek bob to her shoulders. She looked comfortable in slim fitted black pants and a zippered mint green fleece top.

"Oh my, God, Renee, you look amazing." Mikayla pulled Renee into a big embrace. When she pulled back, she looked over Renee's fitted jeans, blue blouse, and brown leather jacket. Mikayla pulled Renee into the foyer that led directly into a large living area. "How is it possible for you to drive almost four hours and look like you just stepped out of a magazine shoot?"

"I feel like I've been in a car for four hours. You on the other hand look...very happy."

Happy was an understatement, Mikayla seemed to glow from the inside with contentment. For the first time in the years that they'd been friends, Mikayla looked completely comfortable in her own skin. A far cry from the shy, fashionably awkward woman who'd first walked in for a job interview at Caldwell Development. Renee had taken one look at Mikayla and seen a fun project. Taking Mikayla under her wing, she'd helped her with fashion, hair, and makeup, and in the process they'd become best friends.

"I am happy. Moving here was the best thing we could have done. No more butting in by the family. We're starting our life together on our own terms. I couldn't be happier."

Mikayla dragged her through the living area filled with large leather furniture and dark wood to the kitchen. The hardwood floors in the rest of the house continued into the kitchen. White glass front cabinets were complimented by dark gray granite counter tops and a beautiful stone backsplash. The savory aroma of hamburgers sizzling on a griddle on the counter filled the air. Renee's stomach growled.

Renee breathed in deep. "You would make hamburgers."

"And you will eat them," Mikayla replied. She picked up a spatula and flipped the burgers. "It's my wedding weekend and you can't claim low carb or nonfat this weekend."

"I also can't afford to gain ten pounds."

Mikayla eyed Renee's slim frame. "Ten pounds wouldn't hurt you."

Renee walked over and leaned her back against the counter near Mikayla. "Easy for you to say. You have the perfect hourglass figure. If I gain ten pounds, it goes straight to my waistline. Not to any of the areas that could use extra padding." She glanced down at her non-existent cleavage.

"Don't fish for compliments, Miss Supermodel Figure," Mikayla teased. "How was the drive up?"

"Uneventful." Except for nervous thoughts of seeing Jonathan again. "I can't believe you're standing there calm as all get out when you're getting married tomorrow. You should have come to the door exhausted and frazzled, begging me to help you get the last minute things together for the wedding."

Mikayla finished with the burgers and laid the spatula next to the grill. She grinned at Renee. "I'm not turning into the bride from hell. I'm not your cousin, remember."

Renee and Mikayla both rolled their eyes. "The only good thing that came from that wedding is you meeting Andre," Renee said. Andre's stepsister had been the biggest of bridezillas, driving everyone crazy.

"Ain't that the truth," Mikayla said. "Like I told you, this isn't going to be a big deal. I don't have to rush around freaking out over the color of ribbons on bubble bottles, and drive half a dozen bridesmaids crazy with stupid demands."

"Excuse me, miss, but you've already demanded that I eat like a pig this weekend. That sounds like bridezilla." Renee pointed to the burgers.

"Eating a hamburger isn't eating like a pig." Mikayla stared at Renee. After a few seconds she reached over, placed her hand on Renee's and squeezed. "I didn't realize how much I missed you until I saw you."

"Funny, because I realized how much I missed you every day." The loneliness she tried to hide crept into her voice. They hugged and tears stung the back of Renee's eyes. Outside of Mikayla, Ryan was the only other person she'd been able to go to with her true thoughts and feelings. Now Ryan was acting like a fool every weekend and Mikayla was four hours away. Renee knew she'd missed her friend, but right then she realized she was also lonely.

Great Woman of the Year material.

They broke apart and Renee hastily wiped the moisture from her eyes. "The house is beautiful. You've got to show me the view. And, yes, I'll admit it. This isn't some back woods cabin."

"I told you that when we moved here. Give me a second and I'll show you around."

"Am I the first person here?" she tried not to sound to expectant. There was an unfamiliar pickup truck in the driveway. It could have been Andre's, but she remembered Jonathan saying he also drove a truck.

"Dad is coming later," Mikayla said while she put the plate with the burgers in the microwave mounted over the stove. "Isaac isn't coming until tomorrow." When Mikayla turned around her eyes were filled with excitement. "Jonathan is here."

"Is there a reason you're wiggling your eyebrows like that."

"You know exactly why. I've tried to get you to meet him for the past year." Mikayla walked over to Renee and tugged on the arm of her jacket. "You two would be so cute together."

"No we won't."

"How do you know that if you haven't met him?"

"I have met him." She filled Mikayla in on the situation with the house and what happened at the game.

Mikayla placed a hand over her heart. "He protected you from gunfire?"

Renee threw up her hands and walked away. "That's all you heard." She shook her head but couldn't help but laugh.

Mikayla pulled Renee back by her arm. "You have to admit that's pretty heroic."

"It was spur of the moment. Any man would have done the same."

Mikayla twisted her lip and frowned as if she were considering the statement. A second later, she shook her head. "Nah. Any man wouldn't have."

Renee tried to picture Daniel LeFranc doing that and came up blank. "Okay, not any man, but that doesn't mean much."

"You can't tell me you weren't a little thrilled to have him sweep you up in his arms and keep you safe?" Mikayla said with all the dramatics of a fairytale princess.

"I didn't get *swept* up. He did what was practical, and smart."

Mikayla gave her a *whatever* eye roll. "Admit it, Renee. You play hard, but you're a sucker for gentlemanly behavior. You thought it was hot."

"No I didn't." Heat crept up Renee's cheeks.

"Not even a little bit?" Mikayla held her pointer and thumb with barely an inch of space between them. "Just a teeny, tiny bit. I'm your friend and won't tell anyone. You thought it was hot."

Strong arms, the faint scent of masculine soap surrounding her, the way he'd immediately shielded her, the hot look in his eyes after. Her body tingled with the same awareness she'd felt in that moment. She shifted from foot to foot.

"Fine!" Renee held up her hands in surrender. "It was a little, *tiny* bit hot."

"Aha! I knew you two would be good together." Mikayla's voice was triumphant.

"No we aren't. I'm still developing his property."

That took the stars out of Mikayla's brown eyes. "Some things are more important than landing a good deal."

"Nothing's more important than securing a good deal."

Mikayla sighed and shook her head. Renee knew Mikayla didn't agree with her on that. "Do you think his aunt really did get into this deal with you without the grandmother knowing?"

Renee was thankful Mikayla saved the argument about love being more important than business. "Who knows? It happens so often in families that it's a real possibility. It doesn't change the fact that I'm pursuing this deal," she said with emphasis.

"I understand. I know how this works." When Renee nodded, Mikayla placed a hand on Renee's shoulders. "It doesn't change the fact that I empathize with Jonathan in this situation."

"He's your friend through Andre, so I get that. Don't worry, we promised not to make this a big deal over the weekend. No shots will be fired until we return to the battleground on Monday."

"I appreciate you putting business aside for me."

"Of course I would. You're my best friend." She bumped Mikayla with her shoulder. "Even if you did move too far away."

They both laughed. Andre walked into the kitchen. "What's so funny?"

Jonathan was right behind him. Renee stifled her laugh. A pair of dark jeans complemented his strong legs and a tan sweater hugged his muscular torso. Jonathan's blue-gray eyes met hers and she was sucked into the memory of being held protectively against his strong chest. The slow dip of his head to kiss her.

She snapped out of the memory, focused on Andre. She needed to concentrate on getting Jonathan to drop any lawsuits. Not contemplate how freaking good his shoulders looked in a sweater.

"Renee was just telling me about how Jonathan saved her life," Mikayla said. She wrapped an arm around Andre's waist.

"I didn't save her life."

"He didn't save my life," they said at the same time.

Mikayla's devilish gaze drifted between the two. "That's the story I'm telling to everyone that'll listen. Before you two go on about what happened not being a big deal, I've got something more important to worry about."

Renee frowned. "What?"

"I have nothing to decorate the house with for the wedding."

Andre looked down at Mikayla. "You said we didn't need decorations. I don't. You standing next to me is the most beautiful thing I'll need."

Mikayla nearly melted in Andre's arms. Renee felt a pang in her chest. She looked away from their obvious affection and caught Jonathan's gaze. He looked as uncomfortable with their display of affection as she did.

"What do you need?" Renee asked, breaking up the tender scene.

"Nothing," Andre said.

Mikayla pushed him with her hip. "Just a few decorations that we can put up to make the place look more like a wedding. Now that you all are arriving, it's starting to feel more real," she said with a happy grin. "Do you mind going by a craft store and picking up a few things?"

"Of course," Renee said. "Do you want to come with me? It is your wedding."

"Umm…you know I should stay here in case my dad arrives." She looked at Jonathan expectantly. "Jonathan, will you go with Renee?"

Renee glared at her friend. The set up was blatant. Mikayla made the offer innocently without a hint of remorse. Renee forced herself to look at the bright side. This would be a perfect opportunity to be nice to Jonathan. Learn more about his motivations to keep the house. Figure out how to keep the deal. She was a Caldwell. It was time to start acting like a candidate for Woman of the Year instead of acting as boy bedazzled as Destiny.

Jonathan's tight smile said he didn't appreciate the attempt to push them together. "I don't know anything about wedding decorations."

Mikayla waved away his protest. "She'll need help carrying the bags."

Jonathan took a deep breath. Renee waited for him to say no. "Anything for the bride," he said with a tight smile.

Mikayla grinned as if she'd just won a major victory. "Good."

CHAPTER 6

Jonathan drove Renee to a craft store not far from Mikayla and Andre's home. The obvious attempt to put them alone together was frustrating, but Jonathan wouldn't do anything to antagonize Mikayla before her wedding. Besides, the trip gave him a chance to see if Renee really meant what she'd said about leaving the fight for the Big House off the table during the weekend, or if she'd try to sway him as Andre suspected.

"What type of decorations are we looking for exactly?" Jonathan followed Renee into the store. The shelves stuffed with craft items and the smell of potpourri overwhelmed his senses. He hoped Renee had an idea of what they needed.

"I'm not sure...exactly. I've never bought decorations for a wedding before, and any event I put together I pay people to handle decorations for me." She didn't say it with any arrogance. If anything, she sounded as unsure as he felt, looking around the vast store. She gave him a sheepish smile that, hard to believe, made her even more stunning. "That's about the extent of my decorating skills."

Her admission surprised him. Renee seemed so put together he'd expected her to be an expert in everything. "Then why did you agree to pick out the decorations?"

"Mikayla asked me too. Even though it was an obvious attempt to put us together, I didn't want to upset her." She grabbed one of the carts near the door. "Decorations are the least that I can do for her before she moves on and doesn't need me anymore."

She pushed the cart away and looked up at a sign hanging from the ceiling that pointed to the various areas of the store. Jonathan considered her words as he followed. Insecure was the last word he'd use for Renee, but uncertainty filled her voice when she talked about Mikayla moving on.

"It bothers you that she doesn't need you." Jonathan followed her to the section filled with white lace and gauze that he guessed was specifically for wedding decorations.

Renee stopped inspecting the various rolls of tulle and glanced at him. "That's ridiculous. What type of friend would I be if that were the case? I'm happy for Mikayla." She turned back to the tulle.

"You can be happy for her and admit to some sadness that things won't be the same anymore."

Renee pulled a role of silver lined tulle off the shelf. Then grabbed a roll of what looked like pearls. "Friends getting married is usually the end of an era. I'll see her even less than I do now. Eventually she and Andre will have kids, which is another major change. I understand she'll have bigger priorities than keeping our friendship fresh. I'm not sad about that. That's life."

Jonathan frowned as Renee continued to pull more fluffy, white items off the shelves. She sounded clinical, as if what she was saying didn't bother her. He didn't believe her. "It's okay to admit that you're a little sad to see your friend move on."

"Are you sad that Andre is moving on?"

"Of course not." Her smirk challenged him. Jonathan shook his head. "I will miss being able to just call up my boy and say meet me at the bar for drinks. It's okay to admit you'll miss the same with Mikayla."

She glanced at him out of the corner of her eye. "I'm fine, okay."

"Fine," he agreed and turned to the rows of decorations.

A second later Renee sighed. "Look. I'm sorry. I don't really get into talking about my feelings with people I don't know."

He lifted a brow and grinned. "You know me. I saved your life."

She shook her head and chuckled. "If you would have let me stand there, your fight for the house would have been easier."

His smile faded. "I'm upset about the house, but I'd never do anything to hurt you or place you in danger." He meant it. He hated her deal with Joanne, but he couldn't hurt Renee. If faced with a similar situation, he'd protect her again.

Her cringe made her nose crinkle in a cute way. "I'm sorry. That was a bad joke. I never claimed to be a comedian."

"Don't give up your day job," he teased.

"It's a good thing I turned down your offer for dinner that night," she said flippantly and studied the decorations on the shelf. "How awkward would that have been to run into each other the next day?"

"It would have only been awkward if I'd gotten what I wanted that night."

Wide eyes met his. "What did you want?"

"I wanted to kiss you. Slow, easy and thoroughly."

She lifted her chin and looked away. "Then it's definitely a good thing I turned you down." Her voice was cool, but her eyes had flashed with something hot and tempting before she'd broken eye contact. "I am purchasing your family's land."

The reminder cooled the thrill of flirting with her. Slightly. He'd never been good at ignoring it when a beautiful woman flirted. That part of him wanted to get beneath Renee's polished exterior to discover if the heat in her eyes burned as hot as he imagined.

Jonathan dipped his head and leaned in, making sure she couldn't break eye contact. "Don't worry, Renee. I'm willing to do everything in my power to stop you."

She swallowed hard. For a second, she looked flustered. "Does that include trying to seduce me?"

"Oh no, sugar. If I seduce you, it'll have nothing to do with the land."

Her tongue darted over her lower lip. "Don't call me sugar."

Warning bells told him not to start something he couldn't, shouldn't, finish with Renee. The dumb part of his brain hijacked his mouth. "Can't help it. That night I dreamed of kissing you, and in my dream you were sweeter than honey."

Her brows drew together. "That sounds a lot like an attempt at seduction." She sounded unimpressed. Almost bored. This time there was no telltale flare of heat. She tilted her head to the side. "Seduction won't work. I'm not ruled by those baser instincts. So please don't waste your time or mine. Now that you're aware, what will be your next attempt?"

In an instant, she was the cool, perfect businesswoman. He liked the warm, flirty Renee much better. "Why should I tell you my war plans?"

She shrugged and turned back to her search for decoration. "Tell me, don't tell me. The results will be the same. I always win."

"But you're not ruthless."

"You don't have to be ruthless to be savvy and successful. I don't see how that changes anything."

"According to Mikayla you also have a heart. You've got a sense of decency and of family pride."

"And?" She was facing him again. Confusion all over her beautiful face. "My family pride is exactly why I don't back down from a sale or a fight."

"But that family pride, that decency in you is also why deep down you know that working with Joanne is wrong. She took advantage of my grandmother and signed that contract with you under false pretenses."

"I don't get in the middle of other people's family dramas."

"But you are in the middle. You will get pulled into the lawsuit and Caldwell Development will be implicated in the nasty business of taking advantage of a sick woman right before she died."

Renee's jaw set with determination. "Your aunt had power of attorney, which means she had the legal right to go into any agreement she wanted with Caldwell Development and whomever else she chose on your grandmother's behalf. You can try as hard as you want to pull us into a smear campaign to make yourself feel better about the fact that your family slipped one over on you." She stepped toe to toe with him. Her dark eyes met his boldly and with angry determination. "I'd like to see you win that one. Many have tried. None have succeeded."

Her challenge awakened the competitive streak in him. Her nearness, the fight in her eyes and the confidence in her voice awakened his desire.

"Is that a warning, sugar?" He couldn't help but throw out the endearment.

"Oh, no, sweetheart," she said, her voice silky, seductive and edged with steel. "That's a fact."

She patted his chest. A taunting gesture, but it still made his pulse buck like an angry bull. She slowly turned on her heels and sauntered down the aisle. His gaze roamed over her back, taking in the sensual sway of her hips. She glanced over her shoulder and cockily raised one brow. The sexy taunt hit him straight in the stomach. He didn't need her, but damned if a part of him didn't want her.

***

Renee hung one of the tulle bows she'd made on the rail of Mikayla's deck then stepped back to admire her handy work. Two hours of internet videos and a couple more practicing, and she was pretty darn proud of her bow. The sun was just rising over the trees and reflected off the mist rising from the lake. Renee pulled her thick cardigan sweater tight to protect against the cold air. Her finger tips tingled, so did the end of her nose, but she wouldn't go back inside until she finished getting the deck ready for Mikayla's wedding that afternoon.

The sliding door behind her opened. No one had been up when she'd crept out here thirty minutes ago to decorate. She hadn't expected anyone to be up this early. She turned and the air froze in her throat. Jonathan stepped onto the deck, two steaming mugs in his hand. The inviting aroma of coffee filled the air.

He held out one mug to her. "You're up early."

"I wanted to get this done before Mikayla and I go for hair and makeup this morning." She eyed the cup he held out. "You brought me coffee?"

She couldn't hide the suspicion in her voice. They'd kept their distance after returning from the store the day before. After they'd drawn the line in the sand. She'd expected to be more annoyed with him after he'd accused her of working with his aunt. Instead, she'd been a little exhilarated by the encounter. More than a little, and not due to the thrill that came from trying to win a business deal. Her exhilaration had come just from being so close to Jonathan. The intensity of his blue-gray gaze, the tingles along her spine when he called her sugar.

"Yes, I brought you coffee. It's cold and you're out here wearing nothing but a sweater and tights. I thought you'd appreciate it."

She did appreciate it. The gesture warmed her way more than the coffee probably would. She carefully took the mug from his hand. Making sure that their hands didn't touch. "Thank you. And I'm wearing leggings. Not tights."

His gaze dropped to her legs. He admired them for a second longer than necessary. She enjoyed the look more than she should. "Either way, they're too thin for a cold morning."

She hadn't thought about the weather when she'd come out here to decorate. Only about getting the work finished for Mikayla's special day.

She took a hesitant sip of the coffee. It was perfect. "This is good."

He shrugged and took his own sip. "One teaspoon of sugar and a little cream. That's all you put in your coffee last night."

Pleasure heated her cheeks. He'd paid attention to how she made her coffee? She took another sip to stop herself from smiling. "I'm surprised you brought it to me. Yesterday we pretty much sealed the deal as enemies."

"Wedding day cease fire," he said. "We know where the other stands on this issue."

They stood on opposite ends of the battlefield. Jonathan wasn't going to back down. Neither was she. Though his accusation that Caldwell Development had worked with Joanne to take advantage of his grandmother had hurt. She would never stoop to something so low, but couldn't say the same thing about her father or Ryan. Everything was fair game when it came to business. That's what made them so successful. Though she hated that he'd called out her sense of family pride and decency as a reason why she'd back out of the deal, he hadn't been far off. The idea of getting the land because of Joanne's deception made Renee more uncomfortable than those too tight shoes she'd worn the night she'd first met him. A discomfort she was trying hard to ignore.

"Good coffee won't make me weaken my stance."

"You wouldn't be the woman I took you for if it did." He strolled over and looked at the two bows she'd hung so far. "I thought you didn't know anything about decorating?"

"I don't."

"These bows say otherwise." He flicked one with his finger then glanced at her with a raised eyebrow.

She shrugged and picked up another bow from the pile on the deck. "You can learn how to do anything if you watch enough internet videos."

She took a sip of the coffee then set down the cup to hang the bow.

"You learned how to do this in one night just from watching videos?" Disbelief and a touch of admiration filled his deep voice.

"Yes."

"Impressive."

"Thank you." She kept her voice cool, hiding the warm rush of pleasure caused by his compliment. He was the enemy. Not the type of guy she wanted to like. She had to remember that.

"What do you do, Jonathan? Outside of fighting developers?" She alternated between taking sips of her coffee and draping tulle between the rails on the deck.

"I work for the conservation district. Mostly with small farmers who want to develop conservation plans that identify ways to help preserve their land and improve the health of their heard. The district provides grants that can help them implement the plan."

"I thought you were just a farmer?"

The skin tightened around his jaw. "Is there something wrong with being *just a farmer*?"

She shook her head, realizing he'd misunderstood her intention. "No. I didn't mean it like that. I didn't realize that you helped people, too."

He seemed to relax and understanding filled his eyes. "Helping people is one of the reasons I like my work. My dad and I raise cows, but we're small. I know how hard it can be for a new farmer or a small farmer to get the help needed to make their farms sustainable, because I'm in their shoes. I get to help the little guy."

As a person who liked giving back, she couldn't help but respect that in another person. "Impressive."

His gaze darted away and he took a sip of his coffee. Renee's lips tipped upward. If she didn't know any better, she'd say he was trying hard not to show how much her compliment pleased him as well.

"That's big coming from a Woman of the Year nominee," he said.

The tightness that liked to take over her body when reminded of her nomination squeezed her. "You know about that?"

"I looked you up after we meet at the Big House. That was one of the things that came back."

Smart move on his part. They were about to get into a legal battle with each other. She'd looked him up too. So had her father.

"It's no big deal." She returned to hanging the tulle.

"It read like a pretty big deal. A big fancy awards dinner and a proclamation at the state house. That's nothing to sneeze at. My Aunt Joanne was once on that nomination committee."

The suspicious note in his voice raised her guard. "That sounds like a shot fired in the middle of a cease fire."

He shook his head. "Just an observation."

She faced him and glared. The morning sunlight seemed completely absorbed by the curly dark strands of his hair. His thermal T-shirt hung like a second skin over his huge, muscled body. Despite her frustration, she couldn't stop the feminine appreciation of his utter maleness.

"Your aunt didn't nominate me. The director of the Still Hopes Family Shelter did. I volunteer there twice a week to mentor the teenage girls on Thursdays, for a book club with the mothers on Tuesdays, and I serve on the board. I'm also the chair of the Caldwell Development Foundation. I used my influence at the foundation to raise funds to build them a new shelter that allows them to house more families. While I appreciate her nomination, I did not ask her to do it. Nor did I partner with your aunt because of the nomination."

"Why do you do all of that?"

"Because I want to." She turned away from him and picked up the last bow. The faster she finished this, the faster she could get back into the house and end this useless conversation.

"I'm sorry. I didn't realize you cared."

Renee spun to face him. "You didn't realize I cared? So, what, you thought I only went down there to get news articles and good press for Caldwell Development? Or because I hoped for a Woman of the Year nomination? Not because women and children, some of whom have been abused or taken advantage of, were threatened to be put into a shelter with men just like the ones they'd escaped from. Oh, no, of course I wouldn't do that. I'm an evil Caldwell who takes advantage of dying old women as well."

She turned away and wrapped the edges of the bow around the last rail with angry, jerky movements. She knew she was cold, calculated when it came to business. She had to be, when she was raised in this family. That view of her typically didn't bother her. Why in the world was it giving her such heartburn because he saw her that way? She needed him to see her like that. He was on the other side of the battlefield. She shouldn't *like* him or care what he thought.

A large hand gently wrapped around her upper arm. Renee froze. In the cool morning air, his hard body was a statue of welcoming warmth. It took everything in her not to lean back against him.

"I was wrong for saying that. I'm trying hard not to like you, Renee. You're not making that easy."

His voice reminded her of bourbon. Warm, husky, just enough of an edge to set her body on fire. She tilted her head to the side and looked at him over her shoulder. He stood so close, just a slight lean backward and a tilt of her jaw upward and she could kiss him. Her eyes dropped to his lips.

He eased her around to face him. His eyes blazed with a desire that both thrilled and terrified her. No man had ever looked at her so intently. As if he could devour her right there and do it so pleasurably she'd beg for it. She wanted to be devoured. She wanted to lay her hand on his chest. Feel if his heart pounded as hard as hers beneath all that muscle. Her fingers twitched. At the last second, she stopped herself. She stepped back.

His hand tightened for a split second then dropped. He stepped back.

His broad shoulders rose and fell with his quick breaths.

Her cell phone rang, breaking the moment. Good, a distraction. They both needed one right now. Renee hurried to where it sat on the opposite end of the deck where she'd started. Ryan's number. The perfect distraction.

"Excuse me," she said to him in a cool, businesslike voice. She didn't wait for his response, just answered and slipped through the back door to talk.

"Good morning, Ryan," she said. She walked into the kitchen.

"How's the wedding?" Ryan's sarcastic greeting scraped across her nerves.

"I hope that isn't why you called. Resentment doesn't look good on you." Renee replied coolly.

"I'm happy for Mikayla. If she wants to tie herself to our arrogant cousin for the rest of her life that's her prerogative."

"Ryan," Renee's voice was full of warning. "I'm hanging up unless you have a point."

"Are you getting anywhere with convincing Jonathan to sell?"

Renee leaned one hand against the kitchen island. The other gripped the phone. "That's not why I'm here."

"It's part of the reason you're there. I know Dad asked you to use your connection to Jonathan through Mikayla to try to change his mind. Are you making any progress?"

She thought of the battle lines they'd drawn the day before. "No. I haven't changed his mind. If anything, I think he's going to fight harder."

"I'm not surprised. He's Andre's friend. Of course he'd be just as stubborn," Ryan said, his tone exasperated. "Doesn't matter how much he fights. We will beat him in court."

"I told him that myself."

"Good. The aunt asked us to meet on Monday. Will that be a problem?"

Mentally she went over her schedule for Monday and couldn't remember any important meetings off hand. "Shouldn't be. I can meet with her, but why?"

"Something about making sure our legal stories are the same."

Renee's lips pressed together. "More like Joanne did a shady deal and now wants Caldwell Development's legal team to help cover."

She shouldn't care. The project was the most important thing. Yet the idea of being the vile person Jonathan accused her of, someone who would ignore a dead woman's wishes, twisted her insides.

"Who cares why?" Ryan said. "We want the land. This project will put us ahead of development in that area. That's what's most important."

Renee chewed on her lower lip.

"Don't we?" Ryan asked.

Renee blinked and shook her head. Guilt was not an emotion worth shucking a lucrative deal over. Not for a Caldwell. "Of course. Getting the Wright property is the most important thing. I'll do what I can on my end."

"Good. I'll tell Dad that we'll handle the meeting on Monday."

"Okay. I'll call you when I'm back in town tomorrow."

The call ended and Renee stared at the blank screen of her phone. She felt off. Wrong even. She didn't like the feeling. She never second-guessed a business decision. Especially not because of what a man would think. An unsuitable man. This was exactly why feelings and business deals didn't go together.

Is it really your feelings or because Joanne's deal is shady?

She heard the shuffling sound of feet behind her. Dang, she'd hoped to be finished with the bows and flowers on the deck by now. She turned to tell whomever it was to stay inside until she finished. Her newfound skill with tulle bow making was her small surprise for Mikayla.

Jonathan stood in the kitchen's entryway. The impossibly sexy smile and warm eyes from earlier replaced with a hard jaw and blue-gray ice chips staring at her. He must have overheard part of her conversation. Guess he wouldn't have any problem not liking her now. That was good. She'd tell herself that over and over if she had to.

That didn't mean she would stand there and freeze under his icy glare. "I'll go finish the deck." She stood and crossed to the door. He quickly got out of her way. "Thanks again for the coffee. Are you coming back out?"

Stupid question. Hanging out with him was not going to change their situation. Only make it worse.

"I'll pass."

She nodded. "Suit yourself." She went back out on the deck and forced herself to concentrate on the decorations. Not how every redrawing of the lines between her and Jonathan bothered her so much.

CHAPTER 7

Jonathan found himself alone with Renee, again. He shifted away from the dishes he was washing in the sink and watched Renee sweep. She still wore the dress from the wedding. Tight, lacey arms, mid-thigh hem. She was the best damned looking sweeper he'd ever seen.

Mikayla was nothing if not persistent. The wedding had been small and simple. Himself, Andre's brother, Isaac, Mikayla's dad and Renee. There wasn't much to clean up after, but since Mikayla and Andre had to leave immediately after dinner to catch a flight to Saint Lucia, Renee offered to stick around and help clean. He should have seen it coming, but Mikayla insisting Jonathan stick around and help out until Renee left had surprised him. Mostly because he'd been thinking along the same lines.

"The wedding was nice," he said.

They'd barely spoken to each other since he'd walked into the kitchen earlier and overheard her declaration that getting his family's land was her number one priority. Not talking was probably better. He liked Renee in the rare moments he saw beneath her ice princess exterior.

But they were the only two in the house. Isaac left soon after dinner and Renee insisted that Mikayla's dad didn't have to stick around to clean up. The silent treatment was kind of stupid, even for adults who were on opposite sides of a business deal.

"Mmmhmm. Very nice." She continued to sweep.

Jonathan turned back to the dishes. She didn't want to talk, fine. He wouldn't force her to talk. Didn't need to hear her gab about what her wedding would be like one day. He'd attended two weddings with his ex-girlfriend Karen and after each, she'd described what their wedding would be like. He hadn't taken her seriously. Maybe that was why she'd cheated.

No thoughts of Karen tonight. Sad and melancholy was not a good look after a wedding. Renee sighed behind him. It was a soft sigh, she probably hadn't realized he'd heard it, but he had. Maybe he wasn't the only one pushing back thoughts of a terrible ex.

Weddings were good for pulling up memories of failed relationships.

"Why are you single?"

Her head jerked up. "What?"

"You heard the question. You being single makes no sense. You're beautiful, you're involved with the community, and you're successful. Where's your man?"

Renee's head cocked to the side and a brow rose. "If Mikayla had her way I'd be looking at him."

Something that wasn't exactly negative stirred in him at the thought. He held up a hand in surrender. Not going there. "Sorry, just trying to make conversation." He turned back to the dishes.

"I just haven't met the right guy yet." A few seconds later. "Where's your woman?"

"With the guy she left me for."

He glanced at her over his shoulder and caught her wince. Bad, *bad* line of conversation.

"Oh, sorry."

He shrugged. The movement was easy. Should be. He'd worked extra hard at making his tone and reactions to his relationship with Karen look like it wasn't difficult to talk about. That she hadn't sent his ego back to pre-adolescent levels. "Shit happens."

"Still, sorry. No one likes being cheated on. You seem like a decent enough guy."

He smirked and shook his head. "Yeah, thanks."

He rinsed the dishes in the sink. He didn't hear her moving behind him. Could feel her eyes on him. Studying him. *Way to go, Jonathan. You should have stayed quiet.*

"Did you love her?"

No one asked him that. Most just went straight into telling him how terrible of a person Karen had to have been to cheat on him. The cheating had been terrible, but he hadn't done much beforehand to prevent her from straying. That's what dug at him the most.

"Yes. Problem is, I realized that a little too late." He placed the last dish in the drying rack then pulled out a towel.

"Is that why she left?"

Left. He nearly laughed except the entire situation hadn't been the least bit humorous. "I didn't ask. When another guy opens the door to your woman's place, you don't stick around to find out why she's sleeping around."

"It's good that she didn't know you loved her." Her voice was matter-of-fact.

Jonathan turned away from the sink. He leaned against it and watched her. Her expression was all seriousness. "Why?"

"There are a lot of things I've done wrong in relationships, but cheating isn't one of them. It's smarter and much more efficient to end a relationship when it's no longer beneficial than to go out and bring in a third party who will only cause confusion or bring drama. If she thought she had doubts about the seriousness of your relationship, she should have asked you. Instead, she sneaked around and exposed you and her unnecessarily to a multitude of problems. Basically, she didn't deserve you or your love."

His mom, sister, even Andre had told him Karen didn't deserve him. Every time, the words seemed like the things they were supposed to say. Renee's same evaluation in her clipped, no nonsense professional tone struck him more. Made a little of the blame he carried in his own heartbreak go away. Made him like her a little more.

Getting the Wright property is my number one priority.

He forced himself to remember those words. Renee was sexy, smart, and dead on about his relationship with Karen, but that didn't take away that on Monday he was dropping the first bomb in the fight. After hearing that conversation, he'd known it was time.

He searched for a conversation he could switch too that would hopefully lighten the mood. "You're really cool with Mikayla's dad."

She'd spent at least two hours with him the night before watching a war documentary Mr. Summers had found on television. Which made the fact that she'd stayed up later watching videos of bow making and gotten up before everyone else to decorate even more impressive. Renee Caldwell was a bit of a machine.

Renee smiled and lifted a shoulder. "I like Mr. Summers. He's always treated me like another daughter. There's no pressure from him, just fun."

He frowned. "No pressure?"

"You've met Andre's dad, right?" she asked.

Jonathan nodded.

"My dad isn't as mean as him, but they are brothers. There's a lot of pressure that comes with it. Mr. Summers just wants to make sure Mikayla and I are eating enough and aren't working too hard. It's nice. Indulging him in a few war documentaries isn't that big a deal."

She turned away and continued sweeping. If Renee's dad had a fifth of the drive that Andre's dad had, then he could understand why she liked to indulge Mr. Summers.

"Still, war documentaries. I'm surprised you didn't fall asleep."

Her laughter was light and airy. It also made him want to hear her laugh again. "If you've sat through enough business meetings like I have, you can stay awake through almost anything. But I don't mind watching them. My great grandfather fought in World War Two. My dad told us some of the stories he remembered, but he doesn't know much. His father wasn't big on passing down family history. The little I do know made watching the documentary and thinking of a family member fighting more interesting. I wish we knew more about him."

Jonathan leaned back against the counter. "A lot of the men in my family, on the Wright side, served in the military. My dad can trace back military service to the revolution. Before Joanne cleaned out the house, there was a picture of the first Jacob Wright who served as a captain in the Confederate Army. My dad's named after him."

"What about your mom's side?" If she heard the bitterness that crept into his voice, he was glad she let that go.

He shook his head "We could only trace back to about the early 1900s. My mom remembers her great grandmother telling stories that the family came to America via the middle passage. But actual records only show that her far removed grandparents lived around Sumter, but were possibly born as slaves on smaller farms. We were never part of a big plantation house."

"One side confederate heroes, the other side slaves. You have an interesting backstory."

"My grandfather didn't see it that way. When Dad met my mom in college at a student rights rally, their histories didn't matter. They fell in love and eloped. My grandfather quickly disowned my father."

"Just because your mom is black?"

Jonathan chuckled. "He never said that in public, but we heard it plenty enough in private. He called me and my sister mutts whenever Dad tried to bring us around for a visit. That was nice compared to the words he threw out to describe Momma. Gigi always tried to make it better. She actually tried to be a grandmother to us when she could and came to visit us a few times. She promised to leave the house to me. Her way of righting the wrong. It should have gone to my father, then to me. The way it had for generations before."

She sucked in a breath. He glanced up. Crap, he hadn't meant to get into that. So much for lightening the mood.

"I had no idea."

"Most people didn't."

He turned around and pulled a plate out of the rack to dry with the towel. It was time to finish cleaning and get the hell out of here. Not spend more time pouring his heart out to Renee.

"Did you ever consider joining any branch of military?" Renee asked.

He was grateful she'd realized the subject needed changing yet again. "For a little bit in high school. My parents are big on public service. I joined JROTC in high school and hated it. Too much structure. I knew the military wasn't for me."

"Hmm, I can't possibly see how you wouldn't like structure. Mr. Biker, farmer, conservationist. You're all over the place," she said, chuckling.

"I'm eccentric. Get it right."

"Okay, eccentric. I joined JROTC in high school and I loved it."

"Really?" He couldn't mask the shock in his voice.

"Structure and order is my middle name. It was the Air Force JROTC. I guess the structure of the military kind of suited my personality because I was going to join the Air Force." A dreamy faraway look filled her eyes. "I even had the poster on my door. I pictured myself flying a fighter jet. Zipping above the clouds and saving the world."

He tried to picture her in military fatigues, but his brain went south and he pictured her in one of those sexy soldier costumes sold during Halloween. Two piece, with her flat stomach out, thigh-high boots and fishnet stockings.

"Why are you smiling?"

Jonathan blinked and snapped out of his fantasy. "Nothing. Just picturing you in the military. You'd probably make a good drill sergeant."

She chuckled. "Probably so."

"Why didn't you enlist?"

"You're a Caldwell and your duty is to this family," she said, deepening her voice. "Not to risk your life trying to fly planes. Seriously, Renee, you're too pretty for that." She smirked. "The last part was from my mom."

"That's insulting."

She blinked several times and her lips parted. A second later, her mouth curved up in a cute smile. "Thank you." Appreciation filled her voice.

He felt like he'd given her something. He wasn't sure what, but he liked the feeling. "You're welcome."

They stared at each other. He got the urge to cross the room, wrap his arm around her waist and pull her body against his. Kiss her like he almost had that night at the school. Like he'd wanted to do ever since seeing her across the hotel parking lot.

She licked her lips. He followed the movement. His skin tightened, along with other parts of his body.

Renee turned away first. Man he was glad she was sensible. Once again, he was forgetting that she was not for kissing.

She bent over to sweep the pile of dust into the dustpan. The back of her little blue lace dress rose and revealed the smooth skin along the back of her thighs. Jonathan's eyes trained on her upturned ass. She stood just as quickly and marched over to the trash.

Jonathan shook his head and turned away to finish drying the dishes. *Not for kissing.* He could not kiss her.

They finished shortly after and Renee locked up the house before they walked to their cars.

"Thanks for helping," she said when they stood next to her Cadillac. "Even though Mikayla kind of forced your hand."

He grinned. "It's no problem. I wouldn't have felt right leaving you here alone anyway."

"I'm pretty sure we're safe from gun men and stray bullets out here."

She glanced around at the dark and quiet surroundings of the lakeside neighborhood. When she looked back at him, she frowned.

"What?"

"I'm sorry, there's lint or something in your hair and it's bugging me." She stepped forward then reached up to pull something out of his hair. "Things on people's faces and in their hair is a pet peeve of mine. I know it's embarrassing when pointed out, but better than walking around looking foolish."

He barely heard her words. Her body was warm and almost brushed his. The smell of her perfume heated his blood. When she moved to step backward, male instinct had his hand out and on her waist before he could even comprehend what he was doing.

Her eyes widened. He expected her to pull back. She didn't. Her body softened ever so slightly. The hand that pulled the lint from his hair had frozen. Slowly, she lowered it to his shoulder. Her touch hesitant, barely a whisper.

He wanted her to really touch him.

Ignoring the plethora of warning bells in his head, he kissed her. Then waited for her to stiffen, pull back, slap him. The hand on his shoulder pressed into the muscle, pulled him forward.

He wrapped his arm completely around her small waist, brought her closer. Renee's other hand came up between them to rest on his chest. A small barrier. A reminder that they both knew this shouldn't be happening. That didn't stop him from kissing her as thoroughly as he could. What was the point of doing the forbidden if you didn't enjoy the moment? If he didn't savor every sweet taste of her lips or commit to memory the confident way her lips pressed to his.

The pressure of her hand against his chest increased. Slight enough he could continue to kiss her and he had a feeling she'd acquiesce. But what would he do if she did? Especially in an empty house with a large guest bed a few steps away.

No, that was a forbidden pleasure they couldn't afford to indulge in.

He eased away from her. Small fingers curled against his chest. For a second he thought she was going to pull him back. Then she blinked away the dazed look in her eyes and hastily stepped back. She cleared her throat and raised her hand to her lips. He expected her to wipe away his kiss. Instead, she pressed her fingers against them. He hoped she kept her hand there to hold on to the feeling. He wanted to hold onto the feeling. His body was tight, hard, and reeling for more.

"I'll follow you out," he said, mostly because he didn't want to do the *we shouldn't have done that* conversation. He knew that already. Didn't mean he didn't want to do it again.

She nodded. "Sure." She turned away and opened her car door.

Jonathan licked his lips. He could still taste her. Cool and sweet, effortlessly seductive. Maybe it was his imagination. Shaking his head, he walked to his car.

"Jonathan," she called. When he faced her, the corner of her lips lifted up in a small smile. "I enjoyed the ceasefire."

Then she slipped into her front seat and shut the door. He lightly ran his fingertips across his lips, then dropped his hand. So had he, no matter how reckless. The ceasefire had ended hours ago. He should have remembered that instead of kissing the enemy, but he couldn't muster even a sliver of regret.

CHAPTER 8

"Great job, Renee," Ryan said.

He'd snapped Renee out of a daydream and back to the present. She sat up in her chair and swiveled it toward her office door. He marched across the room and slapped a stack of papers on her desk. She'd barely heard his words, but she picked up on his agitation.

"What are you talking about?"

She picked up the papers. They'd been served. She frowned and scanned the documents. Shots fired. The ceasefire was definitely over.

"He's put a freeze on the development," Renee said, still scanning the papers. "He's accusing Caldwell Development of working with his aunt to take advantage of his grandmother." She stared at Ryan. "We had nothing to do with that."

He'd accused her of the same. The words had pricked her conscious then. Seeing them in black and white made her blood boil today.

"Do you know what happens if word of this lawsuit gets out?" Ryan asked.

It would be damaging to their reputation. Their dad had worked hard to build their reputation as a strong, family-centered development company. Being better than her cousin's side of the family went deeper than just being more successful. Philip wanted to prove he wasn't the same ruthless, heartless, blackmailing businessman as his brother. This lawsuit would go against every bit of that.

"Has Daddy seen this yet?"

"Not yet, but this isn't something you can hide from him."

Renee's eyes snapped to Ryan's. "I'm not going to hide this from him. I don't hide things from him."

"Sorry, I forgot I was talking to the perfect twin."

Renee stood and glared at Ryan. "What's your problem, Ryan? Do you want to figure out a way to fix this or did you come in here for another reason? If it's not the first, then save it. We're meeting with Joanne in a few minutes and we need a game plan with this new piece of news."

"This is your project. I'm just the messenger. You can figure out how to fix this problem." He turned to walk away.

Renee rushed from around her desk and stood in front of him. "What's gotten into you? You call me on Saturday to remind me how important this development is, and today you're acting like it's my fault we've been sued. Newsflash, we knew it was coming. I don't understand why you're giving me grief."

"Maybe if you'd worked harder for the family at the wedding instead of fawning over Mikayla and Andre, we wouldn't have been served with a lawsuit."

She stepped back. "You're still on that? She's my best friend, Ryan. My best friend that you hurt. You can't get mad every time she moves on and I support her. Don't take your issues out on me. We've got more important things to worry about." She pointed to the papers on her desk.

There was a knock on the door. Renee spun to the administrative assistant. "Joanne Wright-Miller is here."

Renee nodded. "Put her in the conference room. I'll be there in a second." When the assistant walked away, she looked back at Ryan. "Are you going to help me fix this or not?"

"My dedication to this family is just as strong as yours. If not more, considering everything I've done to try to make our father see that."

Some of Renee's anger melted away. Ryan was dedicated to the family, but because he was more emotional, he was always viewed as the screw up. He wasn't, not by far, but lately he'd taken the role of family troublemaker seriously.

"I know that, Ryan." She placed her had on his arm.

He pulled out of her grasp. "We'll tell Joanne that we'll back out of the contract if she doesn't get this lawsuit dropped."

Renee let him drop the touchy subject. Ryan was so volatile lately. Alternating between carefree and happy to angry and brooding. She wished there was a way to get her brother out of this funk.

"Counter sue her for bringing us in under false pretenses." Renee nodded. "I'm fine with that, but I don't want to lose the land. There are two schools going up in that area and a new shopping center. If we drop out and another developer snatches it up, we're behind the ball."

She respected Jonathan for fighting for what was promised to him, but respect didn't change her position on doing what she could to salvage a lucrative deal. If for some reason Caldwell Development lost she'd feel no regrets suing Joanne for wrapping them into her hateful vendetta.

"Let her think we're willing to sue. That'll give her more of an impetus to get this cleaned up with her family. I don't want our lawyers working on the case between her and her family."

"Neither do I. It'll only hurt our image." She bit her lower lip and considered the options. "In public we'll stay out of it, but I can still try to work on Jonathan without having lawyers involved."

"Do you think he'll listen to you? How did things go at the wedding?"

Her face heated. Renee walked to get her tablet off the desk to hide her reaction. Ryan could always tell when she was into a guy. He'd known she was going in that direction with Daniel and warned her off. If only she'd listened, she may have avoided heartbreak and embarrassment. She could only imagine the warnings he'd have about her feelings for Jonathan.

"His grandmother promised the land to make up for his grandfather disowning his father when he married a black woman. I think he wants it because of that promise, but I don't think the property holds much sentimental value. Not if his grandfather was a hateful as Jonathan made him seem."

She turned back to Ryan.

"He's fighting out of spite?"

She shrugged. "Maybe."

"If it's out of spite then there has to be a price to buy him out," Ryan said. "What did you offer him?"

"Nothing. We never got that far in discussions."

Ryan scowled and looked nearly identical to their father. She understood the scowl. That was the main thing Philip asked of her when she was there. Find out Jonathan's selling price. She'd been too infatuated with a pair of sexy blue-gray eyes, and one steaming, but not quite enough kiss.

"I'll find out," she said before Ryan could say anything else about her forgetting the family at the wedding. "You may be right. If he's fighting out of spite, then he's mad about the broken promise, not the sell. Get our lawyers to draft a non-disclosure agreement. When he tells me what it'll take to make this go away I'll get him to sign and the entire thing will disappear."

Ryan nodded. "Good. Now let's go put a little pressure on Joanne to make her family happy."

Renee followed Ryan out of the office and toward the conference room. The plan was solid and typically would work. Jonathan had no real reason to want the house. Not if what he said about his grandfather was true. Still, something in her gut told her that asking for his selling point would only extend, not end, the war.

***

The sun was high, providing a small amount of warmth and bright rays of sunshine behind the various clouds hovering over Jonathan in the pasture to the west of his house. He was putting the finishing touches on the walls of the small corral for his niece's birthday party the next day. He always hosted his niece's party. He thought the pony rides had something to do with it.

His sister Nadine let out a heavy sigh and pushed her curly, reddish-brown hair away from her face. "Maybe we should let Caldwell Development have the place."

Nadine's cool, light brown complexion was clear, and her amber color eyes were darkened with old memories. The chill in the air put a slight red tinge on the tip of her nose and her high cheekbones. Despite the chill, Nadine wore a thin, long-sleeve T-shirt with her slim fitting pants. Jonathan had given her his jacket to try to warm her up.

"No," Jonathan shook his head.

"Why not? The place has nothing but bad memories for both of us. Listening to the terrible things he said about Momma. The way he always offered Dad money if he left the colored whore and her mulatto mutts."

Jonathan scowled at the memory. "Because having the place is the only payback I'll get toward the evil bastard. I hope he turns over a hundred times in his grave when I get it."

"But do you really want to live there, Jonny?" Nadine raised a brow and peered at him. "Do you really want to live day by day with the hurtful memories that place holds?"

"They're not all hurtful." He tightened the last screw that completed the small metal circle. "Remember when we pretended the pecan trees out front were our enchanted forest?"

Nadine's lips curved up in a nostalgic smile. "I was the fairy princess. Even though you said I couldn't be a fairy and a princess."

"It wasn't fair," Jonathan argued. "Especially since you said I could only be a prince. A prince with no magic."

Nadine laughed. "Then there was the time Gigi showed us the trail and small house he built for her off in the woods. I thought it was her playhouse."

"More like her escape house for when he went on a rant," Jonathan said, picturing the small hut built in the woods surrounding the Big House. Gigi had set up the place like a mini home, complete with lace doilies, curtains, and a wood-burning stove. He and Nadine would go to the house when they got tired of sitting on the porch, listening to their father argue with his father.

Nadine sighed and used her toe to dig into the ground. "Fine, there were a few good memories. Not enough to make me want to live there. Besides, you have your own place."

"It's not just about living there. The place should be Dad's. Would have been if our grandfather wasn't a bigot."

"Then it's Dad's fight, not yours, Jonny. If he doesn't—"

"She took advantage of Gigi," he said quickly, his tone sharp with anger. "The only person who cared about us. The one person who wanted to make things right. Aunt Joanne said to hell with what her own mother wanted and signed the place away." He gave one last jerk on the screw and pushed away. "That's not right, Nadine. I can't let her get away with that."

He sighed and ran a hand over his face. Frustration and anger clawed his insides. "I can't let that go. Not getting the place is another broken promise and thinly veiled insult from a family that rejected us."

Nadine walked around to his side of the corral and faced him. "You're right. I hate thinking about our visits there. I wouldn't care if it burned to the ground, but for Gigi's sake, I understand. If you're going to fight for it, then I'll stand beside you."

Jonathan placed his hands over hers on the edge of the corral and squeezed. "Thank you."

Nadine smiled then sighed. "So we're fighting Caldwell Development. That's not going to be pretty, or easy."

Jonathan turned away and packed up his tools. "It would have been just as ugly and hard if Joanne had chosen another development firm."

"I know that. But they're liars and cheats, Jonny. Andre's told you so for years."

He slipped his tool bag over his shoulder and walked to the gate. "Not all of them. Andre's gotten to know his cousins better now that he's with Mikayla. I think they're cool with each other now."

Nadine strolled over to the gate and swung it open for him. "Being cool doesn't wash away the dirt of the past."

"Some of those stories were exaggerated. Besides, his problem was with his cousin, Ryan. Ryan's twin sister Renee is the one handling the sell. I met her at the wedding, and she doesn't seem to be like her brother."

Understatement of the year. Nothing like her brother is what his brain told him. Or maybe it was his hormones. He hadn't been able to get that kiss out of his mind. Which only made his frustration grow stronger. Both at his brain for the continual loop of fantasies about her, and with his body, one part in particular, for craving more of her.

"She's his twin, which means she's just as bad as her brother," Nadine said. "Probably worse, because she's a woman."

He stared at his sister. "You're awfully hard on your sex."

"Because I know us," Nadine said, slapping her chest. "We're worse than men, but better at hiding our tracks."

He couldn't argue much with that. Karen cheated for weeks without him noticing.

They were walking toward his truck when Nadine stopped. "Are you seeing someone new, yet?"

Jonathan shifted and shot a glance at Nadine. "Why would you ask that?"

"I don't know. My comment and your angry scowl, I assumed you were thinking about that bitch Karen."

Nadine always had a knack for reading his thoughts. "Karen has nothing to do with my dating life."

Nadine's snort screamed *bullshit*. "So you're seeing someone?"

He shook his head. "I'm out there. Nothing serious."

"Don't let one skank ruin you for other women."

"I haven't." He stomped toward the truck.

Nadine's quick footsteps followed. "Good. Dad says that Laura is still making googly eyes at you. Ask her out."

He grunted. "I'm not asking Laura out. We work together." He dumped his tool bag on the back of the truck.

Nadine grinned and tugged on the arm of his shirt. "Lots of people meet at work."

"I'm not dating Laura. She's a nice woman. I'm just having fun right now."

Nadine rolled her eyes. "Guy code for I just want to get laid. Fine. Continue your debauched decent into bachelorhood."

Jonathan laughed. "My debauched decent?"

"You're sinking fast and hard. Karen was the wrong one. Find a nice girl, like Laura, settle down, and move on. I'm ready to be an auntie."

"Why? You've got a kid."

Nadine smiled sweetly. "Because you do such a great job spoiling Lilly rotten, I can't wait to pay you back."

Jonathan smiled at the mention of his niece. Nadine had Lilly during her brief marriage right after college. Back when Nadine thought settling down with a guy would make things easier for her family. Five years and one kid later, Nadine finally divorced her husband and confided to her family that she was a lesbian. Something Jonathan had suspected for years.

"I do spoil her pretty good, don't I?"

Nadine punched his arm before she jerked open the passenger door. "Pony rides and princess crap everywhere? Yes, you spoil her pretty good."

They got into Jonathan's truck. "I'm her uncle," he said. "That's what I'm supposed to do."

"How about you have your own kids and spoil them."

Did Renee want kids? He could slap himself for even letting the thought cross his mind. That was a big ole none of your business subject that should be etched in all caps in his brain. He hadn't heard from her. Surprising since his lawyer delivered the paperwork on Monday. He guessed that meant she was gathering her troops. He was actually looking forward to her next move. The fight for the house was serious, but the sparing with Renee was surprisingly fun.

Nadine was talking away. Jonathan tuned back in, shoving thoughts of Renee and kids out of his mind.

"I invited her best friends down for the party," Nadine said. "They remember the carnival you put together last year."

Jonathan laughed and turned the truck around in the pasture before driving to the gate that separated it from the yard of the house. "I know a guy who rents bouncy houses and has a few clown friends. It wasn't a carnival."

"Sure." Nadine's smile faded and lines formed between her brows. "I wonder how Mom and Dad will be tomorrow."

The concern in her voice put Jonathan on alert. "What do you mean?"

"Have you noticed something weird is going on with them?"

"Weird like what?" Other than thinking something was off when he'd met his dad for lunch the other week, he hadn't thought much of his parents' relationship.

"Dad went to Charlotte the other weekend by himself. Momma came up to spend a weekend with me and Lilly."

He shrugged. "That's not weird."

"Momma not calling or talking about Dad the entire time she visited is. And you know he always takes her when he goes out of town. For Dad to leave her behind just struck me as odd."

It struck him as weird, too. But if there were two people who were in love and happy it was their parents. They'd fought too hard to be together to not be happy.

"Don't go looking for trouble where there isn't any," he said. "They've been married for years after going through hell just to be together. I think they're strong enough to survive a few weekends apart."

"I hope so," Nadine sighed. "But something just feels off to me. Kinda like right before me and Luke split."

"You and Luke split because you weren't attracted to him."

Nadine grinned and punched his shoulder again. "You're not funny."

"I didn't say it to be funny. I said it to make a good point. Don't compare mom and Dad to you and Luke. They're fine."

"Fine," she said, raising her hands in surrender. "But I'm still going to watch them at the party."

"Watch all you want. Mom and Dad didn't go through hell to give up after thirty years of marriage. They're okay," he said forcefully to ease Nadine's fears, or cover his own.

His parents had to make it. If they didn't after fighting so hard to be together, then Nadine's advice that he should find a nice woman to settle down with was pointless.

CHAPTER 9

A quick online search using the right tools, and Renee found Jonathan's address. It had taken all week to get the lawyers to agree on a non-disclosure agreement and Philip to agree on the amount of money he would pay to end the entire situation. Joanne had seemed more than willing to do whatever she could to make her family happy so that Caldwell Development wouldn't sue her for breach of contract. She should wait to hear back from Joanne before making any offer to Jonathan. Still, she found herself driving to Spartanburg on a Saturday morning to make the offer to him in person.

She needed a quick resolution of this situation. That's why she didn't wait until Monday. Not because she might have wanted to see him again.

Jonathan's motorcycle sat in the open garage. His truck and an unfamiliar sedan were parked outside the garage. Renee picked up the portfolio that held the paperwork and strode to the door with a confidence she didn't feel. Her insides quivered uncontrollably.

An attractive woman with thick curly hair, more curves than should be legal, and long legs answered the door. The uncontrollable quivers turned into a burning nausea.

He didn't have a girlfriend. A worse thought prevailed, his lover.

Renee forced her mouth upward into what she hoped was a professional smile. "Hello. I'm—"

"Renee Caldwell," the woman said, not smiling. "What are you doing here?"

A scathing return of those same words nearly worked their way up Renee's throat. She swallowed them. "I'm looking for Jonathan. Wright." Renee paused between his first and last name. A petty piece of her wanted to allude to there being more between her and Jonathan.

The woman raised a brow and her lip twisted. Renee cocked her head to the side. "I'm sorry, but do I know you?"

"I'm Jon's sister."

Relief nearly made Renee's shoulders slump. "Then you know why I'm here?"

"To cheat us out of more land?"

Renee's chin tilted up. "I didn't cheat. If your brother's lawsuit allegations are true, then Joanne signed a contract with us under false pretenses."

Nadine, if Renee remembered the sister's name correctly, crossed her arms and leaned against the door. "Are you saying you're on our side?"

"I'm saying we both may have been cheated. I'd like to find a mutually satisfying resolution."

"Mutually satisfying, huh?" Nadine didn't sound convinced. She straightened. "Come on in."

Renee followed her inside. Curiosity about Jonathan made her want to study every inch of his home. See what she could learn about him. Caldwell professionalism kept her eyes forward. Nadine led her to the kitchen. Platters covered in foil lined the counter and table. At the center of the table sat a two-tiered birthday cake in pink and lavender covered with Disney princesses.

Renee froze. "Oh no. I'm interrupting."

"Kinda," Nadine replied. She walked over to stir pink punch in a crystal bowl.

Renee shifted from foot to foot, taking in all the food. This was why impulsive decisions were stupid. "I can come back at a better time."

"That's up to Jon. Your business is with him."

"Where is he?"

Nadine glanced up at Renee. "Didn't you see the bouncy houses going up in the field?"

"No. I didn't pay attention."

"That's where he's at." Nadine nodded toward the door, which Renee guessed was also the general direction of the field.

"Should I go out there and talk to him?"

Nadine took one look at Renee's four-inch Louboutin shoes. "Not in those shoes."

Renee looked down and nodded. "Right."

The kitchen door opened. Jonathan breezed in. All broad muscled shoulders, long jean clad legs, and bright happy smile. "I've got the bouncy house up," he said to Nadine. He lifted the dark blue baseball cap covering his hair and wiped his brow. He hadn't even looked Renee's way.

Renee cleared her throat. Jonathan turned. His bright smile turned into a confused frown. She wanted the smile back.

"Renee? Hey." He sounded surprised. Not angry or upset, maybe slightly pleased if she were to believe the returning flutters to her midsection.

"Hi." Her lips tried to betray her by lifting into a silly grin. She barely squashed it in time.

They stared for a second. Renee thought about the kiss. Her cheeks heated. Maybe he read her thoughts because something hot flashed in his eyes.

"Okay, that's not weird at all," Nadine said. Renee didn't have to look at her to hear the eye roll. "Jonny, Renee is here to offer a mutually beneficial ending to the situation with the Big House."

Eyes the color of a winter sky met hers again. "You want to settle out of court."

She nodded, and forced her mind back to business. "Yes. If it's possible."

"It's possible. Is Caldwell Development ready to drop the contract so that I can handle this with my aunt?"

"I have an idea I'm hoping you'll like better."

He looked interested. Good. Maybe he would be willing to sell out. She nearly cringed. Sell out was probably not the right phrase to use when she made the offer.

The door burst open again and a little girl ran inside in a flurry of pink and glitter. "Uncle Jon, Uncle Jon." She ran directly to Jonathan.

"Princess Lilly." He scooped up the girl in his arms and the sheer joy on his face brought that silly smile to Renee's face.

"I saw the bouncy house, Uncle Jon," Lilly said.

"Bouncy house," he frowned and looked around. "What bouncy house?"

Lilly giggled and tapped him on the shoulder. "Don't be silly, Uncle Jon. The pink one in the field, right next to the corral. Did you get my pony? Does she have pink ribbons in her hair?"

Jonathan hoisted Lilly higher on his hip. "I don't know. Pony's don't like pink ribbon."

"Yes they do. Don't they Nanna?" Lilly looked toward the door.

An older woman with flawless mocha skin and sparkling brown eyes grinned at them both. "I don't know, baby girl. Uncle Jon is the horse expert."

Lilly spun toward Nadine. "Momma, ponies like pink ribbons don't they? The one Uncle Jon got me last year did."

Nadine shrugged and raised a hand. "Oh we're talking to me now. I thought you only had eyes for Uncle Jon." Nadine smiled at the girl.

She wiggled out of Jonathan's arms, ran over, and wrapped her arms around Nadine's waist in a hug. "Mmm. There. Now don't they like pink ribbons?"

Nadine laughed and ran her hand over Lilly's pigtails. "I think Uncle Jon is fooling you."

Lilly ran back and smothered Jonathan in another round of hugs and pink ribbon questions. Renee eased a step back the way she'd come. She had picked the absolute worst day to show up.

The girl's dark eyes swung Renee's way. "Who are you?"

Three sets of adult eyes zeroed in on her as well. Renee felt every bit the intruder. She lifted her hand and waved her fingers. "I'm Renee."

"Hi, Renee. I'm Lilly," she said with a cheeky grin. "Will you tell Uncle Jon that ponies like pink ribbons."

"Of course they like pink ribbons," Renee said using her most brisk businesslike tone. "Everyone knows ponies love pink ribbons."

Lilly bounced in Jonathan's arms and beamed at him. "See, Uncle Jon, Renee says so."

Jonathan kissed Lilly's cheek then set her down. "Well then I guess it must be true." He reached into his pocket and pulled out a handful of ribbons. "I haven't had the chance to put them on the pony yet."

Lilly jumped up and down and clapped her hands. "You're the best uncle in the entire world."

"That's what all the six year olds say," he said with a shrug.

Renee took another step backward. "Jonathan, I shouldn't have intruded. I can come back another day."

Lilly ran over and grabbed Renee's hand. The movement startled Renee and she looked wide-eyed from the child to Jonathan and Nadine. They both shook their heads and grinned.

"Don't go," Lilly said. "You know all about pink ribbons and ponies. It's going to be the best birthday party. Uncle Jon got a bouncy house and a princess cake. All of my friends are coming. It'll be tons of fun."

Renee was at a loss for words. Lilly stared at her with huge dark eyes. Renee felt terrible and she hadn't even said no yet. She got an inkling that very few people said no to Lilly.

"It would be rude to intrude on your party, Lilly," Renee said. "But thank you for the invitation."

"It's only rude if you're not invited," Lilly said with a nod. "I invited you so it's not rude." Her brows drew together. "Are you Uncle Jon's girlfriend?"

Renee nearly choked on her own saliva. She coughed and patted her chest. Her face burned. "Umm. No."

"How do you know Uncle Jon?"

Uncle Jon walked over. "Okay, Lilly, you've pestered Renee enough."

"He saved me from a gunman," Renee blurted out.

Lilly's eyes went wide. Across the room, she heard Nadine and his mother gasp.

Lilly leaned closer. "For reals?"

Renee nodded. "For real. He was walking me to my car when a bad man ran by chasing another guy. When the bad man pulled out a gun to shoot, your Uncle Jon grabbed me in his arms," Renee wrapped her arms around her shoulders. "Shielded me with his body and kept me safe until the police arrived."

Lilly clasped her hands in front of her. "Like a super hero. No, like a prince."

Renee smiled and nodded. "Kinda."

She glanced at Jonathan. His cheeks were redder than before. She'd made him blush. Something jolted between them when their eyes met. She didn't have to tell Lilly the story. It was obvious the girl idolized her uncle enough as it was. But the story sounded much better than admitting she was the greedy developer here to steal the family land.

"You're his princess," Lilly whispered. "Now you two will get married."

Renee shook her head and dropped her arms which were still wrapped around her shoulders. "I don't know about that."

Lilly nodded. "You will. Wont you, Uncle Jon?"

Jonathan's cheeks turned another shade of red. Renee bit her lower lip to keep from smiling. He was saved by the doorbell.

Lilly jumped up and down. "Party time!" She ran to the front door.

Nadine hurried after her. "Lilly, don't you dare open that door until I'm there."

Renee got out of the way for mother and daughter. When she glanced back at Jonathan the blush was gone.

She pointed toward the door. "I really should go. I'm sorry for barging in like this."

"You might as well stay. Lilly will ask about you for the rest of the day if you leave."

"You want me to stay?"

"The party will only last a few hours. We can talk after."

She raised a brow. "So you want me to stay?"

He frowned and shifted his weight to his other foot. His mother came up behind him and wrapped an arm around his shoulder. "He wants you to stay. And since you and Lilly made my very grown up son blush, I want you to stay as well."

***

"Jonathan, please tell me you really didn't block a bullet for *Renee Caldwell*?" Nadine leaned against the fence next to Jonathan where they watched the kids take turns riding the pony.

Renee offered to help keep the kids in some type of order, and she kept the line of fifteen from getting out of hand while his neighbor helped the kids onto the pony that made slow circles around the corral. Nadine had given her a pair of rain boots she kept in the car. Renee had tucked her fancy slacks into the boots and jumped in to help.

Damned if that woman didn't make it hard to dislike her.

"Would you rather say I stood by and let a guy shoot her?" Jonathan asked with a grin.

Nadine bumped him with her shoulder. "Don't be stupid, Jonny. She's trying to buy the Big House and you're playing Superman. News flash, buddy, she's not Lois Lane."

"It was instinct, Nadine. The guy came, a gun flashed and I pulled her down and out of the way. It's not that big a deal."

That silenced Nadine for a few seconds, but, as expected, that didn't last long. "Then explain those googly-eyed greetings you two gave." Nadine wiggled her fingers and batted her eyelashes. "Hi," she said in a breathless voice.

Jonathan laughed. "That was not what happened."

"You didn't see it. You were too busy looking at her like she was the head cheerleader to your high school quarterback."

"Really, Nadine?"

"Really." Nadine said with a firm shake of her head. "I get what you said the other day about her and her brother not being as bad, but they're twins, right?" Jonathan nodded and Nadine cocked her head to the side. "That means they have to share the same asshole gene."

The need to defend Renee stiffened his spine. "Look, I get that you don't like her, but don't call her an asshole."

Nadine's brows rose. "You like her?"

Jonathan scoffed and turned back to the kids. "I just said don't call her an asshole. Don't read anything into that."

"I don't trust her, Jonny. I don't trust that she's not trying to soften you up to drop the lawsuit."

"I'm not dropping a lawsuit just because I said don't call her an asshole," he snapped. "Fixing what they did to Gigi, getting the house, that's what's important to me."

Renee laughed and clapped. Lilly had finished her pony ride and ran over to Renee. Lilly taking an instant liking to someone wasn't new. She was just as quick to take an instant dislike to people as well. The extent of her attachment to Renee was what surprised Jonathan. Lilly treated Renee like her own grown up doll. Playing with Renee's hair, running her fingers over Renee's nails, and comparing Renee's silk blouse to her sparkly princess T-shirt.

Even more surprising, Renee wasn't the least bit bothered by Lilly's attention. Was it all to soften him up, or did she really like talking to Lilly?

"I can't see you two making things work," Nadine said.

Why was on the tip of his tongue. He caught it in time. "We're not together. Not getting together."

"She's not into the same things you are, Jonny." Nadine continued.

"She's a pretty girl, high maintenance, and you hate high maintenance. If Mom and Dad can't make it work, when they are more alike than anyone I know, how in the world will you two make it?"

"Hold up," Jonathan turned to Nadine and held up a hand. "What do you mean 'if mom and Dad can't make it work'? Mom and Dad are fine."

Nadine shook her heard. "They arrived separately, Jonny."

"So?"

"Why didn't they come together if things are good? I think they're separated."

"Don't be ridiculous."

Nadine frowned, a sad look in her eye. Jonathan spun on his heel and marched toward the house.

His parents were talking and laughing while they watched the kids from his patio. They looked happy. How in the world could they be separated if they were laughing together? They stopped talking and smiled up at Jonathan when he reached them.

"Good job on the party," his mom said.

"Are you two separated?"

The smile on his mom's face faded and she shot an uneasy glance to his dad. Jacob took a deep breath then met Jonathan's eyes. "We are."

Jonathan's knees seemed to give from under him. He slowly sat in one of the chairs. "Why?"

Jonathan's mom, Connie, sighed and gave a weary shrug. "We're in two different places. We need some space."

"I don't understand. You two belong together. You fought through so much crap to stay together. You're up here laughing and talking."

His dad nodded. "Just because we're separating doesn't mean we hate each other."

His mom placed her hand over Jacob's. "It's just a little time to figure out what's going on between us."

"What brought this on?"

Connie sighed before her dark eyes met his. "I've accepted a job in Nashville. I'm moving next month."

Jacob shrugged. "I don't want to move to Nashville."

"So you're separating? This makes no sense."

"It makes perfect sense," his mom said. "When they offered the job I knew I would take it. Then I realized that I applied, and accepted, the position without once thinking of what your dad wanted. This was something I wanted. The entire thing was selfish of me, but I couldn't pass up the opportunity."

"When she told me," Jacob said, "I realized that I couldn't ask your mom to turn down the opportunity, even though I don't want to move. We're not ready to talk divorce."

"Divorce?" Jonathan ran a hand over his face. His world reeling.

Connie placed a hand on his knee. "That's why we're separating. We'll see how things go when I'm in Nashville."

"You can't just throw your marriage away."

Connie sat up straight. "This isn't throwing anything away. Nothing is set in stone, yet. Don't worry about something that is ultimately a decision me and your dad have to make."

The *mind your business* was implied. Jonathan slowly stood. "I hope you two know what you're doing. That this separation is just temporary."

"Only time will tell," Jacob said.

His mom's smile was the same smile she'd given him at the age of seven when he found out the Easter Bunny wasn't real. A little sad at the loss of innocence. Maybe it was innocent, or naive of him to think separation was something that could never happen to his parents. Everyone else's parents had problems, but his fought too hard to be together to not make things work. After his break up with Karen, it was his parents' relationship that made him think one day he'd meet a woman worth fighting just as hard to be with. Now, he wasn't so sure.

CHAPTER 10

Renee paused in the middle of passing out juice boxes to the kids at the party and smiled at Jonathan's mother.

"You're doing a great job with the kids today," Connie said, standing behind Renee.

"I'm having a good time."

That morning she would have laughed so hard, she'd snort her latte from her nose if she'd been told that she'd trade in her Louboutins for old boots in order to help kids take pony rides at a birthday party. Much less that she'd be enjoying herself.

Lilly was a sweetheart. Spoiled by her uncle, but not in general. Lilly worked harder than Renee to make sure her friends all got turns on the pony and in the bouncy house. Renee didn't often get the biological clock pangs that made other women want children, but she had to admit that a little girl like Lilly wouldn't be a hardship. Especially if the father was as caring and considerate as Jonathan.

Stop that, Renee! Stop that right now.

"You're just ready to have a passel of your own kids now," Connie said.

Renee dropped the juice box in her hand. Could the woman read minds? "Sorry," Renee said to the last little girl in line and reached into the cooler for another. "Here you go."

The girl ran to join the other kids around a bonfire Jonathan had started to ward off the afternoon chill after the pony rides. The kids were eating hotdogs and making s'mores before cutting the cake and singing happy birthday.

She turned back to Connie, who watched her with a knowing smile. "I'm not thinking about kids right now. I'm so far away from that point."

"But you do want kids one day?"

Renee slid the cooler over on the top of the picnic table and hopped up to sit next to it. A second later, she thought about how the top would likely get her trousers dirty. A dry cleaning bill she was willing to pay.

"Maybe one day. I have too much going on right now to think about settling down and having kids."

"Spoken like a single woman who gets that question a lot."

Renee chuckled. "You've got me there." She reached into the cooler and pulled out two diet colas. She handed one to Connie who shook her head. Throwing the second back in, Renee popped open the soda.

"So you're the one trying to buy the Big House."

Renee stiffened. She'd almost forgotten that she was technically the enemy here. That if Ryan or her dad saw her they'd jerk this project out of her hands and give it to someone more dedicated.

She straightened her spine and met Connie's direct gaze. "I've signed the contract. I'm trying to prevent a messy lawsuit."

Connie waved away Renee's words with a flick of her wrist. "Don't stiffen up because of me. I have no love or connection to that place. It's caused nothing but heartache and bad memories for me."

Renee's business senses perked up. Maybe Connie could help her convince Jonathan to settle. "You're okay with the house going?"

"I am, but—" she held up a finger and stopped Renee from replying. "I understand why Jonathan wants it. I don't have to like his reasons, but I can respect them."

"Why would he want it? He told me a little about your father-in-law's attitude toward you, him, and Nadine."

Connie shifted until she could fully meet Renee's gaze. One dark brow rose. "He talked to you about that?"

Renee almost squirmed under the knowing look in Connie's eyes. "He just let it slip at the wedding the other weekend. I'm good friends with Mikayla. We had to talk."

She emphasized had. Curious looks from a single guy's mother were often followed by unwanted matchmaking.

"You *had* to be nice, he didn't have to tell you about his grandfather."

Renee didn't reply. That was the truth. They'd both revealed personal details about themselves that could have remained hidden. She didn't want to think too long or hard about why.

"Are you hoping he'll change his mind about the lawsuit?"

Connie shook her head. Her gaze left Renee to look for Jonathan handing marshmallows to the kids. "I doubt it. That house means a lot to him. I hate the place, but I think having it will give Jonathan some type of validation that he is a part of his father's family. Whether he's wanted there or not."

"He cares that much?"

"Jonathan cares a lot more than people realize." Connie watched Renee intently. "Why are you trying to settle out of court? Not only that, show up here on a Saturday? You have lawyers who can handle this. Probably much more efficiently and without the threat of mud on your pants."

Connie pointed to a smudge on Renee's cream pants. Renee brushed the spot, but grinned. One kid had accidentally kicked her leg in his haste to get on the pony. The kick hadn't hurt, and the boy's excitement about his first pony ride had made Renee instantly forget the stain.

"Because I like him." The second the words were out, she wished she could bite off her tongue and boil the rebellious thing in acid.

She glanced at Connie who still watched Jonathan. Renee followed her gaze. Jonathan helped Lilly roast a marshmallow. He said something that made the girl giggle and wrap her little arms around his neck.

"I mean. I respect him. I thought he deserved to hear my offer in person."

Connie sighed. "I know what you mean. Be careful, my dear. Normally I would encourage the spark I see between you and my son. But it takes a lot more than spark to make a relationship work."

Renee scoffed. "Relationship. Mrs. Wright."

"Call me Connie."

"Connie. There is no relationship between me and Jonathan. Let me reassure you this spark you're referring to is nothing but professional admiration."

"Is professional admiration behind those hot looks you two are pretending you're not throwing each other? Honey, there's more than admiration going on between you two. Any fool can see. Even if he hadn't jumped in front of a gunman, the blushes and looks give it away."

"Mrs. Wright," Renee began.

The older woman raised a brow. "Connie. Even if there were some miniscule spark of attraction between Jonathan and I, acting on it would be inappropriate and unwise. He's suing my family's company. If he doesn't accept this offer, I can't back down from that."

"Which is why I'm pointing out how things look between you two. If there really isn't anything there, good. I won't press you, or ask you to stay away from my son. You're both grown-ups. Not only that, I think you're a smart woman. I'm confident you'll do the right thing."

Renee opened her mouth to ask Connie what was the right thing. She snapped her mouth closed. Staying away from Jonathan was the right thing. Letting her lawyers handle this was the right thing. Leaving immediately instead of staying and enjoying herself with his niece was the right thing.

What in the world was she doing here? Letting a kiss and an infatuation with a man who was suing her for heaven's sake, twist her mind into making ridiculous choices. No, this was not the right thing.

Renee hopped off the top of the picnic table and wiped her pants down. "I actually should be going. I can have my lawyers call Jonathan on Monday."

"If you're sure." Connie didn't sound the least bit like she wanted Renee to stick around.

Embarrassment burned hot in Renee's veins. How desperate must she look to his mother?

"Renee, Renee, Renee," Lilly's voice interrupted.

Renee turned toward the girl. Lilly ran full speed from the bonfire to Renee. Her eyes bright and a huge smile on her face. "You've gotta make s'mores with us."

"Lilly, slow down. You're going to fall and hurt yourself." The girl's speed didn't stop. If only she could tap into the boundless energy of a child.

"Come make s'mores. Everyone is making them."

Instead of stopping at them, Lilly ran directly for the picnic table. She jumped up onto the seat then in a rush tried to jump onto the top. Both Renee and Connie reached out toward the girl. They were too late. Lilly's foot caught on the table, and she tumbled over the side.

"No!" Renee cried.

She and Connie rushed to where Lilly had fallen on the other end of the table. The girl's smile was gone. A look of shock followed a pained sob. Connie swept the girl up into her arms.

"Ow!" Lilly gripped her left arm. The arm she'd fallen on. "Nana, that hurts."

Connie relaxed her tight hold on the girl, but didn't put her down. In a second Jonathan and Nadine where there. Whenever they touched Lilly's arm she cried out in pain. The next few minutes were frantic scrambling to get Lilly inside where they could look at her arm better. When the girl insisted she couldn't move her fingers, the decision was made to take her to the emergency room.

While the family looked after Lilly, Renee looked after the guests. She passed out the goody bags, thanked them for coming, and promised they'd get an update as soon as they found out something from the emergency room. By the time Jonathan came back in the house after putting Lilly in the car with Connie and Nadine, Renee had gathered most of the discarded food from the party area outside and was covering the leftovers with aluminum foil in the kitchen.

"Are you going with them?" She asked.

He ran a hand over his face. Lines marred his eyes and mouth. "No. Dad is following them. Someone needed to stay behind to wrap things up here." He looked around the kitchen then frowned. "What are you doing?"

"Putting up the food."

He looked at her as if she were an alien or something. Renee's face prickled with embarrassment. "I could have left it all outside for the flies."

He shook his head and blinked. "Sorry. With everything going on with Lilly, I didn't realize you were cleaning up. You don't have to do that."

"Would you rather clean up on your own?"

"I like cleaning up with you." Something hot flashed in his eyes.

The kiss played in her mind. She pushed that aside. "Is Lilly okay?"

Concern once again clouded his gaze. "She may have broken her arm. I'm hoping it's just a sprain. It happened so fast. One second she's making s'mores with me, and the next she's running full speed toward you and the picnic table."

"I should have caught her."

Jonathan shook his head. "I saw the entire thing. Who knew she'd try to pole vault over the table?"

"I still feel awful. I was too late, too slow to stop her."

"Don't beat yourself up. Lilly is a strong kid. She'll be right back asking for her birthday cake before we know it." He sounded like he was hopefully clinging to those words.

"She is sweet. You're good with her."

Jonathan shrugged. "She was upset when her parents split. Her dad is pissed at Nadine and doesn't try hard to be in Lilly's life."

The simply said words provided another hint at how much Jonathan cared for his niece and created another soft spot in her heart for him. "You're being her surrogate father."

"More like the best damn uncle she could ever have."

Renee chuckled and his low laugh joined hers. The look that passed between them made her pulse buzz with the type of anticipation she typically got when she closed a deal.

Kind of like the deal she needed to close right now.

"Jonathan, about the lawsuit."

He lifted a hand. "Not now. Let me get the stuff put up outside before we talk business."

It wasn't smart, but she nodded. Though truthfully, she hadn't wanted to break their current ceasefire.

He went back outside and Renee stayed in, packing up the food and washing the platters. She felt comfortable in his cozy kitchen. Daydreaming wasn't something she indulged in often. Ever, really. But for a moment, she did.

She was the wife cleaning up after dinner while her husband did chores outside. He'd come in. Wrap an arm around her waist and kiss her neck. Her fingers trailed down the side of her neck. The touch was a poor substitute for the soft press of lips. *She would lean into him. Tilt her head to the side for more. He would turn her around until she faced him. The kiss would turn hot and passionate. His arms possessive while the hard press of his erection branded her.*

The kitchen door opened. Renee jerked her hand away from her neck. When she spun around, Jonathan was taking his cap off and running fingers through his dark hair.

"I'm done with the dishes," she said a little too brightly.

Frick, get out of the daydream, Renee.

He met her gaze then quickly looked away at the dishes and the rest of the kitchen. "Umm, thanks." He rubbed the back of his neck.

He looked like he was ready for her to leave. She needed to leave. She didn't want to talk business. A first for her. A first that was a four-alarm fire of a warning that she was losing her mind.

"Jonathan."

His cell phone rang. "It's my mom." He touched the screen then brought the phone to his ear. "Mom? How's Lilly?"

Renee crossed the room to his side. Thoughts of leaving fled as she waited to hear an update on Lilly. Jonathan frowned, nodded, gave way too many uh huhs, before finally smiling. His shoulders relaxed. His eyes met hers. He nodded then ended the call.

"What did she say?" Renee asked in a worried rush.

"Lilly is okay. They went to urgent care instead of the emergency room. Which was good because they got her back for an X-ray quickly."

Renee bit her lip and stepped closer. "What did it show?"

"Hairline fracture. Not a big break. Mom says Lilly's excited about getting a pink cast."

Renee pressed one hand to her heart and gripped Jonathan's arm with the other. "Oh thank, God. I was so worried."

"So was I." Jonathan ran a hand over his face and shook his head. "I freaked out when she flipped over that table."

They both let out relieved laughs. Jonathan placed his hand over hers on his arm. "Thank you for staying. And for cleaning up."

"It was no problem. I wouldn't have been able to think for the rest of the day anyway if I hadn't known."

His hand squeezed hers. "Still. I appreciate it."

He didn't pull away. She should pull back. Bring up the business of why she was there. Make up some line how sticking around gave her the opportunity to talk about the settlement or that she would have stayed for anyone. They were both lies. She stayed because it was him. Because she liked Lilly. Because leaving him in a crisis hadn't felt right.

The atmosphere between them shifted. Awareness of his nearness, memory of their kiss, they all sparked and crackled in the back of her mind. His gaze dropped to her lips. Flicked back up to hers and was nothing but tempting blue fire.

He blinked and frowned slightly. She saw common sense creeping back into his eyes. Common sense she should be siphoning for herself. She didn't want that. She wanted the fire. Renee lifted up on her toes and pressed her lips against his.

His arms wrapped around her with no hesitation. Her pulse fluttered while excitement and need flooded her. She wasn't the only one fighting this. She didn't keep her hand between them as she had before. If she was going to kiss him, then she was *going* to kiss him. She would indulge in this hunger. Her arms wrapped around his neck.

He spun her around and pressed her back against the wall. He was all muscle, melting heat, and masculinity. Before today, Renee would have said she'd been kissed well. She might even have stretched to say she'd been kissed somewhat passionately. She would have lied.

Jonathan's kiss was passionate. Hot and deliberate. He kissed like he knew exactly what he was doing to her. The play of his lips and tongue drove her wild with every brush against hers.

She'd been right from the second she's seen him and guessed he would kiss her like this. Hold her like this. Tightly, possessively, completely. She instantly opened and responded to him. Her fingers dug into his hair. She stretched higher on her toes to better meet his kiss. Her chest was pancaked against his. Never in her life had she felt like she could kiss a man forever.

Jonathan's hand cupped possessively around her nape. Not tight enough to threaten, but with enough pressure to know he was taking control. His other roamed up and down the side of her body. There was a tug at her side, and then her shirt released from the waistband of her pants. The tips of his fingers explored the sensitive skin along her side with light, teasing strokes. Slowly edging their way upward.

Renee pulled back just enough to allow his hand to rise to her breasts. Her bra was nothing but lace covering the petite mounds. Lace that did nothing to temper the heat of his palm cupping her. His hand engulfed the moderate swells completely. One soft squeeze and Renee moaned deeply.

His thumb brushed across the hard tip. Pure, delicious sensation trembled through her. Her hips bucked. Her back arched.

"You like that?" he asked against her lips.

Did she like that? Of course she liked that. Wasn't she practically turning into mush in his hands? Wasn't she ready to rip off her shirt, his pants, and every other stitch of clothing separating them and finally experience the raw, sweaty, passionate sex that she'd wondered about, but was never quite bold enough to experience? Wasn't she ready to forget about the consequences of her job, the deal, and her plan to find a suitable guy to date?

Her eyes widened. Reality slammed into her brain. Her hands lowered to his chest and she pushed. He stopped kissing her and shifted back. His hands remained on her neck and her breast.

"Jonathan, this is…we shouldn't…I don't think…"

His thumb brushed her nipple again. Her knees threatened to give out on her. She pressed harder into the wall and curled her fingers into his chest.

"I'm here to discuss business, not to kiss you again," she said in a rush.

***

It took several seconds for Renee's words to burn through the haze in Jonathan's mind. Mostly because he could barely think after she'd kissed him. The perfect swell of her breast in his hand may have also had something to do with it.

He tried to remember that he didn't like her. That she was the enemy and he shouldn't want her so damned much. Except, he did like her. She was a bit rigid, and a little too perfect, but she had a good heart. When you melted the ice around her.

"Renee…"

"If you'll just let go of my breast." Her hand rested on his wrist.

Every fiber in him wanted to continue to hold, to squeeze. He let go. "Renee, we—"

"I have the paperwork ready for you to review." The woman managed to sound breathless and businesslike at the same time. She tugged on the hand that still cupped her nape.

He released her. She eased aside and out of his grip. "Thank you." She didn't look at him as she went over to the black folder that she'd brought into the house earlier. Papers he really didn't want to read or even think about.

"Renee, we've got to talk—"

"We've come up with what I think you'll find to be a satisfying deal." She pulled out the paperwork. "You'll find the compensation to be very generous."

"Renee, we can't ignore what happened," he said at the same time. A second later, her words sunk in. "Compensation?"

She held out the papers. They trembled in her hands. "Yes. We're willing to pay you very well to drop the lawsuit. All we ask is that you sign a non-disclosure agreement and refrain from discussing Caldwell Development in any negative way after you're paid."

"You're here to buy me out?" His voice rose with disbelief.

Renee smoothed down the front of her blouse then lifted her chin. "I'm here to reach a settlement."

"Is that why you were so nice to Lilly? Why you helped out with the party and cleaned up after she fell."

The smooth, professional mask he'd watched her struggle to retain after breaking their kiss shattered. "Of course not. I would never use you or Lilly that way."

"But you knew the entire time you were here that you ultimately wanted to pay me off." He pointed to the papers she still held in her hand. "When you were kissing me. You knew."

She rushed forward. Her finger pointed directly at his chest. "I did not kiss you because of these papers. I kissed you because I wanted to."

The words sent a rush of searing desire through his body. One that threatened to derail him. Andre's warning at the wedding came back full force. "How do I know that's the truth?"

"Because you drive me crazy and make me feel things I shouldn't be feeling. Things that make me want to forget everything except for the way I feel when you kiss me." Her mouth snapped shut.

Jonathan's eyes zeroed in on her. "What?" His voice was low, surprised.

Renee shook her head. "It doesn't matter. Just sign the papers, or not." She slapped the papers on the counter. "I'll have our lawyers call you on Monday."

She spun on her heel and hurried toward the door. Jonathan was two steps behind her. His hand took hers and stopped her from leaving.

"Why did you say that?"

She tried to pull her arm away. He didn't let her go. "Does it matter? You're just going to think that I'm trying to sleep with you to get you to drop the lawsuit."

Her voice was filled with pain. No, humiliation. Both sounded like they went deeper than just their conversation.

"It matters, Renee." He took a step closer to her. "I need to know. What's real?"

"What's real is irrelevant." Her voice was calm, professional. Her eyes burned with longing, and regret. "We are on opposite ends of a fight. A fight that my family won't give up and one you won't settle out of. Besides that, we aren't right for each other."

"Who cares about being right for each other. This thing between us is hot and fucking hard to ignore."

"We have to ignore it." Spoken like someone trying to convince themselves of the same.

"Says who? Who says because we're business adversaries that we have to be personal adversaries as well?"

A part of him acknowledged that the argument he was making wasn't the smartest. Hell, a large part of him. Something smaller and stronger insisted he fight to keep Renee in his life. Fight to explore the passion between them.

Her brows drew together as she considered his words. "It's not that easy to separate the two."

"It is when we only consider what's firing between us, sugar. We both felt it that night in the hotel."

"Sparks don't make a relationship last," she said in a quiet, faraway voice.

"I'm not talking about a relationship. I'm talking about dealing with what we both feel. Hell, Renee, do you really want a relationship with me?"

She shook her head. "No."

The quick rejection stung. He started to ask why then remembered that she was too polished, too businesslike to be the type of woman he'd consider long term. She'd helped out today, but he couldn't imagine her being happy out here with quiet dinners with him in his kitchen, or waiting up for him to come in after working around the house and in the fields.

Her eyes widened. "I didn't mean—"

He shook his head. "My feelings aren't hurt. I know what you mean."

She crossed her arms and stepped back. "Then what are you asking?"

The hell if he knew. "I want you."

"You want to sleep with me." The words were an accusation.

"And you want to sleep with me."

Her eyes darted away. The tip of her tongue ran across her lower lip. "I'm not sleeping with you to get you to sign the settlement."

His head jerked back. "I wouldn't ask you to. I'm not a jackass." He scrambled for the words to try to express what he wanted that wouldn't make him sound like a, well, a jackass. "Can you take yourself off the project? If you give it to someone else, then there's no conflict of interest if we continue to see each other."

"There's still a massive conflict of interest. You're suing my family."

"Not you."

She frowned and bit her lower lip. He could practically hear the gears churning in her brain as she processed his words. Maybe it was the gears in his brain. Alternating between calling him an idiot and patting him on the back for a smart resolution. The latter had to be the testosterone revving through his bloodstream. She'd brought *settlement* papers. She wasn't here for anything other than that.

"You drive me crazy and make me feel things I shouldn't be feeling. Things that make me want to forget everything except for the way I feel when you kiss me."

Those words had rung with truth. She couldn't be here just because of those settlement papers. She could have called. Better yet, her lawyer could have delivered them. Renee was here because she couldn't ignore what they'd both felt from that very first day, any more than he could.

As long as they both knew this wasn't going to be anything serious, was it really a bad idea? They were adults. He was entering with his eyes wide open. No chance for her to hurt him the way Karen had. In fact, his life had been nothing but quick hook ups with no expectations since then. This would be no different.

Except everything about the way he felt about Renee seemed different.

He brushed his hand over the side of her face. Took a step closer. She turned her head and stepped back.

"I need time to think." She nodded to where she'd placed the papers on the counter. "Review the offer then let me know if you're still interested…in me."

"I can give you my answers now. No, to the offer. Yes, to my interest in you. That isn't going away."

"Still. Review the offer." She took another step back. The conflict in her gaze suddenly masked by the cool professionalism she hid behind. "I'll be in touch."

CHAPTER 11

Jonathan got out of his truck and sloshed through the rain and mud to the service hall of Cedar Grove Lutheran Church for the monthly Cattle Farmers' Association meeting. A group of half a dozen farmers stood on the church porch, finishing their cigarettes and talking, before going in for the meeting. They all smiled and waved as Jonathan hurried out of the rain to the shelter of the porch and then into the service hall.

Two rows of tables were lined up for the twenty or so farmers who normally attended the monthly chapter meeting. In the back of the service hall was the kitchen, where a woman with short brown hair and smiling blue eyes hurried from the kitchen with a large aluminum tray of food in her hand.

Jonathan headed in her direction, lifting a hand in greeting to the other farmers inside. "How's it going, Mary?" He reached for the large pan and she quickly handed it over.

Mary's smile created small laugh lines around her eyes. She pointed to a table next to the kitchen that was topped with food. "Hey, Jonny, is it wet enough for you out there?"

"Not quite, I could take another inch or two." He teased and set the tray where she indicated on the table.

"You would say that. I'd only welcome more rain if I were at home curled up on the couch with a book. Not here feeding you lot." Her words were softened by the humor in her voice.

"You know we couldn't make it through a meeting without you here yelling at us to keep our hands away from your banana pudding." He searched the table for the bowl that he knew would contain her coveted desert.

"You can put your hands on my pudding." Mary winked at him.

"Stop saying that or I just might steal a cup before the meeting."

Mary playfully swatted his arm. "That's the problem with you men. You're intentionally obtuse."

Ever since Saturday, there was only one woman whose pudding he could think of. He still couldn't believe the compromise he'd put out there to Renee.

"I'm going to stay obtuse," he said to Mary. "George showed me his gun collection the first day I visited his farm to discuss his conservation plan."

Mary chuckled. "He won't shoot you. Not when he's trying to get you to run for president of the state chapter this year."

Mary turned to walk away, but he stopped her with a hand to her elbow. "President?" He hadn't thought any more about it since George mentioned it the other week.

Mary nodded. "That's right. I heard George talking earlier about how it's time for you to assume the role. A lot of the members think he's absolutely right, too."

Mary made her way to the kitchen and Jonathan turned to scan the room for George. He was a new member, but he was vocal. Combine that with the quiet push by other small farmers who were members and there may be enough people to actually support his nomination.

George stood talking with a few other board members in a corner of the room. Including the current president of the chapter, Randy Byrd. Jonathan strode their way.

Since raising beef cattle was only a part-time thing for Jonathan, he had no interest in taking a more active role in the organization. Serving on the state board, maybe, but to put his name in for president? An appointment as state president would involve trips to the capital to lobby the legislature. As the state president, he'd be expected to get involved in national politics as the chapter liaison. He may like staying abreast of what was happening regulatory-wise on the state and national level, but he had no desire to dive head first into the same viper pit his grandfather catered to.

Randy looked up as Jonathan approached. His grin wide and welcoming. A bit too welcoming.

"Jonathan, just the man we were talking about."

Jonathan shook Randy's hand and then the hands of George and the other members in the group. "Uh oh, I hate to hear what that conversation was about."

"All good things," Randy said. "Mostly about how good of a job you did heading our government affairs committee while serving as president last year. If you wouldn't have put together the financial impact statement to submit to the state house on the effect that new farm bill would have, then a lot of us would be hurting come next year. You've really got the interests of the association at heart."

"Which is why I'm perfectly happy to continue to serve *our* chapter and keep everyone up to date."

Randy nodded and placed a hand on Jonathan's shoulder. "Your insight shouldn't just be limited to helping us upstate. You could do a lot representing the entire farming community at the state house. Now that's where we need you."

George nodded in agreement. Jonathan held up his hand. "Guys, I'm really not the best candidate. I have no interest in getting involved in the politics of the state house. I've got a lot on my plate right now."

Foremost, the lawsuit against Caldwell Development. He'd read the settlement. They offered a lot of money. Enough to be tempting. Not enough to let go and forget about how Joanne had betrayed Gigi.

"Your word will go far," George said. "Your granddaddy had a lot of influence in the state house before he died. Your parents have a lot of respect around here. If you talk, people will listen."

Jonathan gritted his teeth. He'd gotten this far without using his grandfather's legacy in the state house to get things accomplished; he damned sure wasn't going to start now. The only legacy he wanted from the man was his birthright: the Big House.

The door to the church opened, letting in a rush of damp air as several other farmers entered, including Jonathan's dad. He hadn't really talked to his dad since the party. Not with the separation announcement and Lilly's accident. They'd brought Lilly back to Jonathan's place after leaving urgent care. She'd wanted some of her birthday cake and Jonathan had wanted to see for himself that she was okay. She'd also asked where Renee was; she'd wanted Renee to sign her pink cast.

Jacob came over to Jonathan and the rest of the board. "Evening, gentlemen," he said with a nod then looked to Jonathan. "Got a second before the meeting starts?"

"Sure," Jonathan said and stepped away with his dad. "What's going on?"

Jacob placed his hand on Jonathan's shoulder. "Your mom is worried about you."

Jonathan frowned. "Worried about me? You two are the ones talking separation."

Jacob dropped his hand and fiddled with his baseball cap. "We explained that."

"It doesn't mean it makes any sense. You're letting her go to Tennessee?"

"It's more than the job, son. We fought so hard to be together. Your mom gave up a lot of her dreams to support me and raise you and your sister. Somewhere along the way, the strength of the glue that held us together weakened. I can't deny her this now."

Jacob sounded tired. Bewildered even. The defeat in his dad's voice scared Jonathan a little bit more. "Fighting to make things work now can strengthen things again. Don't just let her go."

Jacob shook his head. "You let me and your mom figure out what's going on between us." Jacob's eyes were blue ice chips. That part of the conversation was over. "You need to be careful with this thing you've got going with Renee Caldwell."

Jonathan couldn't have been more shocked if his dad had started singing the theme song from Lilly's favorite Disney princess movie. "What thing? Who says there's a thing?"

"You're telling me there isn't a thing between you?"

Oh, there definitely was a thing. Jonathan needed to know how his mom figured that out. "I'm suing her company."

"You like the girl. Your mom says it's obvious. Worse, the girl likes you."

"How do you know that?" He ignored the spike of excitement.

"Your mom talked to her. Renee didn't admit anything, but she tried too hard to admit otherwise. Look, normally I'd stay out of your business."

Jonathan snorted. "Didn't you tell me to go out with Laura the other week?"

"Laura didn't work with my vindictive sister to steal the Big House from you. Now I get it. Renee is sleek, sexy, and sweet, but before you get tangled up with her, think about your ultimate goal. If you want to fight for the Big House, you can't get involved with that woman."

"I can keep that separate."

The president of the association tapped the gavel to start the meeting. The other people in the room stopped side conversations and made their way to the tables.

"You can't keep it separate. Don't even try."

"You fix this thing between you and Mom. A marriage possibly breaking up is a lot more important than whether or not I get involved with Renee Caldwell."

Jacob's lips pressed together. Jonathan slapped his dad on the shoulder to stop the lecture. "Let's find a seat."

They sat at the end of a row of tables. Randy called things to order, prayed, and then the group lined up to eat. Dinner always came before the business began. Jonathan mulled over his dad's warning while he stood in line. He may not want to admit it, but his parents were right. The second he'd brought up his idea to Renee, he'd known there were several things that could go wrong.

She had to know too, he'd seen it in her eyes. She'd said she'd be in touch, but she hadn't. Her lawyer had called that morning. Jonathan had told the man to take the settlement and shove it. Maybe her not calling was the answer to his proposition. If so, it was the right answer. That didn't mean he liked it.

A hand slapped his back. "Good luck tonight, Jonathan," an older farmer he'd known most of his life said.

"Umm…thanks," Jonathan said.

Another young farmer patted him on the back and shook his hand. "You've got my vote."

"Mine too," said a guy ahead of him in line.

Jonathan fought not to frown. He'd forgotten the potential nomination just that quickly. The sentiments were soon parroted by other members. Many of them small farmers. The guys who needed someone to champion their needs at a higher level. With each well wish, Jonathan's future was sealed.

He resigned himself to what was happening. He could look like an unappreciative dick, refuse, and turn his back on an organization that protected the interests of so many people he worked to help every day. Or, he could accept the nomination and see what happens.

When they got to the business meeting, he didn't protest when his name was the only one given. With grim determination, he accepted and watched as his peers voted to nominate him for the state chapter president.

He hated the idea of having to stop working behind the scenes and get up close and personal with politicians, but he was honored by the trust put in him by the other members. There was always the chance that he wouldn't get voted in at the state level. He'd accept this and hope for the best.

At the end of the meeting, he shook hands with everyone. Made arrangements with Randy to pull the board together soon to start the list of items that needed to be brought up to the legislature.

His dad waited for him on the porch. Jacob smiled and patted Jonathan on the back. "I'm proud of you, son. This is a good move that'll benefit you in the long run."

"So you say."

"And you know I'm right. With you representing the voices of small farmers, we'll get a lot more accomplished. You and I both know anyone else here would have a hard time arguing the points you put together in our last set of comments to the legislature."

"I get it," Jonathan said. "Believe me, I get it. I may not want to be the president, but I won't turn my back on their faith in me. Besides, it's up to the rest of the state members now. Who knows what'll happen."

"Democracy is a beautiful thing. Whether you win or lose, people will know your name. That's one of the greatest rights we have as citizens, to let our voices be heard. To get involved and shape the world around us."

Jonathan wasn't in the mood to hear the *we are the world* speech his dad was about to give.

"Let's get out of here," Jonathan said and pulled his keys out of his pocket.

"You know, if you're voted in you'll be a big lobbyist in the state house.

You'll make a name for yourself. It'll be good to have something positive associated with the family name on the state level."

Jacob slapped Jonathan on the back, then made a dash for his truck through the rain and mud. Jonathan stood on the porch for a second longer. He'd never thought of things that way. Between being a positive influence and getting the Big House, he could double his efforts to turn the hateful tide his grandfather started. There was a plus side to serving.

He ran to his truck. On the way, he wondered what Renee would think.

CHAPTER 12

Renee walked into her dad's office before the Tuesday morning staff meeting and stopped right before his desk. "I need you to pull me off the Wright property case."

Philip turned away from his computer screen and peered at Renee. "Why? You've never dropped a project before."

"I can't do it anymore." Renee straightened her shoulders and tried to hide the insecurity twisting inside of her. "I have a conflict."

"Conflict?" Philip frowned and clasped his hands together on top of his desk. "That boy, Jonathan?"

She fought hard to say he's not a boy, he's a man. A defense that would put her dad instantly on alert. She knew he didn't mean what he'd said in a derogatory way.

"Jonathan is part of the reason."

"Are you two seeing each other?" Philip's words were blunt.

"No. It's not that. But there is something there. I'm not willing to act on it," she said quickly. "But I don't want the situation to cloud my judgment."

Philip leaned back in his chair. His intent gaze probing. "That serious, huh?"

Renee lifted her hand and waved off the pesky words that struck too close to the truth for her. "It's not serious. I'm acknowledging the problem and being proactive. I won't let this compromise the project."

A pleased look covered Philip's face. "I appreciate what you're doing."

Relief was a whirlwind through Renee. She kept her shoulders square. She'd been afraid he would ask more questions. Dig harder. "I'm glad you understand."

"I do, but I'm not letting you off the project." He turned back to the computer monitor.

Renee barely kept her jaw from dropping. "I'm sorry, what?"

Philip threw her a glance before shrugging. "Business and personal issues should be kept separate."

"I know that." She lived her life based on that. "Which is why I don't understand why you're leaving me on the project."

Philip's sharp gaze hit her like a snap of a whip. "Are you saying you can't keep your personal feelings out of a business deal?"

"Of course not."

His gaze softened and he nodded. "Then you can work on this."

Renee felt like the entire conversation was some type of riddle. She was never good at riddles. "I can't ask him to settle. I know how much keeping the land means to him."

"Do you know how much developing this land means to us?"

Building another successful subdivision in a prime area before other developers were able to get in. That was what drove her dad, what drove her. To be ahead of the curve. To prove Caldwell Development was the best.

"I do," she said.

Philip's gaze probed her again. "Are you putting his needs before the family's?"

"No." Her voice adamant.

"Then what's the problem? You're not dating him. You're just attracted to him."

She wanted to sleep with Jonathan, but that wasn't the only thing. She liked him. Understood and respected why he wasn't likely to back down. Something about him intrigued her. From the earliest fantasy of jumping on the back of his motorcycle, to the daydream of them being together while she cleaned up after the party. Something about Jonathan made her see herself doing things that she never would have thought would interest her.

That wasn't a conversation she wanted to have with her dad.

"That's all," she said.

"Then there's no issue," Philip said confidently. "He's not the right guy for you anyway. You deserve a man who's going places. That man isn't Jonathan Wright."

The need to defend Jonathan sprung like an angry cat inside her. "How do you know that? He loves his job and cares about helping people."

"There's nothing wrong with helping people. But you need a man who'll challenge you and bring something more to the table than the need to help out some small farmers. I know you Renee. You won't be happy with a guy like him."

"A guy like him?" She just kept the frustration from creeping into her voice.

"Yes, a guy like him. A farmer slash conservationist. He's worked at the Conservation Department for years, taught a few agricultural science classes, and coached high school football, but that's the extent of his accomplishments. You wouldn't be happy at his country home discussing cows and conservation plans. A man like Daniel is what you need. Someone who will strengthen you and the business."

Philip turned back to his computer. Renee stood there stunned. Basing her relationships on how they would benefit Caldwell Development was one thing. Actually hearing her dad say the same made her sound cold, calculated. Like the ice tray Daniel had accused her of being.

That her dad couldn't see her being swayed by her attraction to Jonathan made her feel frigid. Of course he wouldn't think she'd let something as silly as a minor attraction to some biker/farmer from the upstate come between her closing a deal. To date she hadn't had a relationship with any man who didn't further her ambitions or those of Caldwell Develop.

"Am I wrong?" Philip asked. She imagined he'd waited for her to process the words.

Renee shook her head. "No. You're not wrong in your observation."

"Good. Don't worry about this little thing you're feeling for the Wright boy. You'll be fine on this project. This is just a little infatuation. You'll get over it."

Philip spoke the words with a confidence that said Renee always did what was right. Always put Caldwell Development above everything. Never took a chance on something that didn't have a direct benefit not only for her, but her image and career.

"Don't you have a Woman of the Year event coming up soon?" Philip threw out the reminder of her ambitions with the blunt finesse of a biker in a ballet.

Philip's lack of subtlety aside, Renee wasn't quite ready to say her father was wrong about her.

"I'll handle the project."

***

The Tuesday night book club at the Still Hopes shelter ended with laughter and excitement to discuss the next section of the book the following week. Renee packed the copy of the sci-fi novel about traveling to different dimensions in her purse. She didn't have the time to read the physical books that she purchased and supplied for the book club, but thanks to audio books, she was able to keep up with the readings by listening in her car while riding to work and meetings.

"Renee, do you have a second?" A voice came from behind her.

Renee turned and smiled at Destiny's mom. "Of course, Adrienne."

Adrienne held the paperback against her stomach. "I want to thank you for talking to Destiny about the boy she asked to homecoming."

Renee had asked Destiny about the homecoming plans after their mentoring session the week before. The girl said the plans were still good to not attend the lake party after the dance, except the more Destiny got to know the boy, the more she was considering going to the party.

"She talked to you about everything?" Renee asked. She'd tried to give the girl advice, but again had urged her to talk to her mother.

Adrienne nodded and pressed a hand to her heart. "She did, and boy was I not ready for that."

Renee placed her hand on Adrienne's arm. "I hope you didn't mind me sending her to you."

Adrienne shook her head. "Not at all. It's never easy talking to your kid about sex. Especially when that kid is thinking about taking such a huge step. But I did it. I wanted the biggest bottle of wine afterward, but I survived."

Adrienne chuckled and Renee laughed too. "What did she say?"

"She told me about your advice. That she shouldn't rush into anything. How this was a big step that she couldn't take lightly. Of course I just want her to wear a chastity belt and not think about boys until she's thirty."

"I can only imagine." Renee actually didn't want to imagine her kid coming to tell her that she was considering having sex. She could barely picture having kids.

"Believe me, it's not easy. I built on what you said. Tried to talk to her like an adult. I had to. The girl is living here with me. She's seen adult life."

Renee didn't respond. She knew their history. The abusive husband that died and left Adrienne and her daughter with nothing. The struggle to keep the house they rented, the loss of a job and finally their decision to come here until Adrienne could get back on her feet. Destiny was a teenager, but she'd seen a lot in her young life. A sugarcoated discussion on sex was insulting.

"Once we talked," Adrienne said. "I think we both realized that even though she does really like him, and is interested in him...in *that* way, she's not ready to make the step. I did try to urge her to let things progress naturally. Even though she's feeling a little tingly for him, she shouldn't force it." Adrienne sighed and shook her head. "As of last night the plans were to stay away from the lake house party."

"Good. I'm glad she came to you and that you were able to help her see things clearly."

"She wouldn't have come if you hadn't have urged her. Destiny thinks I hate men. I can't blame her. After Roy died, I did hate the idea of letting another man in my life."

Renee slipped her purse on her shoulder. "That's understandable. From the way you described him, he didn't seem like a nice man."

Adrienne smiled. They both walked toward the door of the conference room. "That's a nice way of describing him. Way too generous for Roy. He was terrible. Treated me terrible. After he died, and we ended up here," Adrienne looked around the room. "I didn't think I'd ever want to get involved with another man."

"Have you changed your mind?" Something in Adrienne's voice made Renee think she had.

Adrienne shrugged. "I don't know. Maybe. My daughter has a relationship. God help me, but she may even have a sex life by the end of the year. Not that I want her to, or really envy her, but it is a reminder that one day, Destiny will go off to college. I'll be alone. I'm not lonely, but that doesn't mean I won't miss having someone to talk to at the end of the night. Know what I mean?"

Renee did understand. More and more each day since her dad inadvertently pointed out that if she kept choosing men the way she had been, she'd end up alone. Or worse, get married to a guy like Daniel and not realize it until it was too late.

"What am I talking about," Adrienne said. "Of course you don't understand."

Renee's lips twisted in a half-smile. "Believe me I do. I've been single for a long time."

"Maybe we both can take a lesson from Destiny," Adrienne said, taking Renee's wrist to stop her from walking.

"What lesson?"

"Work up the courage to ask out a guy. If a sixteen-year-old can do it, then certainly we can."

Renee chuckled and wrapped her arm around Adrienne's shoulder. "It's easier when you're sixteen."

"That's what we tell ourselves. When it's really just a loss of some of the confidence that comes with youth. I'm pretty sure you can think of one man out there who would respond positively if you asked him out."

Jonathan. His name was the only thing that went through her mind. He'd only offered an affair. She didn't partake in affairs. Sex served a purpose in relationships, but she'd never entered into a strictly sexual relationship just for fun.

Maybe because you're too frigid.

She didn't want to be frigid anymore.

"What about you, Adrienne?" Renee slipped her arm from around Adrienne's shoulders. "Is there a man waiting on you to ask him out."

"I don't know. Maybe I'll work up the courage to find out."

Renee considered the woman's words. Confidence came easy for Renee in the boardroom. Daniel had taken that from her outside her professional life. She needed to get it back.

Renee nodded. "Maybe I will too."

Renee left Adrienne and said good-bye to the program director of the center. On the way to her car, her cell phone chimed with a text message from Mikayla.

Andre invited Jonathan to the tailgate. I hope that's ok.

Earlier that week Mikayla had called to tell Renee that Andre wanted to tailgate for the University of South Carolina Homecoming game. Andre and Jonathan had both attended undergraduate school there, but Andre had never gone back for the games. He'd always been too busy when he'd worked for his father to take time to enjoy himself. Mikayla had invited Renee to join them.

Renee's reply was quick and simple. *That's ok.*

Two words that gave no indication of the rush of anticipation bursting through her system. With those words, Renee accepted that she was one step closer to giving in to her attraction to Jonathan. Business was business. This was just about pleasure. Surely, she was strong enough to keep them separate.

CHAPTER 13

Jonathan stood at the back of his pickup truck in the tailgate spot next to Andre's on the green across from Williams Brice stadium and sipped beer from a red solo cup. Music played in the background from various tailgaters, the smell of food grilling filled the air, and the sounds of hundreds of fans created an energy that took Jonathan back over ten years.

He'd missed college tailgates with Andre. Another good reason for Andre and Mikayla to be together. She'd made his friend realize that there was more to life than work and family duty.

He glanced at Renee talking with Mikayla on the other side the garnet and black tent that marked Andre's spot. Her chocolate brown eyes lifted to his and her lips curved up in a smile that made him feel like a ready-to-conquer-the-world college student again. Maybe because all day she'd shot him shy, flirty glances that created the same thrum of anticipation he used to feel when he'd catch a pretty girl's eye across the dance floor at a college party.

"You're watching my sister pretty hard," Ryan said.

Jonathan turned to face Ryan, who gave Jonathan a look that held all the warmth of a junkyard guard dog. He'd come as Renee's date. Jonathan would have preferred her bring an actual date instead of her brother. They'd never met, but he'd heard the stories through Andre.

"I mean no disrespect. Your sister is an interesting woman."

Ryan tapped his finger against the bottle of some fancy foreign beer he'd brought. "True. She's also soft hearted, even though she likes to keep that part of herself hidden. She's strong, but that doesn't prevent people from trying to take advantage of her."

"I feel sorry for anyone who underestimates your sister's ability to handle herself. Soft hearted or not, she's smart and not easily swayed." He made sure to infuse a little *mind your business* in his tone. Whatever was going on between him and Renee, it was for them to figure out.

Ryan shifted his position until he stood in front of Jonathan. The moved blocked Jonathan's view of Renee. "Did she give you our offer?"

"She did. I'm not accepting it."

Ryan's eyes sharpened, turned calculating. "You really want to fight us in court?"

"I'm not afraid to fight for what's right." Jonathan straightened his shoulders and lined his voice with unwavering steel.

"Your aunt had the authority to sign over the land."

"Weeks before she actually signed it she had the legal authority. Not after my grandmother passed." Jonathan tipped his lips upward but the gesture was far from friendly. "It's why you'll lose."

Ryan's smirk was the confident sign of a man who constantly got whatever he wanted. "Renee never loses."

"There's a first for everything."

"You're confident. Good for you." Ryan leaned in. "Eventually you'll let us know how much it will take to get you to drop this. Every man has a price."

Frustration formed a hard knot in Jonathan's stomach. "I'm not every man."

Ryan didn't seem fazed by the anger creeping into Jonathan's voice. "We know the place holds no sentimental value for you. You have a price. She isn't for sale." Ryan jerked his head back toward Renee.

Jonathan's body froze harder than concrete. "I'm not asking for her."

"Good. Renee deserves happiness. Not another guy using her for his own means." Ryan lifted the fancy beer and took a sip. "Remember that when you name your price." Ryan tipped his beer at Jonathan and strolled away.

Anger flowed down Jonathan's spine like lighter fluid. One more word from Ryan and Jonathan was likely to burst into flames. Had Renee told her brother that was his asking price? Had she taken his request for her to acknowledge the sparks between them as an offer to drop the lawsuit if she slept with him? The idea made his skin crawl.

What kind of man did she think he was? He wanted her, against all rational thoughts and good sense. But not because having her meant he would be closer to winning the lawsuit. If anything, sleeping with her would make winning that much harder.

His gaze focused on her with the precision of a laser. She stopped in the middle of a sentence and looked his way. Her smile faded away. Confusion clouded her beautiful features.

He took a determined step in her direction. There were several things they needed to get clear.

A hand slapped Jonathan on the back. "What the hell did Ryan want?" Andre barely kept the animosity out of his voice. Jonathan knew that respect for Mikayla's friendship with Renee was the only thing that kept Andre from telling Ryan to leave.

"Wanted to know my selling price for the Big House."

Andre's scowl would've scared a python. "Of course he'd bring that up today. The man has no class."

If Andre and Mikayla heard what Ryan thought was Jonathan's asking price, they'd accuse Jonathan of having no class. He needed to clarify things with Renee. Withdraw his crazy suggestion altogether. No woman was worth his integrity.

"I'm more pissed they think they can buy me out."

"I can't really blame them on that. I used to believe every person had an eventual selling price." Andre gave one of those *what can I say* shrugs. "Most of the time the people my dad went to with a bribe eventually took it."

"I'm not most of those people."

Andre bumped Jonathan with his elbow. "I know that. I'm just saying don't take it personally that they think you have a price. It's part of the Caldwell family nature to try to buy our way out of a bad situation."

"Maybe that's true, but I don't have to like it." He took a step in Renee's direction.

Andre touched Jonathan's arm. "What are you going to do?"

"There are a few things Renee and I have to get straight." He gave Andre the *I'm good* head nod.

Andre lifted his hand and stepped back. Jonathan crossed the tent and interrupted Renee and Mikayla. "Hey, can we take a walk?"

Renee was statue still for a second before she blinked. "Of course." She looked to Mikayla, who smiled brighter than a dozen LED lights.

They walked for a few minutes in silence, looking at the other tailgaters. When they reached the end of the row of vehicles, they turned and strolled down the next.

"How is Lilly?" she asked. "I wanted to call and ask you but…"

But there was the big dancing elephant between them. The suggestion he'd thrown out without thinking.

"She's fine," he said. "Got a pink cast that she's decorated with glitter and sparkles." He thought about the picture Nadine had sent of Lilly's improved cast and smiled. He pulled out his cell phone and called up the picture so Renee could see it. "She keeps asking when she'll see you so you can sign it."

Affection filled Renee's face as she looked at the picture. She laughed and shifted closer to him. "I'll have to get a special pen to sign such an awesome cast." She handed his phone back to him.

"She'll love you even more for that," Jonathan said.

They walked a little more when Renee sighed. "What did Ryan say that pissed you off?"

"What makes you think he pissed me off?"

"He has that effect on people. Plus, I saw the scowl on your face when he walked away."

Jonathan stopped walking and faced her. Renee met his eyes directly. No more shy, flirty smiles. She watched him with the straightforward focus of a businesswoman.

"Was it about the settlement?"

"What did you tell him?" Accusation turned his voice into a whip.

"Nothing."

A woman walked into his periphery before he could speak. "Jonathan, is that you?"

Jonathan's body tightened. He could have gone the rest of his damned life never hearing that voice again. His neck stiffened as he turned his head to face her, as if his body was rejecting what his ears heard.

Karen. He hadn't seen her since their breakup, and she looked just as good. Not that he expected her to age much in the past few months, but it would have been nice if the next time he saw her, she was wearing rollers and a bathrobe in the grocery store. As if she'd be caught dead that way.

She wore a garnet sweater dress and heeled black boots. The material clung to every one of her curves, highlighting an hourglass figure he'd adored the entire time they were together. Light brown eyes watched him warily. He held her gaze for several seconds until she glanced away and tucked a strand of dark hair behind her ear. Her lips pressed together in a tight, awkward smile that brought out the dimples in her round cheeks.

"Karen, you're the last person I expected to see here."

"Likewise." Her eyes, the same color as cognac flicked over his body. "You're looking good."

Jonathan refused to let his eyes give her the onceover again. "Likewise."

Karen's lip quirked up but then fell, as if she were trying to smile but couldn't quite get there. "I've been meaning to call you."

As if they had anything to talk about. "Where's your lawyer?"

She didn't even flinch when he brought up the other guy. "Around." Her voice said she didn't know and didn't care.

Renee cleared her throat and shifted next to him. Karen's eyes were razorblades when they cut to Renee. Jonathan wanted to kick himself for being so startled he'd ignored her. Renee glanced at Karen, and then at him expectantly. Karen didn't deserve to be introduced to Renee. She was nowhere near her league.

"If you'll excuse us," Jonathan said.

He placed a hand on Renee's back, which was stiff.

Karen took a step forward. "I need to talk to you."

"There's nothing to say." He tried to usher Renee away.

Karen shifted again. "I'm sorry. About everything. The things I said, the way we ended."

He didn't think it was possible, but Renee stiffened even more. He didn't want to do this now. "Karen." Her name was a warning on his lips.

Ever bold, Karen kept talking. Funny how he used to love that about her. "I hope we can be friends again. That there are no hard feelings."

"I don't even care anymore. If you needed to come over here and apologize to make yourself feel better, then fine. You've done that, but I've moved on."

Karen's gaze met Renee's in a challenge. Jonathan expected Renee to say he didn't move on with me, or walk away and leave him in ex-girlfriend purgatory.

Instead, she relaxed and leaned closer to him. Her hand slipped into his and her head tilted just a little to the right. "Oh, *you're* Karen," Renee said. "Jonathan's talked about you."

***

Renee watched as the smug challenge in Karen's eyes turned to wariness. Typically, she didn't play these childish games, but the woman had completely overstepped her bounds. Renee and Jonathan may not be together, but the way Karen had ignored Renee and made her *heartfelt* plea for them to be friends again, had scraped Renee like glass-coated sandpaper.

"You've talked about me?" Karen asked.

"Of course," Renee said filling her voice with the cool confidence she used in the boardroom. She held out her hand. "I'm Renee Caldwell."

Karen's handshake was weak. "Nice meeting you," she said, with all the authenticity of a million-dollar bill.

"Are you here with friends?" Renee had to admit Jonathan's comment about Karen's lawyer had piqued her interest. She guessed the lawyer in question was the guy.

"I'm here with my boyfriend. He's a lawyer." Karen's shoulders lifted and her voice held enough gloat to tell Renee she liked to tell people that her boyfriend was a lawyer.

"That's nice," Renee said.

Karen looked over Renee's shoulder and waved someone over. "Here he is."

Renee recognized Karen's boyfriend, Jared Knight. Renee and Jared hung around in the same circles. He and Ryan had been pretty good friends in high school and their families knew each other. He was a nice guy, handsome, and successful enough to be considered a catch.

"Hello, Jared," Renee said.

Jonathan's hand stiffened in hers. He was so still, she wondered if he were breathing. Jared must have been the guy. She rubbed the back of his hand with her thumb and hoped he understood the gesture was supposed to be comforting.

"Renee," Jared said with a warm smile. He slid his arm around Karen's waist. "Long time no see. Do you two know each other?" He looked between her and Karen.

"Actually, we just met," Renee said. "Karen is an old friend of Jonathan's." Renee tilted her head to Jonathan. "Jonathan, this is Jared Knight. Jared and Ryan were once close friends. Jared, this is Jonathan Wright."

Jared's gaze turned to Jonathan. "Any friend of Karen is a friend of mine." He held out his hand toward Jonathan. "It's nice to meet you."

Jonathan didn't hold out his hand. "We met once."

Jared's hand curved back in and he looked genuinely confused. "Sorry, I don't remember."

Karen tugged on Jared's waist. "It doesn't matter. Let's go."

Jared didn't move. A second later realization struck on his face. "Oh. We did meet." His friendly smile turned wary and he leaned back. Though Jonathan had made no movement toward him. The hard glare on Jonathan's face would have made Renee lean away as well.

"If you'll excuse us," Renee said with a calm she didn't feel.

Jared shot her a relieved smile. "Good to see you again, Renee."

"Likewise," she said to be polite.

Jonathan said nothing else as he navigated her back toward their tailgate area. He didn't talk and she didn't press him for conversation. Though curiosity ricocheted inside of her harder than a gumball machine bouncing ball.

"You dated him too?" Jonathan asked after they walked closer to Andre's set up.

"No. Jared is a friend of the family, but that's all."

Jonathan's tight hold on her hand loosened. She hadn't realized they were still holding hands as they walked until he lessened his grip. She didn't pull away.

"Would that have mattered?"

He shook his head. "Not really. Still."

"Still what?"

Jonathan's deep sigh carried a ton of regret. "I lost one woman to him."

"You wouldn't me to Jared. You wouldn't lose me to anybody."

He stopped moving so suddenly that Renee nearly tripped because of their clasped hands. A million pinpricks of heat rushed up her cheeks. She wasn't sentimental. Where in the world had the statement come from?

"I mean," she stammered. "If you were my type. If...we were together, but we're not."

His winter-sky eyes held hers in a captive hold. *Son-of-a-biscuit.* She was an idiot. She lifted her chin. The slow smile that spread his lips sent more heat spreading to lower regions of her body.

"You wouldn't let me go, huh?"

Renee pulled her hand from his. "Don't get big-headed about it. I already told you I'm not a cheater. That's the only point I was trying to make."

The grin on his face said he didn't believe a word. Renee didn't want to think too hard about what she'd really meant. Sleeping with Jonathan was one thing. A thing she still wasn't sure she was ready to do. A relationship with Jonathan was out of the question. They didn't have enough in common to consider something serious.

Mikayla ran up before Jonathan could say more. "Renee, did you know Ryan was bringing a date?"

Renee tore her gaze from Jonathan's to Mikayla's and frowned. "No. He brought me here."

"Then you don't know that he invited Eva Drake?"

"What?" Renee snapped. Her gaze cut to the tailgate area.

Sure enough, Ryan stood there laughing and what looked like flirting with Eva. Renee had nothing against Eva. Her design company decorated all of Caldwell Development's model homes. She didn't even care that Eva was ten years Ryan's senior. The problem was Eva's husband, a businessman rumored to be as ruthless as her Uncle Curtis, and two teenage children.

"He said he invited her in a purely professional capacity," Mikayla said, concern filling her voice. Mikayla and Ryan may not have made a good couple, but Mikayla had been Ryan's friend before their failed relationship. Renee had filled her in on Ryan's recent crazy behavior.

The way Eva used her thumb to wipe Ryan's bottom lip after he sipped his beer screamed unprofessional.

"This is ridiculous." Renee marched the remaining way to the tailgate. She kept her smile as cool as possible, though her stiff cheeks protested the forced nicety. "Eva, what are you doing here?"

Eva slid closer to Ryan. "Just enjoying a game with my client."

"Where's your husband?" Renee asked tilting her head to the side and filling her voice with false sweetness. "And kids?"

Eva's beautiful smile faltered for a second. "Stephen didn't want to come. He lets me handle my clients my way."

Renee looked to Ryan. "Can we talk?"

"Of course, talk." Ryan shifted his weight and took a sip of his beer, clearly not planning to move an inch.

"Ryan." Her voice filled with warning.

"How about you continue to hold hands with Jonathan, and I'll entertain Eva, okay?" Ryan placed his hand on Eva's lower back. "Besides, Eva has an extra seat for the game. I think I'd rather discuss business with her there instead of hanging with the *happy couple*."

He ushered Eva from under the tent. Renee clenched her teeth to keep her jaw from dropping. "Ryan, are you coming back here after the game? You're my ride."

"You'll be good. You've got a date." Ryan threw a look at Jonathan, then walked away with Eva.

CHAPTER 14

Renee lived in one of the smaller homes built by Caldwell Development mainly because she didn't need a lot of space for herself, and with the smaller lot the yard was easier to maintain. She didn't do the yard work herself, but she did try to make her place feel welcoming with seasonal touches, such as the autumn themed wreath hanging on her front door and pumpkins in baskets on the porch.

"Nice house," Jonathan said pulling his truck into her driveway and parking.

"Thank you. For the compliment and for the ride."

She still couldn't believe Ryan had left her at the game. For Eva Drake. What could he be thinking? Sneaking around with a married woman was foolish; sneaking around with a married woman whose husband was suspected of having gang ties was downright stupid.

Ryan rarely thought things through. It was one of the reasons their dad didn't trust Ryan's judgment over Renee's. Ryan always went for what he wanted without thinking of the consequences.

She glanced at Jonathan out of the corner of her eye. What would it be like to go for what she wanted with no thought to the consequences?

"Do you want to come in?" She tossed out the question hard and fast.

Jonathan turned off the truck. "Yeah. We need to talk."

A mini earthquake of nerves racked her midsection. She opened her door and concentrated on walking normally to avoid giving any indication of the turmoil going on inside. Was she really doing this?

Inside, she led Jonathan down the entryway to the open living and kitchen area. The blinds were drawn which made the inside dark. The dim lights increased the severity of her internal tremors.

She crossed the room to open the blinds covering the French doors that led out to her patio. "Do you want anything to drink?"

She walked to the other windows to let in more light. The task offered a distraction and time for her to think about what she was about to do.

"No, I won't be here long."

Renee turned away from the last window to face him. "You won't?"

"We need to get a few things straight." He took a few measured steps toward her. "Ryan wanted to make it very clear that you are not part of the payoff for my family's land. Not that I expected that."

So that's what caused the angry look after Jonathan talked to her brother earlier. "That's good to know." Not that she expected Ryan to want to offer her up.

"What I need to know is why he would think I'd expect that in the first place."

She wanted to say overprotectiveness and leave it at that. Surprisingly she wanted to tell him the truth. "Because it's happened before."

He stopped crossing to her again. "What?"

Renee lifted her chin and met his eye. "His name was Daniel LeFranc. We dated about a year ago. I thought it was because we both saw a mutual benefit if we were to date. His family is rich in land but they hadn't let go of so much as an acre in years. They're well respected and Daniel had political connections. It wasn't until after we slept together that he made it known that he'd gotten what he wanted. A taste of me and a few million dollars for the land. Apparently, he was about to file for bankruptcy."

She didn't include the jibe about her being cold and unfeeling in bed. She'd tried to fake passion with Daniel. Told herself that less passion with a perfect man was worth a lot more than passion with an imperfect one. After her dad's call on her relationship status, her way of thinking seemed even more jaded.

"He ended our relationship shortly after that."

"Did you tell your family?"

"I told Ryan, and Mikayla. I couldn't bring myself to tell my parents. They became friends with the LeFrancs in the short time Daniel and I were together. The connection is beneficial to them. No need to mess that up because Daniel and I aren't compatible."

"There's every reason to mess things up." His voice was razor sharp. "He used you."

Renee shook her head. "People close deals in bedrooms all the time."

"It's different if both parties know what's going on. He only decided to let you know about that afterward. He's a bastard that didn't deserve you."

His words sent comforting warmth through her. She took the next few steps to stand in front of him. "Maybe he and Karen learned about relationships from the same terrible book."

Jonathan flinched and took a heavy breath. "Maybe."

"Was it difficult to see her today?"

He ran a hand through his hair. "It damn sure wasn't easy."

Renee sat on the edge of her cream colored sofa. Jonathan sat next to her and leaned back on the cushions. His long legs spread out in front of him while he stared at the ceiling.

"Do you still love her?"

"No. In fact, her lets be friends routine before Jared walked up only proved that I dodged a bullet."

"We both know you're good at dodging bullets," she teased.

Jonathan's low chuckle was like warm silk against her. "I guess I am, huh, sugar."

The endearment made her heart clench. "I think she wants you back."

"Too bad for her." He turned his head and winter blue eyes met hers. "What you said, about not losing me. Why did you say it?"

Renee looked away. "I told you why."

His hand covered hers on her lap and squeezed. He sat up and faced her. "Why, Renee? Because when I first saw you I couldn't let you walk away without talking to you. When I kissed you the first time, I knew that one kiss wouldn't be enough. I've got a feeling that once you're mine, sugar, I'm going to have a hard time letting go."

Her stomach flipped and her heart jumped haphazardly in her chest. Time to step out and take a chance at going for what she wanted. She leaned forward and pressed her lips against his. The kiss was soft and fleeting before she pulled back.

"Don't let go, Jonathan."

His hands rose, cupped her face. He leaned in and covered her mouth gently with his. His lips were firm and warm. They glided across hers with aching tenderness. Her midsection tightened with need. Renee pressed her hands onto his chest and pushed him back.

"Upstairs," she whispered.

***

Jonathan followed Renee upstairs to her bedroom. He got a feel for tasteful furnishings and surprisingly bright colors before he forgot everything and pulled her into his arms. Her fingers tunneled through his hair the second his lips touched hers.

She wasn't hesitant, or coy, her lips parted and her tongue met his in a long, deep kiss. He wanted to taste her, every inch of her. Starting with the silky caramel of her skin, then her hard little nipples that he hadn't been able to erase from his mind, and end with the sweet essence between her legs.

Renee wrapped one leg around his and twisted her hips in a slow seductive motion. His toes curled and raw sexual hunger blazed in his blood. Her small breasts glided across his chest behind the thin material of her top. The tips hard points running lines of sensation across his chest. Gripping her ass, Jonathan pulled her forward until the heat of her sex seared him.

Renee broke the kiss. He groaned the semblance of disapproval until her lips pressed soft, sweet kisses down his neck. Jonathan pulled off the T-shirt he'd worn. He hated letting her go for just that brief instant. Renee's near silent gasp and the appreciation in her eyes as her gaze caressed his body gave him more pleasure than he'd ever expected to feel from a simple appraisal. Slim, feminine fingers ran through the hair along his chest.

"I've wanted to touch you all day." Her tone was quiet, hesitant, as if she were afraid to admit to her desires.

Never that. He wanted her to always admit her desires with him.

Her fingernails lightly scratched the muscles of his chest. His thoughts scattered. Her lips were warm drops of pleasure following in the path left by her fingers. He looked down, her tongue flicked his nipple, and his balls tightened. Pleasure exploded through him and he groaned.

"You like that?" Her low and sexy voice was also unsure.

"Oh, yes," he said through clenched teeth.

Warm feminine lips surrounded his flat nipple. Her tongue danced around the tip then she sucked deep. Jonathan's head fell back; his hand grasped the back of her head and his fingers splayed through the soft strands of her short hair.

"How about this?" Her plump lips brushed against his nipple.

There was a tug at his waistband and he couldn't even think to talk. She'd unhooked the buttons. Cool air surrounded him followed shortly by the delicious heat of her hand wrapping around him.

"You're so big, and thick," Her voice was sultry, sexy, excited. "I knew you'd be thick."

Slim fingers grasped his hard flesh. Her palms were smooth, her hands small but strong as she stroked him while her soft lips and warm mouth moved to his other nipple.

Jonathan's knees nearly buckled. "You've been thinking about my dick."

Her thumb brushed across the swollen tip. Sharp pleasure scattered like a thousand shards of glass through him. Her other hand went into his pants to cup his balls. "I have thought about it. Along with all of the things I could do to it."

Heaven help him. If Renee kept this up, he wouldn't make it to the main event. "I wouldn't have expected you to focus on that part of my body."

She squeezed him gently. Her hand gliding up and down. Her fingers trailed over him as if she were committing his entire length to memory.

"It's the best part. Next to your eyes."

Sweet heaven, she was wicked. Jonathan's hand fell to her shoulder. She continued to work him with her soft, delicate hands. He wanted to push her down to her knees. Pull out his dick and watch as her lips surrounded him. See her tongue come out to tease and flick across the head. He groaned low and deep.

Renee's thumb made a slow circle over the very tip of him. "You want me to go down, don't you?"

Hell yes he did! His hand tightened on her shoulder. He didn't push. He wouldn't force it. Wouldn't insist. Even at this moment, when Renee held him literally in the palm of her hand, old insecurities crept in. Karen saying he was obsessed with that. That he asked her to do it too much. She seemed to forget that he loved giving as much as receiving.

"Do whatever you want," he said through gritted teeth. His arm tensed as he fought the urge to get her on her knees.

Her hands slipped away. Jonathan clenched his teeth to prevent from begging her to hold him again, except then her hands were at the waistband of his jeans, pushing them down, her body following.

"Are you sure?" Renee didn't seem the type. She wouldn't want him holding her head, directing her how to suck, when to lick. She'd be turned off, disgusted.

Then her mouth was on him and fireworks exploded behind his eyelids. Her tongue slid over him like he was the most decadent of treats. She started at the base, slowly moved up to the head. All the while, her hand played with the heavy sac beneath, testing him out.

Her lips parted then the heavenly heat of her mouth was hot and wet all around him. Up and down. She started nice and easy with long, wet movements, then she pulled hard. Jonathan's eyes rolled to the back of his head as a kaleidoscope of pleasure took his body on a joy ride.

Her hands worked in concert with her mouth. Her tongue did voodoo magic tricks with each decadent pull of her lips.

"Mmmm." Her moan filled the room. Seriously, was she trying to make him cry like a baby? Her moan along with her heavy breathing, the sounds of her efforts had his spine trembling.

He dragged his lids up. Her eyes were closed, but her face was filled with pleasure. Hell, delight. Pleasure that matched the excited sounds of her moans.

His hands dug into her hair, but he didn't push, he just wanted to feel her work. She didn't go fast and hard, wasn't slow and timid, but perfect. If she kept this up, he wouldn't make it.

"Renee," he ground out. "You've got to stop."

She didn't.

"Renee," his voice strained. "If you don't stop…"

She sucked harder. His eyes crossed. "Renee … you've…" her tongue lapped the underside.

Shit, too late. He exploded, gripping her head, his body jerked and trembled with his release. Still, she didn't stop.

Fuck, this woman was perfect. With each tremble of his body Renee not only got under his skin, she got into his blood.

***

Renee stood at her bathroom sink, rinsing her mouth out, her knees shaking. What in the world had gotten into her? She usually hated doing that. Only did it as a last resort, or when the guy she was dating asked enough. She read enough books to know how to do it right, but never did that for her own pleasure. Yet, the second her hand closed over the hard length of him, she'd wanted nothing more.

She turned off the water and a strong arm wrapped around her waist. She turned her head to the side and rested against his shoulder.

"My turn," his whisky warm voice in her ear.

His lips ran along her neck with light kisses. One large hand covered her breast. She briefly wondered if he thought them too small. He pulled and tugged until her jeans were unbuttoned then pushed them past her waist. Thoughts of the size of her breasts dissipated. Renee kicked the jeans off and to the side.

His fingers slipped between her slick folds. All thought fled.

Gripping the edge of the sink, Renee moaned and parted her legs. His hands weren't soft. They weren't the manicured hands of a man who pushed papers all day. They were the rough, callused hands of a man who worked hard every day. The coarseness added to the sweet friction of his fingers against her sensitive clit.

"Can I have you how ever I want you?" His voice was deep, demanding.

His hips pushed forward. The heavy thickness of his erection pressed into the cleft of her backside. A thrill of excitement went through her. "Yes."

"Good."

He spun her around and picked her up. He carried her back into the bedroom. Lowered her on the bed. His body covered hers. His mouth plundering her with a slow deep kiss.

Raising on his knees between her legs he slowly pulled off her panties. After flicking them over his shoulder, he took her hands in his and pulled her into a seated position. Swiftly he removed her shirt and bra. Once those were gone, his hands clasped her face. His eyes were hot and bright in the muted light of her bedroom. He stared at her for a second that held an eternity, then kissed her hard and long.

Renee's hands explored every inch of his body. He was so big! Every part of him. She could touch him, *rub* him, for days, and still not get enough. Her fingers immediately sought out his erection, but he brushed her hands aside. Pushing her down into the mattress, his large hands engulfed her breasts.

"Too small?" she asked.

"Bite sized," he said with a sexy grin. His body covered hers and his head dipped to do just that. His teeth nipped the protruding tips before he sucked one deep into his mouth.

Renee arched up, offering more.

Jonathan groaned. "Perfect size." His mouth opened and took in nearly her entire breast.

"Oh my God, yes," she moaned, her head twisting. Her fingers plunged in the silky softness of the curls on his head, pulling him closer.

His fingers slipped back between her legs. Not slow and playful, but confident and sure as they parted her folds before slipping what had to be two fingers inside.

Her head pressed back. Her eyes squeezed closed as pleasure washed through her. Spreading her hips as much as she could with him covering her, Renee lifted her hips to get him deeper.

His fingers pulled back then pushed in harder. Renee cried out. Jonathan went still. "Too much?"

She shook her head. "If you stop, I'll kill you."

His chuckle was decadent. He shifted to lie beside her instead of on top of her. Her legs popped wide and he grinned before lowering his head back to her breast. His hand continued to push hard and deep into her.

Renee's hips bucked. Her walls clenched around him, and her moans filled the air. As good as this felt, she wanted more, needed more. Her hand reached down until her fingers brushed the tips of his erection. He pulled back.

"Not yet," he said.

"I need that. I need you." She panted, not caring that she'd begged.

Swiftly, Jonathan shifted lower. He grasped her knees and pushed them up then out. Exposing her to his hot gaze. Fire licked over every inch of her body.

"You're so slick and beautiful," his voice was low. His molten gaze locked on her sex.

He licked his lips. Renee bit her lip. "Lick me," she whispered. A command she'd never made before. Most of the guys she'd dated weren't thrilled with reciprocating.

The happy grin that split his face made everything that was female in her sing. "My pleasure."

He settled his broad shoulders between her thighs and slowly eased his tongue across the protruding pearl of her sex. His long, languid licks turned her into a stuttering fool. Every moan she made was answered with a deep excited groan of his.

There was nothing practiced or premeditated about her reaction. Her body went on autopilot, her hips grinding, her hands pulling his hair and her cries of pleasure filling the room. His actions drove her mad, until her body shook and her legs trembled.

Suddenly he lifted. Renee's hips tried to follow. "No, don't stop!" She all but sobbed.

"Now, I'm ready for you. Condoms?"

She pointed to her nightstand. "Top drawer. It's been awhile. Not sure how old."

He reached into the drawer and pulled out a condom. He glanced at the wrapper. "Not too old."

Her sex ached for him. Renee lowered her hand between her legs, and played with her wet flesh. Jonathan's eyes narrowed. He pulled his lower lip between his teeth and watched her while easing the condom on. Her eyes were glued to his hands working. She knew he was thick, had felt his thickness, tasted it. But to see his wide, blunt, erection ready for her was another thing. The thought of him filling her made her core clench. She increased the pressure of her fingers until her eyes closed and her head fell to the side.

Jonathan's large hands grasped her hips, lifted them. The thickness of his erection pushed against her sex. Over and over, back and forth across the bundle of nerves that touched every fiber of her being. Renee jerked. She was so close, her toes curled into the mattress. She clutched his forearms.

"Jonathan! Yes, do that again."

He did, pushing and sliding across her, building her need until she knew she'd burst. Then he was at the opening. Pressing inside, slowly. "Perfect," he groaned. "You're so fucking perfect."

She hated when people called her perfect, but the word on his lips sounded right. Felt right. She wasn't trying to be, wasn't playing the role of perfect lover, and therefore the words only filled her with joy.

"More, Jonathan. Deeper." She pressed her nails into his arm.

Jonathan's hips surged forward, filling her hard and fast. She gasped, cried out. *He* was perfect! "Harder."

Jonathan's hips pistoned, deep, hard, and fast, pounding until her shoulders slid against the bed with each thrust, taking her closer to the other edge. She didn't care. Only cared about how great he felt inside of her.

"You want more?" he asked.

Was he kidding? How could this possibly get better? "More."

He worked harder. Pushed faster, his dick going deeper. She broke, her orgasm shattering through her. She shouted, clawed his arms, tears streamed. She was spent. Couldn't move, could barely breath.

Jonathan's hips slowed but didn't stop. He thrust in unhurried, easy strokes as he lowered her hips and pressed his body against hers. His big hand brushed the tears from her cheeks. She dragged her eyelids up and met his gaze.

He raised a brow. "Again?"

She still trembled from her orgasm, but the sensual, easy glide of him deep inside of her stirred her desire. "Do you even have to ask?" She panted, her voice hoarse from her cries.

Jonathan grinned. He reached down, gripped himself, and slowly pulled out. Renee whimpered.

Then he flipped her over, lifted her onto her knees, and pushed in deep.

CHAPTER 15

When Jonathan came out of Renee's bedroom the next morning, the smell of coffee brewing and eggs cooking greeted him. He took a deep breath and followed the smell of food. He'd pulled on his jeans from the day before after washing his face and brushing his teeth with the spare toothbrush Renee had laid out for him. Even though he was relaxed and sated from a wonderful night, he felt...off balance.

He'd promised himself to never again get attached to a woman he couldn't trust after Karen cheated. No, he could be honest with himself. After Karen broke his heart. He'd done a shit job of being in a relationship then, but he had loved her, and after she hurt him, he had no intention of ever being some other woman's chump.

Yet, here he was. Damned near skipping out of Renee's bedroom, anxious to see her and pull her into his arms after she'd thoroughly pleased him the night before.

He wasn't sure he could trust her completely, but he wanted to see her again. Not just because of last night. She'd held his hand when seeing Karen and Jared had brought back that kicked in the nuts feeling from a year ago. She'd opened up to him about the jerk in her past. What they'd done last night had not felt like a one-night stand. Last night felt like the start of something substantial, and that scared the shit out of him.

He found her in the kitchen. The silky material of a pair of conservative navy blue pajamas poured over the soft curves of her small breasts and slim hips. His fingers would slip and slide easily across her nipples through the material. She'd gasp, her eyes would get that far-off dreamy look she'd had last night. Her hands would clasp his arms. He wouldn't be able to stop himself from lifting her onto the counter...

He cut the fantasy short. He could keep his dick in his pants at least through breakfast. He hated having *the* talk in relationships. Hated going through the will-we-won't-we phase, but he needed to know. He hadn't lied yesterday. He was going to have a hard time letting Renee go.

"You're making me breakfast," he drawled, strolling barefoot across hardwood floors to where she stood scraping eggs from a nonstick pan onto a plate.

She glanced at him over her shoulder. Her brown eyes sparkled in the morning sunlight pouring in from the open blinds along her French doors.

"I'm only scrambling a few eggs. That's about as far as my culinary skills go."

Jonathan wrapped his hand around her waist and pulled her body against his. He couldn't help it. She was so damned beautiful and sexy with her morning-after glow. He palmed one of her breasts, the tip hardened, and smiled.

"Good thing I love scrambled eggs." He kissed the side of her neck, breathing in her luscious scent.

Renee's contented sigh made him think, hope, she was just as swept away by this as he was. He toyed with the hardened peak in his hand and her ass pressed against his semi-hard dick.

"Stop, I'm trying to make breakfast."

He glanced at the eggs on the plate next to the stove. "Looks like you're done to me."

"Well you need to eat."

He ran his finger in circles around her nipple and her head fell back. "I'd much rather play with you."

Renee moaned and twisted against him, then suddenly turned and maneuvered out of his arms. "We did it enough last night. Now it's time for food."

Jonathan grinned and reached out to unbutton the top button of her silk pajamas. "If you insist."

He popped open the next button until the slight swell of her cleavage appeared. Renee swatted his hand away, but she didn't button her shirt. "I do insist. I cooked for you. I don't cook for anyone, so you better enjoy it."

"Who's the last person you cooked for?"

"Other than myself, no one recently. I'm not that great of a cook, there are only a few things I can make that are edible."

She reached into her cabinet and pulled out white ceramic plates. The toaster dinged and two slices popped up. She added the toast with the eggs onto the plates.

"I think I made eggs for Ryan right before he asked Mikayla to the infamous wedding. He spent the night, told me all the reasons why he thought he was ready to settle down. We talked into the night and the next morning I made breakfast."

She sounded happy about the memory so he didn't snort his disbelief. If Ryan had been ready to settle down, he wouldn't have cheated on Mikayla that very weekend. Renee put the plates on the table, before pulling a glass pitcher with orange juice from the fridge.

"Where are the glasses?" he asked.

She motioned to another cabinet and he grabbed two glasses while

Renee got silverware.

"If he cared so much, why did he cheat on her?" Some of his bitterness crept through.

Renee shrugged. "I never said Ryan wasn't impulsive. He thinks through big decisions, but he also tends to jump head first with his first instinct in other situations. That's what often creates problems."

"Do you think things through, or go with your gut instinct?"

"Mostly I think things through." She sat at the table. Jonathan joined her. "Impulsive decisions typically lead to disaster."

He knew she'd thought through sleeping with him. Someone had to because he obviously hadn't when he'd given the suggestion. Right now, they needed to think through their next steps. He didn't want to. If they thought about the future for too long, they'd probably agree Jonathan needed to go.

Renee picked up her fork, but froze with it hovering over her eggs. A pensive expression covered her face.

"You okay?" He shoveled a forkful of eggs into his mouth.

"Will you hate me if Caldwell Development wins the lawsuit?"

The food stuck in his throat. Jonathan picked up his glass of juice and drank it all. Her question and the very real possibility of that happening pounded through his head.

"If I thought you used unethical means to win, yes." He looked into her eyes. Thankfully, there was no guilt there. "But if, for some unforeseen reason, the judge is in favor of my aunt, I can't really blame you. My issues with my family started years before I was even born."

"Your grandfather?"

He nodded and took another bite of eggs. They were almost gone. Briefly, he wondered how many she'd cooked. "Gigi promised to leave the house to me, and I know she did so because she felt guilty."

"Guilty?"

"She made the promise after my grandfather kicked me out of the house. My dad would try to visit, mostly because of Gigi. My mom only came to the house once or twice, but my grandfather was so hateful toward her, she eventually refused."

You could only take being called ugly names so many times before you started to internalize them. That's what his mom had said after his grandfather's last rant.

"If your granddad was so bad, why did your dad take you?"

Jonathan dropped his fork and let out a heavy breath. He ran a hand through his hair. "I think my dad hoped that one day his father would accept his grandkids. Instead he called us mutts, half breeds, and any other vile thing that came to his mind." Resentment was a noose around his neck. He'd felt like a kicked dog every time his grandfather spoke to them.

"Gigi tried. She'd play with us, bring us candy and cookies, and try to distract us from my grandfather's rants. The day she promised me the land was after he threw me out on my college graduation. I knew I shouldn't have gone over there, but Gigi missed graduation because my grandfather was sick. So I went, in all my cap and gown glory, so she could take a picture."

"What happened?" Renee's fork was down, she'd stopped eating. Her hand was on the table, reaching toward him.

His chest hurt with the memory. He slid his own hand toward hers until their fingers brushed. Her touch grounded him in today instead of the pain of the past.

"He was sitting on the porch. Looking frail and evil as hell. I remember being surprised. By the frailness, not the evil. I was used to the evil. He took one look at me and snorted. 'I had more respect for that school when they didn't allow niggers in,'" he said in the hate-filled, nasal voice of his grandfather.

Her touch went away. She'd balled her hand into a fist. "That's terrible." Her voice trembled with anger. "For someone to say that to any person is horrible. To say it to your grandchild..." Her hand pounded the table.

Jonathan covered her fist with his hand. Her dark eyes sparked with fire and met his. She was so damned beautiful. Ready to fight to defend him. In that second, he knew that if he were her man, she'd always fight for him, support him. And he'd want her to.

"Like I said, my grandfather had no love for his grandchildren. I turned to leave, but Gigi came after me. Cursing a blue streak at him the entire way." He grinned at the memory. "It was the first time I'd seen her actually talk back to him. Maybe it was because he was dying, maybe she really was fed up. Either way, she told me he was leaving the house to her and that she'd then leave the house to me. She said it was my birthright, and that I deserved to come anytime I wanted and that my kids should feel welcome there one day."

"That's why you want the place? To turn it from a place of pain to one of acceptance."

"It's not just that. I hate so many parts of my family history, but everything they did wasn't terrible. There was some good. They served their country and they helped shape this state. But there was the bad, which can't just be swept under the rug. Writing my dad and his family out of the inheritance does that." He took a deep breath and thought of that day. The anger and hurt in Gigi's face. The sorrow in her eyes when she'd said the place was his birthright. "More than that, Gigi wanted to make things right and Joanne stole that from her."

He met Renee's eyes. "If it hadn't been Caldwell Development, it would have been another developer. Joanne did this. She took advantage of the trust Gigi placed in her and went against my grandmother's will. All because she's just as hateful as my grandfather. I can't let that go."

Renee's brows drew together. "I wouldn't expect you to."

"So you understand that I won't settle out of court. That I won't drop this. Not for anything." Not for us, the meaning inherent in his words.

She nodded, and slid her hand away. He started to let her withdraw but couldn't. He leaned forward and clasped her hand. "That doesn't mean I don't want you."

The smile on her face was a sweet, sad, second-place smile. An I've-got-to-be-graceful-even-though-this-sucks smile. "I know why you have to fight. I even agree that you should fight. My family is all about the business. Outside of taking care of his family, turning a profit and making Caldwell Development stronger and more successful is the only thing my dad cares about. He'll even understand why you won't drop this, but that doesn't mean he'll bow out. Our reputation is threatened by the lawsuit. That's something he won't let go."

"We knew this wouldn't be easy," he said.

"Nothing worth having ever is." Her eyes were calm and collected as they stared into his. "The question is, if the fight is worth it."

"I don't know," he answered truthfully. She once again tried to pull away, but he didn't let her go. "But the regret of not trying would be worse."

The smallest hint of color tinged her caramel cheeks. The edges of her mouth lifted in the simplest of smiles, but the radiance shining from her eyes said everything he needed.

"I agree." Her hand opened to squeeze his back.

Just like that, everything shifted. Something that he was almost afraid to admit was the precursor of deep affection shifted in his chest. Renee presented as a cool, professional businesswoman, but all of that hid a caring heart. He'd seen behind the mask to a woman he liked, the woman he wanted.

Her cell phone rang. Renee took a deep breath then gave him an apologetic smile. "Excuse me," she said with perfect manners before getting up and lifting the device off her counter.

"It's Ryan," she said, her smile going away. A concerned frown marred her beautiful features. "I should ignore him for leaving me, but I need to make sure he's okay."

"Why wouldn't he be?"

"Eva isn't the right woman for him. He could do better." Renee answered the phone, "Hello."

He wondered if she realized her family would probably say the same about him. He couldn't imagine Ryan or her dad pushing her to explore a relationship with him. Well too bad, he had her and he wasn't letting go easily.

She was still as she listened to Ryan then frowned. Her shoulders stiffened and she glanced at Jonathan. She mouthed *be right back* and pointed to the French doors. Jonathan nodded and Renee slipped through the doors to the balcony.

He glanced at his empty plate. She'd made him breakfast. Oh yeah, he was keeping Renee.

Even though he appreciated her efforts, he was still hungry. She must have only made three or four eggs for the two of them. Jonathan chuckled and stood. Of course, someone as tiny as Renee wouldn't know he typically ate three or four eggs just himself.

He took more eggs from the fridge to make more when his cell phone vibrated in the pocket of his jeans. He pulled it out and found a text message from Nadine.

Aunt Joanne wants to meet with us.

Jonathan frowned and rubbed his eyes. His good mood slowly eroded at the thought of meeting with his least favorite family member. *For what?*

A second later, his phone chimed again. *About the Big House.*

Jonathan wished he felt some optimism, but knowing Joanne, this meeting would be another chance for her to try to settle out of court. *Who's us?*

Me, you, and Daddy. She didn't invite Momma.

Not surprising, but anger still flared in Jonathan's gut. *When?*

Up to us. I say sooner the better.

True. Okay, I'm in Cola. He used the abbreviation for Columbia. *I'll call when I'm home. We'll set a date/time.*

K. A second later a second text came through. *Why r u in Cola?*

He wasn't answering that question. Lilly may like Renee, but Nadine hadn't weighed in either way. He didn't plan to keep their relationship a secret, but it wasn't something he wanted to reveal via text message. *I'll tell you when I get home.*

Fine. Keep your secrets.

Jonathan sighed and reread the text conversation. He only wanted to see Joanne in the courtroom, but if there was even a remote chance they could settle this peacefully, he'd take it. The sooner they met, the better. Even though every fiber in him knew the meeting wouldn't result in a peaceful end of this situation.

He glanced at Renee out on the patio. Her hands moved in jerky motions, her brows creased and her body tensed. He wondered if the argument was over the Eva woman or him. Either way, he didn't like seeing her angry.

After pouring coffee into a mug he got from the counter, Jonathan sweetened it then crossed the doors to take it to Renee. Renee's back was to him and she kept talking without turning around.

"Once again, it's not like that Ryan. Maybe I am being naive, but I like him, okay. You on the other hand are just being plain stupid." Renee's body stiffened and she sucked in a sharp breath. "Don't you dare say that."

Jonathan crossed the patio and touched her back. She jumped and spun to him. Anger and frustration marred her features. Jonathan held out the coffee mug with one hand. She relaxed and smiled before taking the coffee. Jonathan moved in close and rubbed her lower back .

Her expression was thankful and apologetic as she leaned into him. "I'm not listening to you anymore, Ryan," she said. "It's your life." Her eyes dropped as she listened to Ryan. A heavy sigh released some of the tension in her shoulders. "Fine. I promise I'll be careful, if you do the same. I'm more worried about you and Eva than what I'm doing with Jonathan." Another pause, a sad smile. "You too. Bye."

She ended the call and rubbed her head.

"I take it that didn't go well."

She snorted, a very un-Renee like gesture. "To say the least." She took a sip of the coffee. "He's so stubborn."

"I think you're a little stubborn too." His fingers pressed into her lower back, bringing her closer to him. "Want to talk about it?"

"Nope," she said, but rested her head on his chest. She gazed silently at the trees behind her house.

Jonathan watched the way the sunshine brought out the red highlights in her short hair and the golden undertones in her smooth brown skin. Struck once again by how sexy she was, how she'd made him breakfast, the way her body responded to him, and mostly, her simple declaration that she liked him.

"You like me."

"I think that's obvious," she said, with a soft laugh.

"That's cool, because I like you too, sugar." He kissed the top of her head.

Her shoulders relaxed. The sweet smile returned to her face and she looked at him. Jonathan was struck speechless for a second, dumbfounded that this woman was with him.

"Good," she said.

He grinned. "Even if you only make enough eggs to feed a toddler."

"I made four. Two for each of us."

"I'm a big man. I need more than two eggs."

Renee faced him and ran a hand over his shoulder. "You are a big man. It's what I like about you." Her hand came down over his chest and her nails scratched across the hairs on his chest. The way she'd done the night before when they were lying on the bed, breathless and sweaty.

He took the coffee mug out of her hand and placed it on the patio table.

Then he leaned down and kissed her, pulling her close, and nearly losing himself in the sweet taste of her. "I think I can wait for more eggs." He leaned down, gripped her hips, and lifted. Renee's legs wrapped instantly around his waist. "I want something else right now."

Renee grinned. "Frick, Jonathan, if we have sex right now my eggs are going to get cold."

"Frick?" he said with a laugh.

"I told you, I think cursing is vulgar," she said in her haughty, sexy tone that was starting to drive him wild.

He leaned in and whispered in her ear, "So, I can't say that I want to fuck you again?"

She shivered. Her eyes melted into deep chocolate centers. "Well, maybe it's okay when you say that."

Her smile warmed him inside and out. He kissed her and hurried back inside before he fucked the hell out of Renee right there on her patio for all her neighbors to see.

CHAPTER 16

Jonathan sat in the porch swing of the Big House and watched as Nadine and his parents drove separately down the long drive and parked next to his truck. Of course, Joanne wasn't there on time for the Tuesday afternoon meeting. He wondered if she was looking forward to blowing them off the same way she'd blown him off when he first tried to talk about the house. She didn't care much for keeping her appointments with this side of her family.

Nadine waited for their parents to get out and the three of them came up the steps to Jonathan. His mom's face was grim. Her face always was when she visited here. His dad's expression was unreadable. Nadine's was sad.

"I still expect to see Gigi come out and greet us before we make it to the door," Nadine said. The pain of the loss of the one family member who'd shown affection for them in her voice.

Their mother sighed and ran her hand over one of the large porch columns. "Your grandmother did try. I'll give her that much."

Jacob squeezed Connie's shoulder. Jonathan watched them. His mom was moving to Tennessee later that week. He'd heard nothing else from either of them about stopping the separation. Jonathan couldn't understand. They'd fought to be together, but now were happy to let go. If they couldn't make it, what were the chances for him and Renee?

Joanne's silver Lexus came down the drive next. Jonathan pushed thoughts of Renee aside. Today he had to deal with his family.

Joanne got out of the car and briskly made her way to the porch. Her Southern Belle good looks were marred by tight lines around her lips and the dislike in her eyes. "I'm glad you all could make it," she said, with not a drop of sincerity in her voice.

Jacob glared at his sister. No brotherly affection in his gaze after all these years. Jonathan hated that almost as much as what Joanne had done. His dad had told him stories of how close he and Joanne had been as kids. Her betrayal had hurt his dad more than their father's had.

"Let's get this over with, Joanne. You didn't call us out here to pretend like you're happy to see us."

Joanne's chin lifted. "Very well. We can do this inside."

She turned and unlocked the door. Jonathan chaffed that he had to wait for her to let them in. That he was in this position because of the way she'd betrayed Gigi.

The tension rose when Nadine and Jacob took in the bare walls and empty rooms. Proof that not only had Joanne deprived them of the house, she'd more than likely cashed in on the antiques in the house.

They settled in the back parlor. That was the only room that still had chairs. Jonathan stood in front of the empty fireplace.

"Why did you ask us here?" Jonathan asked as soon as everyone was still. He was in no mood to prolong this.

"I want to find a way to settle this entire mess," Joanne said.

Jonathan shrugged. "That's easy. Break your contract with Caldwell Development and honor Gigi's will."

Joanne shook her head. "It's not that easy."

Jacob crossed his arms and shifted forward in his chair. "Sounds simple enough to me, Joanne."

Nadine nodded. "Me too."

A sneer crossed Joanne's face. "You all make it sound so simple. Breaking a contract isn't something you just do with a snap. I can't afford to break the contract."

"Why not?" Jonathan asked. "Your husband left you with enough money."

"If he had, do you think I would be selling the Big House?" Joanne spit out the angry words. "I don't want you to have the house. I'm not going to lie about that. Daddy didn't want you to have it and Momma was wrong to go against his wishes, but that's not the only reason I signed that contract. I need the money."

Silence followed Joanne's admission. To say he was surprised would be an understatement. Joanne had not only inherited everything their grandfather had, but her late husband had been a successful surgeon.

Nadine spoke first. "*How* could you need money?"

Joanne brushed her shirt with her hand and sniffed. "Daddy didn't have a lot left after hospital bills. What was left, he gave to Momma. Which I had to go through when she was sick. My *husband*, God rest his soul, was a gambler. When Momma died, I realized I was land rich but cash poor."

"So you signed the Big House away." Jonathan's voice dripped with anger. "You went against Gigi's wishes to line your pockets."

Blue eyes so similar to his dad's snapped to his. "I went with my daddy's wishes, and I worked it out so that the Big House wouldn't be torn down. The deal with Caldwell Development is to build around the house. It was a smart move."

"No, it was a selfish move," Jonathan replied.

Connie, who'd been silent through the entire thing shifted and looked to Joanne. "That explains why, but not why we're here."

Joanne leaned back. "I'm offering you a cut. Well, not you. Jacob, Nadine, and Jonathan."

Jacob's eyes narrowed to slits. "If you weren't my sister."

Connie placed a hand on Jacob's knee and shook her head. "She's not worth it, Jacob."

Joanne sniffed as though affronted by the statement, but wisely kept silent.

"What do you mean, a cut?" Jonathan asked before the volatile situation got any worse.

Joanne looked back at him. "Re-work the contract with Caldwell Development so that you all get a portion of the proceeds. Jonathan, since you *were* in Gigi's will, I'll also concede some involvement on your part in the development. My input to help preserve the character of the land was included in my contract with Caldwell Development. That way it's not a total loss for you, and you'll make money."

"No," Jonathan said instantly. "This isn't about money."

Joanne smirked. "Oh, I forgot. It's about your hurt pride." Joanne stood. "I can't apologize for my daddy and I won't. He laid down his beliefs and that's the way it is. Fighting for this house won't change that. Won't take back how he felt, or make a difference in what resulted from his choices. I'm tired of this entire situation. Getting rid of this house closes the door on the past." She looked at Jacob. "For all of us." She sighed. "That's my offer. Take it or leave it."

She walked out of the room without another word. Jacob stood and paced to the other side of the room. His body was tense with anger. Connie studied her hands in her lap. Nadine got up and crossed over to Jonathan.

"I hate to admit it, but she's right, Jonny. This can be the end of it."

Jonathan looked at his mom. Her eyes said she agreed with Nadine. He understood their sentiment. This could put the past behind them. Shut the door on all the hurt, anger, and disrespect shown to them by the family.

Agreeing to the deal felt wrong. Forgetting the past opened the possibility to relive the past. It meant saying what Joanne had done was okay. That Gigi's wishes to make things right were fine to forget.

Jonathan looked across the room at Jacob. "Dad?"

Jacob's wide shoulders lifted and lowered with a deep breath. Slowly, he turned back to face Jacob. "To hell with her deal. I'm not letting my family's hatred take everything." He glanced at Connie. "I've lost enough."

Jonathan hoped that meant his dad was going to fight to keep his mom. He'd ask about that later, but for now, he was motivated by his dad's words.

"Then let's not lose anything else. Let's prepare for court."

CHAPTER 17

Even though Renee, Ryan, and Philip worked together, they didn't see much of each other outside of the office. There was always some social function for her parents to attend and Renee and Ryan had their own engagements, their own lives. Hence, the reason Victoria insisted the family block off one night a month so they could all get together. Renee always looked forward to dinner with her family. She just hoped Ryan was in a decent mood. He'd been dreadful ever since the game on Saturday.

"Are you sleeping with the Wright boy?" Philip Caldwell demanded the moment Renee entered their spacious and comfortable sitting room.

Renee paused in removing her coat and gloves. Her gaze went first to the angry face of her father and then to the disappointment in her mother's brown gaze. Ryan stood by the window. He avoided her eye. Traitor.

"Well, hello to you, too." Renee finished taking off her outerwear and folded the coat over the edge of one couch.

Philip did a frustrated shuffle of his feet, the highball glass of bourbon clenched in his hand. "Don't avoid the question. Are you or are you not sleeping with Jonathan Wright."

The coating of disappointment in his voice was exactly why she hadn't wanted to tell her parents about her and Jonathan. They needed to know, but would they understand or respect her decision?

Firming her shoulders, she lifted her head and met her father's gaze. "Jonathan and I are seeing each other."

Her mother winced. Philip downed the rest of the bourbon in his glass. "Renee, I thought you said this little attraction with him wasn't serious."

"No, Daddy, you said that. I asked to be taken off the project."

"If I'd have thought you'd fall for this game of his I would have," Philip said. The frown on his face was not only disappointed but concerned.

"I didn't fall for anything."

"Are you sure he's not with you just to change your mind? Ryan says he's using you."

Renee's eyes jerked to her brother. Ryan didn't bother to look away. He was so quick to blab on her. She wanted to be petty and bring up his relationship with Eva, but wouldn't. Ryan would have to deal with that mess on his own later.

"Why do you think he's using me?" she said in a cool voice.

"I don't want to believe it, but he had to say something good enough to make you turn your back on your job and settle."

Anger whipped through Renee like a gale force wind. "I'm not turning my back on my job, nor am I settling. Can't you just accept that for once I'm doing something that makes me happy? That I like him and he likes me."

Philip's face twisted and his lips pressed tightly together. Holding back from cursing at her. She recognized the sign. Philip spun and looked at his wife. "Victoria, talk to the girl."

Victoria sat forward and met Renee's eyes. "Of course we want you to be happy, Renee. That's all we ever want, but this Jonathan guy isn't the type of man you typically go for. He's not for you."

"He's employed, successful, and treats me with respect. What else could he possibly need? A trust fund?"

Victoria's lips thinned. "Don't snap at me for saying the obvious. You've been very selective about the men you date, Renee, and have made no secret about it. Forgive us if we're a little confused when you suddenly claim to care for a part-time cattle farmer and pseudo government employee."

The words were a truthful dart that pierced and deflated Renee's anger. "I can't explain why I like Jonathan. I just do. What's wrong with giving this a try?"

Philip snorted. "He's suing us, that's what's wrong. And don't you forget that we're suing him back."

Renee's eyes widened. "We're trying to settle out of court. We have no reason to sue him."

"For defamation," Philip said firmly. "His lawsuit implies that we willfully took advantage of his grandmother. I will not let him drag our name through the mud."

Similar words Renee had spoken to Jonathan. "Talk to him first. Understand why he's fighting so hard. It's not about us, it's about his family."

"Then he should have kept the fight between him and his family. Or taken the money."

"He's not going to take the money, or drop the fight to keep the land." Renee lifted a hand when her dad's mouth opened to interrupt. "But, maybe he will drop the accusations against us."

She hoped he cared enough to consider that option.

Philip's eyes narrowed. "Are you sure you know what you're doing with him? I asked you to use your friendship with Mikayla to change his mind, but I didn't mean…"

"Daddy!" she snapped. "I met Jonathan before I knew anything about this fight. I felt this for him then. Getting to know him only strengthened that. Even if we weren't embroiled in this battle, nothing would change."

She glanced at her mother, who looked disbelieving. Renee could hardly blame her. Hadn't she turned away Mikayla's match making efforts and attempts to get Renee to meet Jonathan for the same reasons her mom had just brought up? She didn't want to date a part-time cattle farmer.

"Please, just talk to him," she said.

Philip and Victoria studied her then shared a glance. Judging whether or not she was telling the truth. The fact that they didn't immediately take her at her word made her feel even worse for her snobby dating history. What had that gotten her? Humiliation and hurt from a man she'd thought was perfect.

Victoria stood and crossed the room to Renee. "I want to meet him."

Renee eyed her mom warily. "You do?"

"I only want you to be happy, Renee. If you like Jonathan, and he makes you happy, then I'll be okay." She placed a cool hand on Renee's cheek. "But remember, you went down this road before. I don't want to see you hurt again."

The guy in college. The customer service clerk her family had scared away after one family dinner. The reason she'd started being more *selective* with the guys she dated.

"This is different, mom. He's different."

Victoria nodded and dropped her hand. "If you say so."

Renee looked to Philip, who walked over to the bar in the corner and poured himself another bourbon. "And you, Dad. Will you meet him?"

Philip turned around and strolled over to stand next to Victoria. "Fine. *If* I'm convinced that he likes you for you, then we'll reconsider reassigning the Wright project to someone else."

She had a sense that her giving up a project for a man still disappointed her dad. Worse, she didn't want him to view her as emotional and irrational as Ryan. She'd hate for her father to lose some sense of confidence in her if this entire thing went sour.

"Thank you," she said with forced contentment.

"Besides," Philip said. "He may have some prospects. He's just been nominated for president of the State Cattle Farmers' Association. From what I've heard, he's done a good job as part of his chapter's government affairs committee and was their past president. He's more than likely going to be voted in, which will mean he'll be in town lobbying the legislature, even serving as a liaison on the national level. We can't deny a statehouse connection is always beneficial."

Renee eyed her father. Once again his sources hadn't let him down. "He hasn't mentioned any of that to me."

"It just happened. If he plays this appointment right, he'll have a strong hand in agricultural policy. He might be able to one day take back the seat his grandfather lost."

The begrudging approval in Philip's voice spoke the words her dad hadn't. *This has the potential to be a successful matchup.*

Old habits didn't disappear overnight. Her mind went in the same direction. Dating the president of the Cattle Farmers' Association would not necessarily be a bad thing.

Stop thinking strategies and angles with him, Renee.

"I'm not sure if he wants the seat," Renee said. "Besides the Big House, he's not interested in his grandfather's legacy."

"That can change with a little *persuasion*," Philip said. Meaning, if she was going to insist on dating him, then insist on pushing him to new heights.

Renee nodded instead of speaking. Her throat was too tight to agree out loud. Would Jonathan pull away from her if he realized she would try to push him to take his grandfather's seat? Would he consider it her way of saying that would make him a better boyfriend?

How would you view it?

Wait until he's president of the CFA then go from there. Jonathan hated his grandfather and she doubted he wanted the old man's seat in the legislature, but he was big on re-writing his family's legacy. If he were to eventually run, and win, he could do that.

"I'll invite him to dinner."

"Then it's settled," Victoria said. "Now let's eat."

Renee glanced at Ryan, who watched her with a blank expression. Probably not the outcome he'd expected.

Dinner went as usual. All talk about the Woman of the Year nomination and the upcoming luncheon where the judging panel would interview each of the candidates. Her parents were excited about the nomination, and what it would do for Caldwell Development.

The pressure to be perfect closed in on Renee. A constant reminder that she represented Caldwell Development. That her job was to help the company. Including encouraging her brand new boyfriend that one day, he'd make a good state senator.

She wished she had Jonathan's motorcycle to jump on and speed away from the house by the time dinner ended. Instead, she stayed for coffee, more chit chat, and then kissed her parents good-bye. Ryan left with her.

"Why did you tell them?" Renee asked when she and Ryan stood on their parents' front step.

His look wasn't the least bit repentant. "I thought they needed to know. I was worried about you." He scoffed "I should have known you'd convince them you were right. Renee does no wrong."

He moved to go down the step and Renee grabbed his arm. "This isn't about me not doing wrong. You told on me like there was something unsavory with my relationship with Jonathan. I don't appreciate that, Ryan."

Ryan pulled his arm from her grasp. "I don't trust him, Renee. For all we know, he's another Daniel. Just out to use you."

"Am I so cold and frigid that the only way men would want me is because of what I have to offer?"

"That's not what I mean."

"It's what you're implying. Stop thinking I'm too stupid to know what's real and what's not."

"Do you think he's the one?"

Renee stepped back. The question threw her off. She wasn't ready to think that far in the future with Jonathan. "He's the one I want to be with right now."

"Then why hook up with a man who's suing our family? A man who's ready to drag our name through the mud? Good sex isn't worth betraying the family for."

The words were a slap in her face. "Being happy isn't betraying the family. Everyone I date doesn't have to be the love of my life. That's part of your problem. You're so quick to fall for the wrong woman you end up making stupid mistakes, like losing Mikayla. At least I enter relationships with my heart guarded and my mind open."

Ryan's jaw clenched. His nostrils flared and he ran a hand over his face. Her words had gone too far, but she didn't care. Not after his insult. "You know what," he said in a surprisingly calm voice. "Don't worry about me. I'm good. I'm taking a lesson from my sister."

"What lesson?"

"Relationships serve a purpose. For you it's helping the business, for me it's just about fun. Go ahead, have your fling with Jonathan. I'm done giving my advice."

His cell phone rang. He pulled it out, looked at the screen, and smiled. "There's fun calling now."

Eva's name showed on his cell. There was fun and then there was suicidal. Renee reached out. "Ryan, don't."

He stepped out of her reach. "You do you. I'm doing me." He pressed the button to answer. "Just the woman I wanted to hear from." Ryan turned away and strolled down the stairs. "Is your husband around?"

Renee sucked in a breath and balled her hand into fists. This wasn't good at all.

CHAPTER 18

Jonathan placed forks, knives, and spoons around the fancy, pearl rimmed in platinum plates set out on Renee's dining table. He would most likely break something by the end of the night. Fancy china was not his normal. Fancy china with fancy parents was definitely not his normal.

Renee entered the room with an efficient click of heels and the scent of her light and sexy perfume surrounding her. She'd coordinated Lilly's pony ride for him. He'd have a fancy, awkward dinner with her parents, whom he was suing, for her.

She looked like a sexy secretary in her starched white button up and a black skirt decorated with gray and blue cranes. Of course, Renee would make cranes look elegant. He certainly wished there was a desk he could prop her up on so he could play beneath that skirt.

"No, Jonathan, the forks go on the left. The knife and teaspoon on the right." She put four crystal water goblets on the table and switched the setting.

She'd been nervous from the second he'd arrived.

"Renee, why are we doing all this? It's just dinner with your parents."

She let out a heavy sigh. Jonathan's lip twitched with amusement. He rearranged the settings on his side of the table.

"I want things to be perfect. So many things can go wrong tonight. You're suing them."

"The company, not them personally."

The frown on her face didn't go away. "Does it matter? What are we doing? Should we be doing this?"

Jonathan slipped his arm around her waist and pulled her closer. "Are you ready to let me go?"

Her body softened and the worry in her eyes drifted away. "Not really." She played with the button of the dress shirt she'd insisted he wear. "So much isn't resolved. We only slept together once and already we're meeting my parents. Are we doing too much?"

"Renee, this gives me a chance to talk to your dad face to face about the lawsuit. Who knows, something good may come out of this. Don't over think things."

"But—"

He cut her off with a kiss. Her lips were soft and willing, but also clung to his with a little bit of the nervousness that hummed in her body. He shared her fears, her concern that they were moving too fast. Except, when he was with her, something said she was worth the fight. Jonathan really hoped he was right and not just going with the testosterone that drugged his system whenever she was near.

When he broke the kiss, her smile filled him with the same awe and wonder typically reserved for dazzling sunrises. "Thank you," she whispered.

"For what?"

"Reminding me why this is worth it."

He squeezed her just a little tighter. He would kiss her anytime to make her smile at him like that. "We may need to remind each other over the next few weeks."

"Years," she said with a sigh. "Lawsuits can go on for years."

The thought of dragging the lawsuit out for years soured his stomach. The same worry filled her eyes. He brushed his lips across hers again. "Kissing you for years might not be so bad, sugar."

The concern lifted from her face and she grinned. "You're such a tease." She pulled out of his arms. "And don't call me sugar in front of my daddy, okay?"

She turned back to the table and picked up the water goblets around a setting. "These go on the right side of the plate but just a little to the left of the butter knife." She re-positioned the goblets then clasped her hands in front of her and studied the table. "Good. Now the wine glasses."

She marched toward the kitchen. She looked sexy in her determination. Jonathan hurried to block her way. "You keep marching around in those heels and I'm going to knock those goblets off the table and eat you on it."

Her body trembled and she pressed her hips forward. "Seriously, Jonathan, stop saying things like that." Her eyes were warm pools of chocolate, her voice just as hot.

The doorbell rang, and Jonathan fought back a curse. "Later." He kissed her quickly.

"Later," she said, her voice a promise of many things to come.

Philip and Victoria Caldwell were exactly what he'd expect from a handsome, successful couple. They came in with broad smiles, air kisses, and firm handshakes. With one look, he knew they both sized him up and judged if he were good enough for Renee. Though he wanted her parents to like him, he didn't care if they thought he was good enough. That was for Renee to decide.

Renee was the perfect hostess. Taking their coats and getting everyone settled with wine and appetizers she'd set out. Then seamlessly moving them to the dining table. She'd ordered the food and she and her mom brought out the platters for the buffet table against the wall while he and Philip wasted time discussing the weather.

No one said anything wrong. Everyone was polite and approachable. Yet Jonathan's tension rose with each minute. They were moving the conversation to anything but the lawsuit. Which meant that was coming later. This was the calm before the storm.

"Renee, are you ready for the Woman of the Year interview the week after next?" Victoria asked.

Jonathan shot her a surprised look. Since the wedding, she hadn't mentioned anything more about the Woman of the Year nomination. He'd forgotten it, with everything going on.

"That's coming up?" he asked.

She nodded. "Yes, a week from Tuesday. I'm as ready as I can be." Her smile said she was confident, the rigid set of her shoulder disagreed.

He placed his hand over hers at the table. "It's normal to be nervous."

Victoria's little laugh was slightly condescending. "Renee doesn't get nervous over things like this. She's a natural leader and one of the most successful business women in the state."

Jonathan detected the barest hint of a warning in her words. Whether the warning was for him or Renee, he was unsure. Renee's position in life had nothing to do with how he felt about her.

Renee leaned forward in her chair. "I am a little nervous," she said. "If I wasn't nervous then that would be a problem. I do well under pressure. The nervousness is what keeps me grounded."

Victoria didn't respond to that. Jonathan squeezed Renee's hand. "I'm sure you'll do well."

She smiled. "I hope so. The more I thought about what it means the more I realized that I kind of want to win."

Before Jonathan could ask what it would mean, Philip spoke up. "Your winning will go a long way toward improving the integrity of Caldwell Development. As we know, some would like to ruin our good name."

First shots fired. Jonathan met Philip's direct gaze. Saw the challenge in the older man's eyes. A challenge he had no plans to back down from.

Philip leaned forward and rested his elbow on the table. "Tell me, Jonathan, what will you do if you're elected president of the Cattle Farmers' Association?"

Jonathan frowned, confused by the abrupt change in subject. How did they know about that? "I'm not sure I'm going to win."

"Don't be modest," Philip said. "From what I've heard you're the likely nominee."

"I'm not sure what you heard, but I'm not assuming I'm going to be elected president. If I am, I'll be happy to serve and bring forth the challenges faced by the small farmers in our state."

"That's all well and good, but wouldn't you go farther if you represented the larger farms?"

Jonathan shifted in his seat and eyed Philip warily. "I'm not trying to go farther. I'm only trying to help people and serve if asked."

"That's nice, but let me be blunt. My daughter is about to be named Woman of the Year. She is one of the most well respected businesswomen in the state. She deserves a man who is equally respected."

Renee leaned forward. "Daddy!"

Jonathan squeezed her hand. This was his battle. "I believe I am well respected."

"In small circles," Philip said. "If you are named president, that'll give you the chance to become respected in larger circles. Larger and more lucrative circles. Renee and I even discussed a possible Senate run one day."

The blood in his veins ran ice cold. His eyes swerved to Renee. A stricken, guilty look flashed on her face. Her calm mask hid it. "You did?"

"Dad mentioned it, but it was far from a discussion." She looked to her dad. "I told you I'm not thinking about that."

"And I told you that if you're going to forget that the man beside you is suing our family and dragging our name through the mud, then it better be for a good reason."

"The fact that she wants to be with me isn't a good enough reason?" Jonathan asked.

Philip met Jonathan's gaze dead on. "Frankly, no. I can't say that I'm happy that she's with you. I won't even lie and say I respect the fact that you two make each other happy. Renee may be too caught up to think about all the reasons you two should have kept your distance. We do have a contract to buy your land. I don't care why your aunt signed it or what her motivations were, I've got enough time, money and lawyers to keep you in court for years. I will do that, because I don't trust you. I don't think you're sincere about my daughter and I won't stick around and watch her get used by you."

Renee stood so abruptly her chair nearly tipped over. "Stop it. Just stop."

Philip's dark eyes rose to her. "Renee, I'm doing this for you."

"I think you should go," she said. "Before I say something I'll regret later."

Philip looked ready to argue. Victoria touched his shoulder. When he glowered at her, she shook her head. "Let's go, Philip. You've said what you needed to say."

Renee and Jonathan were silent as her parents stood. Victoria walked over and placed a kiss on Renee's cheek. Philip leaned in to hug Renee but she held up her hand and stopped him. Hurt flashed briefly in his eyes before he hit Jonathan with an accusatory glare. Victoria took Philip's arm and led him out. Renee and Jonathan remained silent until her door closed.

"I'm sorry for that," Renee said. She was still standing and leaned over to place her hands on the table.

"You said he wouldn't stop fighting," Jonathan said grimly. That wasn't what had his stomach churning like an overloaded washing machine. "Did you two really talk about me running for Senate one day?"

"It wasn't like that." Her voice was tired.

"What was it like? Because it sounds like you had to debate what I brought to the table."

Renee dropped back into her seat with a huff. "Jonathan, I'm going against my family for you. Of course they're going to ask me what's the benefit of this relationship."

He turned in his seat and stared at her. "What's the benefit? Is that how you judge relationships?"

She took a deep breath then reached for the wine glass next to her plate. "Yes. That is how I typically judge relationships."

"And you did the same with me."

"Not before we slept together. I had no idea about your potential…" She flinched and her hand tightened around the wine glass.

Jonathan's laugh was humorless, caustic. "My *potential*. And here I thought you were just into me."

She turned to him. Her stare said he was being ridiculous. "Of course I'm into you. Otherwise the idea of there being no benefit from dating you would have told me to stay away."

Jonathan blinked and shook his head. "Is that supposed to be a compliment?"

"I'm saying this wrong." She rubbed her temples.

"No, it sounds like you're saying this right. You're with me, even though you didn't think I brought any *benefits* to the relationship. Now you know about my nomination and you can see a future with me in the Senate. A future I never said I had any intention of pursuing, yet you still consider me to have more *potential*."

"You're trying to make it sound bad."

"It sounds bad because it is bad."

"What do you want me to say, Jonathan?" She asked quickly, frustration punctuating every word. "That I was jumping for joy because I'm attracted to a part-time cattle farmer who's suing my family? That I'm ecstatic about fighting with my dad over this for a sketchy future I don't even know that I want?"

"Yes," he said, his body tight with tension. "I'm with you because I want you. What we feel is all that matters."

Renee sighed and took a sip of her wine. "You sound like Ryan. Emotions in everything." The words were not spoken like a compliment.

"I don't like Ryan, but at least he knows that you don't treat relationships like a business arrangement." Jonathan pushed his chair back and stood. "I'm not a deal you can broker. I'm not going to be your future senator, or cater to large farmers to work my way up in the statehouse. Take me as I am or not at all, Renee."

Her wide eyes lifted to his, confusion, pain, and a little bit of frustration in her gaze. "What are you doing?"

"Leaving, before I say something I will regret." He took a step backward. Waited to see if she'd ask him to stay. Say that she understood what he meant. That she didn't care about the land, lawsuit, or his future *potential.*

Her mouth remained steadfastly closed. Her silence sliced him deeper than any cutting remark Karen had thrown.

"Good-bye, Renee." He turned and left. She didn't call him back.

CHAPTER 19

Renee hated apologizing.

Most people didn't like to admit they were wrong. That was natural. She was usually right when it came to business dealings. She gave to her family, friends and the residents of Still Hopes with very little argument or question. Therefore, she rarely had to apologize for being herself.

The cold, calculating, what's-the-benefit-in-this-for-me self. The self that had ruined things with Jonathan. That's the part of her that had messed up and warranted the need to apologize.

Just because she didn't like admitting she was wrong, didn't mean she wouldn't. So she took a deep breath, lifted her chin, and rang his doorbell.

She'd picked six in the evening on a Thursday night. She hated to cancel the mentoring session at Still Hopes, but thankfully, another board member had offered to step in. Jonathan should be at home. As long as he wasn't out on a date.

The thought took hold and twisted her stomach like a typhoon right before his front door opened. She puffed out a relieved breath and smiled. He wasn't on a date.

"Hi," she said.

His large body filled the doorway. His hair was damp, and curly. From the shower she guessed. A gray T-shirt hugged his wide shoulders and a pair of jeans sat low on his hips. Everything in her ached to touch him. She'd come to apologize, and in that second she knew even more that she'd been wrong to let him go.

"Renee, what are you doing here?" He didn't smile. Didn't invite her in. What was worse, she couldn't blame him for either.

Dozens of words whizzed through her head. Variations of her apology speech that she'd practiced on the way here. Now it all felt inadequate. Wrong.

He raised a brow. Gave her a look that bordered on hurry the heck up.

"You were right," she blurted.

He shifted his weight. Watched her with surprise. "About what?"

She took a deep breath and squared her shoulders. "Everything. I shouldn't have thought about what you bring to the table. Before or after we got together. I've been living my life that way for so long that it's almost second nature. I do these things without even realizing it. Except, when it came to you, even though *normal* Renee would have said no, I couldn't. I couldn't say no to you, Jonathan."

"Renee, I'm not a guy that plays the power games your family likes to play." His voice was low, but iron clad.

"This isn't a game for me, either." She took a step toward the door. "I'm going against everything I know, my family and it's scary."

"Is that why you let me leave? Because you were scared?" He sounded doubtful.

She told him the truth. "Jonathan I'm petrified."

He shuffled back a step. "You're what?"

"Scared out of my friggin' mind. I want it all, okay? I want a husband, and kids, and a house with a white picket fence, but guess what, I'm probably not getting that. I'm expected to marry a doctor, lawyer, or senator. A guy who walks in the same calculating circles as my family. I tried to ignore the expectations. I met a guy everyone said was unsuitable. I even had friends of my mother tell me I could do better, but I didn't care. I was in love. He met my family, and they laid out their grand plan for me and my life in all their glory. Just like they did the other night at dinner. You know what happened. He broke up with me the next day."

Her hand clenched into a fist that she placed over her heart. "Daddy used him leaving as proof that I didn't deserve a man who hadn't already proved he had something to offer, and I believed it. *Lived* it. I dated suitable men, but none of them made me want them. Mikayla and Ryan thought I was just picky, but the fact was that I wanted the same fire, and heat, and love that I'd had once. When Mikayla fell in love with Andre, I knew I'd never have what she had. I gave up on finding it. That's why I let myself believe that things would work out with Daniel." Her laugh was caustic. "I've already told you how that worked out."

"Renee," he reached for her.

She pulled away. "Let me finish." She was on a role, baring her soul and insecurities. She had to finish before he told her to leave.

He lowered his hand and crossed his arms. She swallowed and lifted her chin. "When my parents said everything they said to you, and when I heard the anger in your voice after they left, I thought we were through. That's why I let you walk away. The last guy did. Why would you be any different? Except you are different, Jonathan. You reminded me that I can feel that way. I can have those fantasies I don't allow myself to have anymore. I can feel the heat and passion that I didn't think I'd find. So even if you are totally done with me, even if you want me to leave and never come back, I had to come here and tell you that I'm sorry. That I don't care about you being a part-time farmer, I don't care if you become president of the Cattle Farmers' Association, I could not care less about you running for Senate. I only wanted you."

She breathed hard to catch her breath. Her throat was so dry it could have been lined with parchment. She'd dumped so much of her personal baggage, felt so much lighter, she would fly if she could. Jonathan looked a little dumbfounded. Heat rushed up her neck and cheeks.

Frick! Good job, Renee. Show him you're the emotional basket case all men love to date.

She didn't know what else to say. The silence grew until she wanted to snap her fingers and disappear into thin air.

"I'm going to go now." She spoke slowly and pointed over her shoulder with her thumb.

He blinked as if he'd just come out of a trance. Before he could reply, she spun on her heels. She'd barely taken a step before his hand was on her arm and he turned her around.

"You drive me crazy, Renee."

Then he kissed her. A long, deep kiss that made pleasure float through her like thousands of champagne bubbles. He pulled her inside. She used her foot to kick the door closed. He lifted her up and carried her through the house and to his bedroom.

In his bedroom, he cupped her head with one hand, the other gripped her butt before his mouth covered hers in another soul-caressing kiss. Renee's hands clutched his arms. The muscles beneath her fingers flexed and her heart skipped.

Jonathan only lowered and released her to pull off her shirt and bra. The warm air in the room caressed her skin, followed shortly by his large hands. His thumbs brushed over the taught peaks of her breasts. Sensual sparks penetrated every pore of her body.

"Keep doing that," she moaned against his mouth.

"I'd rather do this." He grabbed her hips and lifted her up in one swift motion.

Renee yelped, then laughed and clasped his broad shoulders. When was the last time she'd laughed during sex? Had she ever laughed during sex? She hadn't. Jonathan brought her pleasure, and so much joy. Why had she fought this?

Jonathan's lips closed over one of her breasts and she didn't care about why she'd fought this. She had him now. Her fingers tunneled into the softness of his hair, her legs wrapped around his hips.

"Yes," she panted while his tongue teased and lips pulled. He held her easily, one arm around her waist, the other splayed against her back, pushing her forward so she couldn't pull away. As if she'd try.

"Jonathan," she moaned. Her plea for more vibrated in her voice.

He pulled back and walked toward the bed. He kissed the hard tips of her breasts as he moved. "Your breasts are so fucking cute."

Big, beautiful, sexy were all words she knew she'd never hear when it came to describing her breasts. Cute wasn't one she'd ever thought she'd hear and like. Jonathan saying that while sprinkling small playful kisses and nips across them turned her bones molten.

He bent over until her back pressed into the mattress. "Unlock your legs."

She rotated her hips, bringing the heat of her center against his thick erection. "Are you sure about that?"

The groan he made was so deep it could have been a growl. "Renee." His voice was part exasperation, part decadent desire.

She chuckled and unwrapped her legs. Jonathan's hungry eyes devoured her. "Slide over."

She quickly scooted to the other side, kicked off her shoes, and pulled off her pants and underwear. Without any flair, he removed his clothes. He didn't need to make a display. The quick, efficient reveal of his tall, muscular body was better than any strip show. He left on a pair of blue and green plaid boxers. The blunt tip of his erection pushed against the opening. Talk about a cock tease.

He pulled a few condoms out of his nightstand and threw them on the bed. Renee thought about using all of them and wanted to giggle in delight. She opted for a huge grin instead.

Jonathan climbed on the bed. He didn't lie on top of her, but sat on his knees at her side. His fingertips ran down her chest between her breasts, over her stomach and stopped at the top of the neat triangle of hair covering her sex. Renee clutched the comforter beneath her with one hand, the other glided up the hard muscle of his thigh until her fingertips brushed the edge of his boxers.

She tugged on the thin cotton barrier. "Why are these still on?"

"They'll be off soon enough. I want to touch you first."

His fingers traced light circles along her outer and inner thigh. The rough tips left burning trails in their wake. Her legs trembled, spreading farther apart. His other hand toyed with her breast. She arched her back, thrusting into his hand. Two fingers delicately pinched her nipple while his other hand skimmed over the slick, wet folds of her core.

Renee gasped and jerked. Her hand tightened on his thigh. Every nerve in her body ached with need. "Jonathan, please," she begged.

Long fingers parted her and made light circles across her slick sex. Her hips jutted upward. Her eyes squeezed closed. Her mind focused on nothing but the delicious feel of Jonathan's hands on her body.

"I love the way you feel when you're wet," he said in a gruff voice. "So hot and sleek." His finger pushed into her. "So tight." He slowly pulled out his finger, gliding it over her clit.

"Jonathan," his name was long low moan.

"Mmm, you like that." He repeated the movement. Pushing deep within then easing out. A thin sheet of sweat covered her body and her breaths came in short, urgent bursts. Her moans of pleasure filled the room and her legs fell far apart.

The heat of his hand on her breast disappeared. Renee's eyes opened to narrow slits. His blue-gray gaze was honed in on his hands between her thighs. His lips pressed tight, one hand in his boxers stroking himself. The muscles of his chest bunched and played beneath his tan skin. He was so big, masculine, and magnificent.

Longing and need squeezed her heart. Her breath lodged in her chest. He was hers.

Her eyes dropped to the hand in his boxers. She slipped her hand into the opening and pushed his aside. Slowly, she took over. The thick, rigid length of him grew harder in her hands. Fiery eyes jumped to hers. Excitement lit a blue flame in his gaze.

Jerking down his boxers until he sprang free, Renee shifted up on her elbows and took the wide tip of him between her lips. Jonathan's body shuddered, the hand between her legs slowed, but didn't pull away. She took as much of him as she could. Moaning at the taste of him, the press of him against her tongue and the rich smell of his desire. His fingers between her thighs moved again, gliding in and out of her in tandem with her deep strokes.

Fire built in her veins. Her body tightened. Her climax drew closer.

Jonathan jerked away. Her mouth fell open in a silent cry. Her tongue ran across her now swollen lips. She blinked. "What are you doing?"

Jonathan jerked off the boxers and positioned himself, on his knees, between her thighs. He took her knees into his hands then pushed her legs back then out, the movement raw, and erotic. One finger trailed down the middle of her sex, dipped into her opening. Renee clenched around him, twisting her head from side to side. He slid his finger out and trailed lower.

She stiffened, her eyes popped open. His finger paused at the tight opening no one had ever touched before. Shock warred with desire at the slight caress.

He glanced up at her, a slow sinful smile spread his lips. "Not today, Renee." His finger eased ever so slightly into the tight opening. "But one day you'll let me take you here."

The need to protest doing something that seemed so against anything she'd ever done rose. Then his hand twisted until his thumb caressed her clit while the tip of his finger still teased her most private opening. The protest died on her lips. The combined pleasure sent a wave of sensation through her.

"Will you let me, Renee?"

Her head nodded automatically. She couldn't say the words aloud. She couldn't believe she even wanted to. His hands left her and he picked up one of the condoms he'd thrown on the bed earlier and slid it on.

He pulled her hips off the bed until her shoulders pressed into the mattress. "Hard and fast, or slow and deep?"

Her body trembled. "Start slow, then make me cry."

He bit his lower lip. Excitement became a bright glow in his eyes. "You are fantastic," he said while slowly pushing into her.

Renee's mouth fell open. Her eyes narrowed into heavy slits. She could cry from the wonderful pleasure of it all. Instead, her body exploded with a glorious orgasm after he did exactly what she told him she wanted.

***

Renee turned over in her sleep and draped her arm across Jonathan's chest. He pulled her closer against him and smiled. He'd never had a woman pass out cold right after sex. He couldn't lie. His ego was well pleased.

His happy glow wasn't just from her screams of pleasure. Though that was fantastic. Her whole hundred-mile-an-hour confession on his doorstep had gotten him. Even before Karen, he would have freaked out by a woman dumping her dating history on his doorstep after only a few weeks of dating. Most women weren't Renee.

She'd put her heart on the line for him. He could have rejected her, laughed at her, or scorned her. Yet she'd trusted him with her insecurities. That was something he didn't think she would have done with any man. No matter his *possibilities* or what he brought to the table.

More and more, being with Renee felt so right, so natural. Renee felt like his woman. Not just for now, but forever.

Jonathan's heart rammed in his chest. His face heated; a cold sweat broke out. He rubbed his forehead. He was getting forever feelings about Renee. Forever feelings that went a lot deeper and stronger than they had with Karen. Karen had crushed his heart. Renee had the power to liquefy it.

Renee wanted him now, but would she be happy living out here away from everything? No cocktail parties or charity balls to attend. Eating steak almost every night and watching Netflix with him after he came in from tending the cows.

Jonathan sucked in a deep breath and counted to six. Slowly he released the breath. His heart rate barely slowed. No freak outs just yet. Regardless of how he felt, he couldn't forget that he was suing her family. Her dad promised years of fighting. That might kill any forever feelings.

Renee snuggled closer and snored. Jonathan raised a brow. *She snores?*

He chuckled and imaged the denial she'd go into when he told her that.

"What's so funny?" she mumbled against his chest.

"You wouldn't believe me if I told you."

She rubbed her nose and crossed her leg over his. "Are you laughing at me?"

"Yes. You snore."

"Oh that." She smiled, but didn't open her eyes. "I know about that already."

"You did?"

"Yes. Ryan teased me constantly when we were kids. It's my one flaw."

Jonathan laughed. She sounded so sure of herself. "I'll add falling asleep immediately after sex to be your second."

Renee groaned and pressed the heels of her hands to her eyes. "The words from that Ice Cube song just ran through my head. About his Jimmy running so deep it put her to sleep, or something like that."

"What do you know about Ice Cube?"

"I occasionally unwind with nineties gangsta rap. Along with a few less than savory songs of today."

"Are you serious?"

Her eyes cracked open and she held up three fingers. "Okay, make that three flaws."

She moved away and stretched her arms above her head. He couldn't help but palm one small breast.

"Mmm, I can't take another orgasm, Jonathan."

He only moved over to kiss her neck. "I think you can."

Her grin was pure feminine seduction. One of her hands lifted to his hair. "When my head explodes, I'm going to come back as a ghost to see how you explain that to my parents."

He chuckled and brushed a kiss across her chin. "Hey, I'm sorry."

She frowned and looked at him fully. "For giving me mind-blowing orgasms?"

He shook his head. "For leaving the other day and not calling. I'm an adult, but I can occasionally act like a temperamental teenage boy. I should have talked to you instead of storming out."

"I understand why you left."

He lifted his hand to trace across her lower lip. "I won't leave you like that again. I won't just walk away, and I won't be intimidated by your family. I thought you didn't think I was good enough. That shit hurt, so I left. It was a punk move, and I won't repeat it. If we have an issue, we'll talk about it. Deal?"

"Deal." She nodded, and her smile warmed him ten times over.

The words *I love you* bubbled up in his throat. Jonathan's heart coughed in his chest. He kissed her, slow and deep. Maybe if he kept his mouth busy with other things it wouldn't spout off words that shouldn't be spoken too soon.

CHAPTER 20

She'd called out of work on Friday. The receptionist had sounded more than a little surprised before clarifying that Renee *really didn't* want speak with Philip directly. She had not. She deserved a personal day. What better way to take one than in bed with a sexy man?

Jonathan had gone to put together breakfast. Last night had been so perfect she'd almost gotten up and made breakfast again. The thought had fled when Jonathan kissed her shoulder, said he had things to do, and told her to sleep in. She lay there, happy, sated, and lazy, on blue flannel sheets in a farmhouse and couldn't be more delighted. Three months ago, she would have scoffed at the idea of it.

She must have fallen asleep, because she jumped later when Jonathan's hand ran up her thigh and she had no clue when he'd entered the room.

"Shh," he whispered in her ear. "It's just me."

"You smell like coffee," she mumbled. Closing her eyes, she dropped her head back on the pillow.

"I brought coffee." He kissed a lazy trail from one shoulder to the other. "And pancakes, bacon, and toast. You ready to eat?"

Jonathan kissed across and down her back. His lips teasing as they lightly pressed against her skin. Renee sighed and stretched. "Mmmm, I won't want to eat if you keep that up."

"Oh, really?" His voice was wicked. He shifted on the bed, moving her until she lay completely on her stomach.

She peeked at him over her shoulder. "What are you doing?"

Jonathan straddled her hips and massaged her shoulders. "Touching you."

His fingers were magical as they eased and massaged her shoulders and upper back. Renee let out a low moan. "Mmmm, okay."

His hands worked first her upper back then moved lower. Warming her muscles and turning them into mush beneath his skilled fingers. His body slid down over hers. His strong hands gripped her buttocks. He kneaded the flesh, gliding his hands down to where her thighs met her rear. He gently pushed her legs wider.

Renee stiffened at the intimate exposure. "Jonathan?"

"Shh, relax," his voice was low and soothing.

Renee forced the stiffness out of her muscles and took several deep breaths. His thumbs brushed the dampening folds of her sex. Wanton pleasure burst through her body. Her lips parted with a silent gasp.

Tension overtook her for another reason this time. He massaged her thighs right beneath her butt, his thumbs lightly caressing her damp folds with each squeeze of his hands. Renee pressed her hips up and tried to widen her legs, but his legs straddling her prevented her from going further.

Lowering his body, he covered her until his chest brushed her back. He kept the full weight of his body off her with his right arm. Warm lips kissed her cheek, ears, and neck. Renee lifted her upper body to push more firmly against him. His left arm snaked beneath them and cupped her breast. Long fingers gently squeezed and rubbed her nipple until it pebbled in his hands.

"You're killing me," she moaned. Renee twisted her arm back until her fingers dug into the soft curls on his head.

He squeezed her breast. "You like it." He murmured against her neck.

"I do." Renee cocked her head further to the side so he could better kiss her neck.

His hand left her breast, trailed down her body, and cupped her mound. He repositioned himself to the right but not so much that his chest wasn't still pressed against her back and Renee's legs spread. His fingers surrounded her slippery lower lips and swollen clitoris. "You like that too. Don't you, sugar?"

She nodded. "Yes."

His hips moved back and forth. The long length of him pushing against her backside. Renee's own hips moved in tandem. Causing her clit to slide across his fingers. Waves of pleasure crashed through her body. His erection slipped; the tip of him pressed against her most intimate spot.

Jonathan's groan was both hungry and desperate. *You'll let me take you there.* His whispered words in her brain. She'd never thought about doing that. Never wanted to, but right now the thought only made her body even more liquid.

Renee pushed her hips further backward. Jonathan moaned against her shoulder. "You don't know how bad I want to do that."

"I want you to," she whispered.

Another deep groan. "Damn, Renee, you're perfect. But not today. I don't have lube and there's no way in hell I could ever hurt you."

The simple statement gripped her heart. Wrapping it so tightly in emotion that Renee knew she was falling in love with Jonathan.

His arm reached out to grab a condom and put it on. He spread her legs and pushed slow and deep into the slick heat of her sex. Renee cried out. Her hands clutched the sheets. Jonathan lifted her hips.

"Heaven couldn't feel better than this," he said.

He slid in and out with long deliberate strokes. The hand that had caressed her clit went back to work. Renee's body trembled.

"Oh, God, Jonathan. Just like that." She moaned.

The glide of his body in hers was exquisite. Better than anything she'd had before. Better than the last time. She squeezed around him. Savoring the feel of him so intimately inside her.

The thumb of his other hand pressed against the opening of her rear. The touch was so foreign, yet erotic at the same time. Her stomach clenched. For the love of everything, she liked that.

The wave of sensation was too much. His cock pummeling deep, his hand rubbing her clit, his thumb with its darkly intimate caress. Renee's body shattered with an orgasm that stole her breath and tightened the hold on her heart.

***

Renee smiled, as much as she could while brushing her teeth, when Jonathan leaned against the door of the bathroom. Wishful thinking made her pack a bag before coming up the night before. For once, wishful thinking worked out.

"I'm going to put out a few bales of hay for the cows this morning. I usually do it in the evenings, but since you twisted my arm into calling in, I might as well do it this morning."

Renee pointed her toothbrush at him in the mirror. "Hey, you twisted my arm into calling in."

He chuckled. "You're too cute to argue with. Either way, it shouldn't take long."

Renee rinsed her mouth then turned to face him. His gaze lowered to her bare breasts and his eyes grew hot. She propped her hand on her hip and tilted her head to the side. Might as well pose, since he was enjoying the view.

"No woman should look that damn good in the morning," he said.

She strolled over and wrapped her arms around his neck. The rough material of his Carhartt coat grazed her breasts. Her nipples turned to hard peaks and wetness slid between her thighs. There was something obscenely sexy about being half-naked in strong arms.

"No man should be that good in bed. You're going to get me hooked. Then I really won't let you go."

Jonathan slipped his hands into the back of her blue and green polka dotted hip huggers and gripped her bottom. "Maybe I don't want you to let me go." His voice and eyes were all seriousness.

The love that blossomed in Renee's chest stretched and grew even more in response to the promise in his words. "Don't say it if you don't mean it."

He brushed his lips across hers in a quick kiss. "I don't say things I don't mean."

Renee barely stopped herself from jumping and throwing her legs around his waist. His words weren't a confession of undying love, but it was enough to keep the hope bubbling up inside her. Hope that maybe she could have everything she never thought she'd get. "I'm going to remember that when you say I'm here too much."

Jonathan's hand tightened on her butt. "Sugar, if you keep prancing around my house topless, I'll never say you're here too much."

She gripped his jacket and tried to shake him. "Don't call me sugar."

"You know you like it." Jonathan teased. He kissed her nose then let her go and left the bathroom.

She did, but she wasn't about to tell him about her heart's silly flutter whenever he drawled the endearment. Bad enough she blushed like a kid caught passing notes in class whenever he looked at her with that come-here-so-I-can-lick-you-all-over heat in his eyes.

Would they make a relationship work, though?

Once her dad figured out she'd ditched work to be with Jonathan, he'd do one of two things: accept that she'd found a guy who made her happy and give her his blessing, or the more likely choice, do everything in his power to drag out Jonathan's efforts to win back the house until Jonathan cracked and broke up with her. Something in her believed Jonathan wouldn't crack, but could they survive a continuous assault from her family?

Renee shook the thought from her head. Today she was going to pretend they could work and enjoy the happy high. Today was about jumping on the back of the motorcycle and riding into the sunset. Reality could wait until Monday.

She pulled on one of the dozens of plaid button up shirts in his closet. As much as she loved the idea of Jonathan coming in and finding her naked in his kitchen, she couldn't do it. He'd pick her up and probably make love to her on the kitchen table. Which was great, but she kind of wanted to spend the day doing something besides having sex. Maybe learn more about the cows.

She frowned and shook her head. Nope, sex all day was preferable to cows.

She left the shirt on, but unbuttoned. Her breasts may not be huge, but he liked them and getting a glimpse or two when he came back in would surely get him excited. She went into the kitchen to cook more eggs. By the time they'd gotten around to eating, the breakfast had been cold, and she'd only nibbled on the toast. Now her stomach begged for more food.

The door from the garage opened as she flipped her first omelet at the stove. "Don't worry, I know you eat more than one egg. Your omelet has two."

"Renee, you're back!" Lilly's voice.

Renee spun around and met a pair of light brown eyes in an adorable face framed with pigtails. Renee's mouth opened then closed. She snatched the front of the large shirt closed.

"Lilly?" Renee squeaked. Nadine came in right behind her. "And Nadine. What are you doing here?"

Nadine's eyes went wide. "Teacher work day at school today. Lilly wanted to see Jonathan at work. They said he called in sick."

Lilly held up a white paper bag. "We brought him soup."

Heat seared Renee's cheeks. "Umm, he's out doing something with hay and cows."

Nadine's head bounced in a jerky nod. "Lilly, go out to the fence and see if you see Uncle Jon. Let him know we're here."

Lilly frowned. "If he's sick why isn't he in bed?"

"I'm sure he's been in bed," Nadine said with sarcasm that thankfully wouldn't register with the little girl.

Nadine pushed Lilly toward the door. "Take the soup with you, dear."

"Okay." Lilly beamed at Renee. "Since you're here, you can sign my cast."

Renee clutched the shirt tighter. Despite her utter humiliation, she was glad to see that Lilly was okay. "I'd love to."

Lilly grinned and skipped out the door. The smell of eggs burning filled Renee's nostrils. *Frick! The omelets.* She spun and slid the pan away from the heat and turned off the stove.

Renee turned back to Nadine. "Has Jonathan told you about us?"

Nadine pointed toward the hall. "Perhaps you should get dressed before we continue." Her frown also said she really didn't want to have this conversation.

More heat burned Renee's cheeks. "Right. I'll be right back."

She turned and hurried to the bedroom. She pulled on a pair of jeans but left on Jonathan's shirt. Buttoned this time. When she came back in the kitchen Nadine was making coffee.

"So, you and my brother are a thing now," Nadine said in a voice that wasn't brimming with congratulations or well wishes.

Renee crossed the room and stood next to Nadine. "Something like that."

"I figured it was going in that direction." Nadine turned away from the coffee maker. Her eyes were one hundred percent don't-screw-with-me. "Jonathan had his heart ripped out before—"

"Karen. I met her," Renee said.

Surprise filled Nadine's light brown eyes. "You know about her?"

Renee nodded. "He told me about her, and we ran into her at the USC homecoming game."

"Then you know that she hurt him."

"I do. I have no intentions of hurting your brother."

Nadine snorted. She turned back to the coffee and crumpled one of the filters in her hand. "No one ever has intentions of hurting another person."

"I love him," Renee whispered.

Nadine did a double-take. "You... Does he?"

Renee shook her head. She wasn't sure if the question was *does he love you* or *does he know.* "I don't know. I haven't told him, but I will." When she knew he felt something deeper for her.

"Why are you telling me?"

"I want you to know that I'm serious about Jonathan. I know we're in a really awkward place with the land, the lawsuit, your aunt. The way I feel has nothing to do with any of that. I just want him."

Nadine studied Renee for several seconds. Renee met her gaze dead on. She worked to keep her face calm while internally her heart pounded her ribs. Nadine's blessing wouldn't stop her from seeing Jonathan, but it would be nice to have. Nice to know that someone in their families wouldn't think they were just idiots in lust.

The garage door opened again and Jonathan came in with Lilly in his arms. His concerned gaze whipped from Renee to Nadine.

"Everything okay?" His voice was uneasy.

Nadine pushed away from the counter. "Everything is cool." She looked back at Renee and gave her an encouraging smile. "Really good. I like your girl, Jonny."

Renee's shoulders relaxed. She returned Nadine's smile. "Thank you."

Jonathan still eyed them warily. "Okay...I think I missed something, but I'm not going to pry."

Nadine and Renee both laughed.

Lilly bounced in Jonathan's arms. "Uncle Jon said we can go to the zoo today. Renee, will you come with us?"

Renee and Nadine both looked at Jonathan with bewildered expressions. "The zoo?" Renee asked.

Jonathan's sheepish grin and lazy shrug were evidence that once again he was playing best uncle in the world. "She wants to see the monkeys. I may have said whatever in my *rush* to get back in the house." He emphasized the last part. His eyes darted from Nadine to Renee.

"Will you, Renee?" Lilly said. "Come to the zoo with us. Please?"

Renee couldn't say no to such a sweet request. "The zoo it is."

CHAPTER 21

The Tuesday morning staff meeting passed by remarkably quick and easy. Renee sat at the conference room table barely hiding her nervousness. The Woman of the Year luncheon was today. That wasn't what had her stomach in knots. Neither her dad nor Ryan had said anything about her calling out on Friday and staying out of town all weekend. They'd greeted her as normal and asked if she was okay, but that was it.

Something wasn't right.

Philip tapped his pen on the table. "Before we wrap up I'd like to get an update on the Wright property." His dark eyes zeroed in on Renee. "Has the pre-trial date been set?"

Her dad knew the answer to that. She'd asked Alicia to take over working with their legal department on the particulars of the case and give Renee a weekly update. That was the same update Renee sent to Philip on Monday mornings.

"It has," Renee said. "Our team responded to the complaint denying any liability or wrongdoing on our behalf. We're looking at a pre-trial in about a month."

Philip nodded. "And still no interest in settling by the Wright boy."

Renee just stopped herself from glaring at her father in the middle of a business meeting. "Jonathan Wright has refused our offer. According to Joanne, he's also refused her offer to be included on the contract."

"I see," Philip said. He looked to Ryan and gave a short nod. Ryan had arrived at the staff meeting on time for the first time in weeks. That too had raised the hairs on the back of Renee's neck.

Ryan returned Philip's nod then tapped out something on his iPad. Renee's shoulders tightened. They were up to something.

"That's all for this morning," Philip said. "Let's everyone wish Renee well as she has the Woman of the Year luncheon this afternoon." The other managers clapped and offered congratulations. Philip spoke up again. "Renee, I am so proud of you. I know we don't always agree on everything. I can be difficult and demanding, but everything I do is because I love you and your brother. You are my legacy. You are my greatest accomplishments."

Tears stung the back of Renee's eyes. Philip Caldwell never neglected to tell his children that he cared, but this was the first time he'd showered either of them with emotion in front of non-family members.

"Thank you, Daddy."

The meeting ended after that. Renee took time collecting her things, waiting until the room cleared so she could talk to her dad about the look he shared with Ryan. Her brother had the same idea.

"Daddy, can I talk with you alone?" Renee asked.

Philip walked over to his desk and picked up his messenger bag. "Later, Renee. Ryan and I have something to do this morning."

Renee glanced at her brother. Ryan's face was stoic. A little too stoic. His tight jaw and grim but determined expression brought to mind a solider who'd just been given orders that went against their very principles, but had to be followed. Ryan was never stoic, and he never mindlessly followed orders.

"What's going on?" Renee asked.

Philip gave her an innocent look. "I don't know what you mean. Ryan and I have a meeting this morning."

"A meeting with whom?"

Ryan's eyes met hers. "Renee, we've got this. You have other things to worry about." He glanced at his watch. "It's nearly eleven."

Renee checked her own watch. He was right. She needed to be at the luncheon by eleven thirty.

"You aren't the only kid that can handle business with Dad," Ryan said. His voice wasn't mean, but it hurt all the same.

"I know that."

"Then go to the luncheon. We'll give you an update on the meeting when you get back," Ryan said.

Renee looked to her dad. Philip nodded. She still felt uneasy about them not telling her about the meeting, but she didn't have time to argue with either of them. "Fine. I'll go."

"Good luck," Philip said, pride all over his face. "Remember that I do love you."

"I love you too," she said before leaving Philip's office.

Alicia stopped Renee on her way out of the office. "Renee, can you sign this before you go."

Renee turned to Alicia and looked at the paperwork in her hand. "All of that? I don't have time to read that."

Alicia shuffled from foot to foot. "I know, I really hate to do this right before the luncheon, but the lawyers say it's something they need for the pre-trial."

"Have you looked it over? Is it changing anything related to our response?"

Alicia's nod was stiff and jerky. "No. It's just routine." She cleared her throat. "They said it's just routine."

Renee looked at her watch, and then at the stack of papers. She really needed to get out of here. "If you've read it, I trust you. Give me the signature page."

Alicia handed it over with a blue ink pen. Renee quickly signed her name on the line. "Put a copy on my desk. I'll go over it this afternoon."

"Okay," Alicia quickly stacked the papers and held them against her chest. "Good luck, today."

Renee smiled. "Thank you. I need it," Renee said then hurried out of the office.

Her dad's words bugged her the entire way to the luncheon. She knew her dad loved her. He never gave her a reason to doubt that. Even when he was being pigheaded and stubborn, he never once took his anger out on her and always considered her opinion. Even with the Jonathan situation, she didn't think her dad would do anything to deliberately hurt her. The threat to prolong the lawsuit was an attempt to scare Jonathan off, not to get back at Renee.

What her dad would eventually realize is that Jonathan wasn't a man that could be scared off. He'd fight to the very end to keep the land. Renee doubted Jonathan had the time or the resources to engage in a long, drawn out property suit. She didn't want him to bankrupt himself over this. Which meant Renee was considering something she never would have even a month ago. Dropping a deal and letting the land go.

Renee arrived at the luncheon and immediately sought out the Still Hopes executive director. Nominees and their sponsors would spend the next hour and a half mingling and getting to know the each other before the votes were cast. The actual winner would be announced at a banquet in two weeks where the governor would hand out the award.

Renee smiled, discussed her work and projects, and was congenial all through the luncheon. The judging panel had already read up on her accomplishments and eased in pointed questions in the middle of polite conversation with the sleek efficiency of cat burglars. Having grown up in a family that mastered subtle interrogation, she wasn't thrown off by their tactics.

Even though she sized up the competition, deemed them all just as worthy of the title as her, and relaxed enough to enjoy herself, irritation scratched at the back of her mind. The entire week had been...off.

She didn't want to talk to her dad or Ryan about her weekend with Jonathan. They wouldn't appreciate how much fun she'd had with him and Lilly at the zoo on Friday. Or laugh about the ribbons Lilly tied in Jonathan's hair when she convinced him to let her sleep over Friday night.

They wouldn't understand how she could no longer care about a project and fall in love with the guy holding it up.

But they should have asked something. Her dad wasn't one to keep his opinions to himself. He would have opinions about this. Why hadn't he said anything?

Toward the end of the two-hour luncheon, movement near her foot at the table got her attention. Renee glanced down. Her cell phone sat on top of her purse at her side. She always kept it in view in case of important calls. The phone vibrated with an incoming call. Jonathan. She almost bent down to pick it up. Except that would be rude when she was in the middle of the Woman of the Year luncheon.

The dread that something was very wrong tickled her senses again. A few minutes later, her phone vibrated again. She looked down. A text message.

Renee turned back to the table of women. "If you'll excuse me, I have to take this call."

Sandra Snyder, one of the judges who also worked in the governor's office and was a good friend of the family, nodded. "Of course, but do hurry back. I'd like for you to tell the ladies about the new facility you worked to have built for Still Hopes."

"This will only take a minute." Renee grabbed her phone then walked out of the room to check her phone.

You're suing me?

Renee scanned the simple message a dozen times. Her heart ricocheted against her chest. A cold hard lump dropped into her stomach.

The pieces all came together. Renee gripped the phone. She called Jonathan back, but it went straight to voice mail. She needed to talk to him, now.

"Renee, is everything okay?" The Still Hopes director asked.

Renee turned and took a slow, deep breath. She could not run out of here. She'd deal with this as soon as the luncheon was over.

She nodded. "Yes. Just…unexpected news." She walked back toward the door. "But everything will be okay." She would fix this.

***

One call to the office after the luncheon and she found out that both Philip and Ryan were still at their meeting. If Renee had any idea where their meeting was being held, she would hightail it straight there and confront them. That would come later.

Jonathan hadn't answered a single one of her calls. That's why her Cadillac hit I-26 right after and went straight upstate to clear the air. She was not going to have this conversation over the telephone.

Thanks to GPS, she found the Conservation Department. It was three-thirty, so he should still be at work. Briefly, she realized she was being the crazy emotional woman who showed up at the man's job, but she didn't care. This was important.

Renee strode up the concrete walkway to the double glass doors of the building. Her head high and shoulders straight. She may have been quivering on the inside about this situation, but she would not show her stress outwardly.

She swung open the door and her heart nearly plummeted. Jonathan stood right there, smiling and talking with the cute blonde behind the receptionist desk. He could ignore her calls, not answer her texts, but he had time to flirt with the receptionist.

They both turned her way. The blonde gave a welcoming smile. Jonathan's own smile morphed into a mask of angry disappointment. A heavy pain twisted her heart.

"Can I help you?" the woman asked.

Renee shook her head. "I'm here to speak with Jonathan."

The receptionist glanced at Jonathan. One look at his face and her own smile turned into a questioning frown. "Jonathan?"

Renee heard the question in the woman's voice. The one that asked do-I-need-to-invent-a-meeting-to-get-you-out-of-this. Any good receptionist knew how to ask that question without ever saying the words.

"I'm good, Laura," he said. "This shouldn't take long."

Laura nodded. "Okay, don't forget you promised to have Mr. Gregory's plan ready by the end of the day."

Renee nearly snorted. Laura was good. She'd easily given Jonathan the excuse he needed to kick Renee out.

"Thanks, Laura." He nodded to Renee. "Come on back." He picked up a clipboard and rolled up papers that looked like construction plans.

She followed him down the hall to a decent sized office with a large metal desk and wooden chairs. Agricultural magazines covered the desk. A few framed articles were on the walls. A picture of his parents and one of Nadine with Lilly were on a bookshelf.

Jonathan dropped the clipboard and plans on the desk then walked around. Instead of sitting, he stood on the other side. He pulled off a Conservation Department baseball cap and ran his hands through his hair. His hair was damp on the edges.

"I'm surprised you're here, Renee," he said. He pulled off his jacket and put it on the back of the chair. He crossed his arms. The flannel of his shirt stretched over his wide shoulders.

"I don't see why. Your text message was rather alarming."

"Alarming," he said with mock surprise. "You signed the papers."

"What papers?"

"The papers filing a counter suit against me for defamation."

Renee's chin cocked to the left. "I didn't sign…" The papers Alicia handed her this morning. "Let me see."

Jonathan grabbed a yellow envelope from his desk and tossed it to the edge. Renee picked them up. She flipped through to the last page. Indeed, there was her signature from this morning along with the date.

"How did you get these so fast?"

"Would it have been better for me to get them later in the week?" His voice dripped with betrayal.

Renee's head shot up. "No. I just signed these this morning. I didn't even know what it was."

He scoffed. "You expect me to believe that? Renee, you're the most respected business woman in the state." He threw out her dad's words with mocking. "I'm supposed to believe you signed papers that you didn't read."

She threw the papers on his desk. "How could you believe I'd sue you after this weekend?"

"Because that's your signature right there on the paperwork. Hand-delivered to me this afternoon by your own brother. His smirk was something to behold as he told me the official summons would be coming later."

Renee's nails clawed into her palms. The meeting they wouldn't tell her about. Her dad's remember I love you comment. They all made sense.

"I didn't know anything about this." She didn't raise her voice, wouldn't come undone, but anger vibrated throughout her body.

"But you blindly followed their lead, signed the paperwork regardless of what it said. Sue the guy you just spent the weekend in bed with."

"That's not how it goes."

"Then tell me how it goes, Renee. What's the next blow I'm going to get with your signature on it? Are you going to add Joanne to the next countersuit that comes my way?"

"Stop it, Jonathan." She took a step forward and pointed at him. "I was wrong for signing the papers without knowing what they were. My problem was trusting my staff when they tell me it's just routine. Trusting my dad and brother to talk to me instead of going behind my back. I've been betrayed today, and that hurts. But you promised me that you would talk to me. That we'd work these things out instead of jumping to conclusions."

"That was before I knew you'd blindly go with anything your family put in front of you. I can't trust you, Renee."

The words punched and bruised her heart. The fantasy she'd lived over the weekend evaporated. This was why she didn't go with her emotions. Emotional decisions led to situations that were best avoided. If she'd ignored her feelings for Jonathan, she never would have slept with him, never would have opened her heart to him, never would have loved him.

Renee lifted her chin and took a step backward. "If that's what you believe, then there's no more to say."

The sharp pain of tears cut the back of her eyes. She spun and walked away before he would notice. By the time she passed the cute receptionist, Renee was wiping them from her cheeks.

CHAPTER 22

Ryan and Phillip entered Renee's office just before noon on Thursday morning. They both wore impeccable gray suits and dark gray ties. They were so different personality-wise, but all too often they arrived at work dressed similarly. She would have teased them as she typically did, if she didn't want to throw bricks at their heads.

"Why is my legal team calling me to say we're dropping the lawsuit against the Wright boy?" Philip demanded, his fists on his hips and his legs spread in a defensive stance.

Renee saved the notes she'd been adding to the report on her computer and slowly turned in her chair toward her dad and brother. She leaned back in her seat and crossed her arms. "His name is Jonathan Wright. He's thirty-two years old. You can stop calling him a boy."

"I'll call him whatever the hell I please."

"You're sounding a lot like his late grandfather with those comments," Renee said coolly.

Philip's nostrils flared with his deep breath. Ten seconds passed before he spoke again. "Renee, don't play with me this morning."

"Why not. You had no qualms about playing with me earlier this week."

Ryan took a step forward. "Renee, that wasn't about playing with you. Your head wasn't in the game."

She raised a brow to her brother. "You haven't been in the game for months. No one is butting into your personal life."

"Ryan's personal life isn't compromising this company," Philip countered.

"If he continues to be seen with Eva Drake, then it will compromise this company when her husband finds out."

Philip glared at Ryan. "What? You and Eva?"

Ryan held up a hand. "We'll talk about that later. This is about Renee dropping the Wright project."

"Hell yes we'll talk about *that* later." Philip's statement dared Ryan to argue. He turned back to Renee. "What's gotten into you? Why would you tell legal to drop the lawsuit?"

"Because it's the right thing to do."

"Don't give me that. It's because this boy got into your head."

Renee's eyes narrowed. "That *man* and I are no longer together. After my family worked so stealthily to trick me into signing the paperwork to sue him, he didn't think he could trust me anymore."

Philip leaned back on his heels. "So he is weak. I knew he wasn't good enough for you."

"No, Daddy, he was perfect for me. I was ready to stop the project, find another location, and let his fight with his family play out however it needed to. Not because he'd gotten into my head, or I wanted to betray my family, but because I love him."

Ryan sucked in a breath. "Renee?"

She calmly turned to Ryan. "Don't sound so shocked. I am capable of falling in love. I've just chosen not to. The last time I fell in love my family scared off the guy. It was easier to focus on the business after that. Silly me for thinking that things would change later." She leaned back in her chair. "You will do this for me. I've given everything to Caldwell Development. I've asked you for nothing, but you will let this project go. You will drop the lawsuit, and end the contract with Joanne. After that I'll go right back to dating the *perfect* men that can bring more wealth and prosperity to our family."

All the arrogance left Philip's face. "Renee, I want you to be—"

"I know, happy." She interrupted. "But your kind of happy. Not my kind. I'll accept that if you drop this. Otherwise, I'll quit."

Philip turned away and flicked his wrist. "Don't be ridiculous."

"I am not. Andre walked away from his family business and he's much happier for it. I'll do the same."

Philip spun back to her. "I'm not letting you walk away from this. I built this for you two."

"Then if you want me to have it, do this for me. Don't break my heart again." Her voice nearly broke with the last words. She cleared her throat and lowered her eyes. It took several blinks to keep the tears back. When she was composed, she swallowed hard and lifted her chin.

Pain covered Philip's face. "You really love him."

"And you really ended us," she said coolly. "I love you, Daddy. But this is going to take a while to get over. No worries, though. I'm a Caldwell. We're good at hiding emotion." She glanced at Ryan. "Most of us anyway."

Philip watched her for several seconds. "It's dropped."

Relief rushed through her, but it was accompanied with so much pain she couldn't even force herself to smile. Pain at her family's betrayal. Pain for Jonathan's inability to trust her. Pain for living her life afraid to listen to her heart. Not anymore. She may not ever feel the way she felt about Jonathan with anyone again, but she wouldn't let her unyielding dedication to the family direct her anymore. She saw what that got her. "Thank you."

Philip watched her for another long moment. "Maybe if you talk to him."

Renee shook her head. "Stop it. Just...stop."

Philip's nod was resigned, his eyes sad. He turned and left her office. Ryan stayed behind.

Renee peered at him. "What?"

"If he's breaking up with you because you have a family of assholes, then you don't need him."

She crossed her arms and raised a brow. "Excuse me?"

"You heard me. People come with baggage. Guess what? We're your baggage. We're selfish, inconsiderate, and pigheaded, but we love each other. Sometimes we show that love in stupid ways. Hurtful ways. He should understand that."

"I thought you'd be happy that Jonathan and I are over."

"I'm not that much of a jerk, Renee. I didn't like him. I didn't trust him, but you wouldn't admit to me and Dad that you loved a guy if he wasn't worth your love. You're too damned stubborn to fall in love with just anyone."

She almost smiled at the backward compliment. Almost. "Well, it's done now. We're over and we're out of the property fight. Let's move on."

Ryan grunted and walked toward the door. "Everyone always says that after a break up. Move on." He glanced back at Renee. "That shit isn't easy. I don't think even for you, baby sister."

Ryan was older than her by a few minutes, but occasionally he called her that. Usually when he was being silly or trying to show her some affection. He hadn't used the endearment in a very long time. Ryan had once been her best friend. Then Mikayla joined their group and she'd had so much love and affection surrounding her, she didn't notice how lonely she was when they weren't around. Now it struck her that over the past year, she and Ryan had grown further and further apart.

"I'll be fine," she said. She missed their closeness, but what he and their dad had done was too raw.

He nodded and took a deep breath. "Spoken like a Caldwell."

CHAPTER 23

Jonathan was leaving work on Monday afternoon when his cell phone rang. Briefly, his heart sped up in anticipation that maybe it was Renee calling. Just as quickly, he remembered that she had no reason to call. He'd thrown her trust back in her face. She wasn't the type of woman who would call and beg for them to try again.

Joanne's number was on the screen. He considered ignoring the call. She called every week asking him to change his mind about settling. Each call a little more desperate. If she hadn't been so hateful to him and his family over the years, he would feel bad about her financial situation. Except she had been.

"Hello, Auntie," he said sweetly, just because he knew it would piss her off.

"Gloating already, I see," was her scathing reply.

Jonathan frowned and powered down his computer. "What are you talking about?"

"Caldwell Development has backed out of the contract. They're paying me what's agreed upon in the breach of contract terms."

Jonathan leaned forward and rested his elbow on his desk. "Come again."

"The deal is over. The contract is null and void. My lawyers are also admitting now that it's unlikely that I'll win against you in court. I can't sign the property over to another developer. I have to go with the terms of the will."

"If they knew you weren't going to win, why did they advise you to fight anyway?" Jonathan asked.

"We had a better chance to win with Caldwell Development backing us. I don't know what play you pulled, but I'm done. If you want the house, take it. I've sold nearly everything in it already that was worth something. That much was left to me. Do what you will with the place."

The call ended. Jonathan stared at his cell phone. They broke the contract. Not they, she broke the contract. He had no doubt this was a Renee move. Why? He'd said he couldn't trust her. Accused her of being manipulated by her family. Anyone would have kept the suit going out of spite.

Most people aren't Renee.

Jonathan navigated to his dad's contact information and called him. Jacob answered on the third ring.

"I just got off the phone with Aunt Joanne. She's giving the Big House to me."

"What the hell? Are pigs flying?" Jacob sounded surprised.

"I don't know if pigs are flying, but that's what she just called to tell me. Caldwell Development pulled out of the contract. Her lawyers are telling her she can't win. She's got to go with the will."

"Well I'll be damned." Jacob chuckled. "Congratulations son."

Jonathan didn't feel much like celebrating. Had it all been worth it? He didn't want to think about that now. "Thanks."

The beeping sound his dad's truck made when he didn't put on his seatbelt came through the phone. "You in your truck?" Jonathan asked.

"Yeah. I'm on my way to Tennessee."

"For what?"

"To get your mom back," Jacob said.

Connie had moved two weeks ago. Jonathan hadn't believed his parents were actually separating, but he'd respected his dad's wishes and stayed out of it. He couldn't begin to understand the struggles his parents faced, being together that long. He'd only been with Renee for a few weeks and it seemed like the world was against them. In actuality, it had only been their foolish pride.

"You came to your senses?"

"Your mom seemed like she really wanted that job. No, she did really want it. She gave up so much to make things work with me and raise you kids. I didn't have the heart to tell her to stay."

"Don't you think she wanted you to ask her?"

"Hell if I know. You can never tell with women."

Jonathan had to agree. "So you're going anyway."

"I fought for her years ago. I'm going to fight for her now. Your mom loves me and I love her. Even if I have to move to Tennessee, we'll make this work."

Jonathan grinned, elated that they were finding a way to make this work. "Go get her then." The beeping continued. "And put on your seat belt."

"Doing that now." The beeping stopped. "I'll call you when I get there."

"Do that."

Jonathan ended the call and stared at his phone, this time smiling at it. Anything worth having was worth fighting for.

***

Jonathan's lawyer, Donald Rider, grinned and slid a set of keys across the card table Jonathan had set up in the kitchen of the Big House toward Jonathan. "Congratulations, Jonathan, the house is yours."

Jonathan waited, but the immediate satisfaction he expected didn't come. He picked up the two nickel keys and stared at them. Still nothing.

"Thank you for all your hard work."

Mr. Rider chuckled. "This wasn't nearly as hard as I expected it to be. I still can't believe Caldwell Development dropped the contract with your aunt. This is a prime spot for development. You're going to have a lot more people coming to you to purchase it."

There was only one development company that he would even consider selling to. Seemed crazy to even consider that now. After how hard he fought to keep it out of their hands. "No one is getting it now." He waited again for the thrill of victory, the satisfaction. Still nothing.

Jonathan stood and Mr. Rider followed. "What are you going to do with the place? Are you planning to live here?"

Jonathan looked around the kitchen. He could count on one hand how many times he'd entered before his grandfather died. No, he wasn't going to live here. Now that he had it, he felt empty. He'd made sure Gigi's wishes were respected, but he didn't want to live here. The Big House was too full of bad memories for him to sleep in every night. "I'm still figuring that out," he said.

They walked out into the cold and stood on the front porch and talked for a few more minutes about what Mr. Rider would do to finalize the documents. Nadine's car came down the long drive when Mr. Rider was getting into his. She got out of her car and held up a bottle of champagne in one hand and waved at Mr. Rider driving off with her free hand.

Jonathan smiled. "You brought champagne."

She reached back into the car and pulled out a plastic bag before coming over and up the steps. "I figured we'd celebrate your victory."

"Hard to call something a victory when you didn't fight a battle."

"A forfeit of the opponent still counts." Nadine crossed her arms as best she could with the stuff in her hands and bounced on her toes. "Let's go inside. It's freezing."

Jonathan took the bag from her then led her inside and back into the kitchen. "So," she said. "Now what?"

Jonathan paused peeling off the foil around the cork of the bottle to look at Nadine. "We drink, I guess."

"You know what I mean. What are you going to do now that you finally own the Big House? Tear it to the ground? Go through and remove every piece of un-valuable furniture Joanne left behind that reminds you of granddaddy? Burn the old slave quarters back in the woods?"

"No, no, and, good idea, but no." He pulled the cork out of the bottle. Nadine whipped two champagne glasses out of the plastic bag.

"Well, guess I shouldn't have brought matches."

He laughed and poured them both a drink. They clinked glasses and he looked around the kitchen. "Despite how horrible our granddad was, there is a lot of history here. Maybe I'll turn over the upkeep of the place to the historical society or something."

Nadine frowned. "You whined about losing the place, just to turn it over to some non-profit?"

"I don't know. It's a thought. I just know I could never live here."

"Which is why I don't know why you fought so hard to keep it."

"Because it was what Gigi wanted. She lost her son, never got to really show love to her grandkids. I couldn't take her attempt to make things right away from her. Even in death. I hate the bad memories, but this is the place where Dad was raised. His brother is buried here and his grandparents. I couldn't let the place turn into a cookie-cutter subdivision."

"I don't know. Caldwell development makes some pretty nice houses. There's nothing really cookie cutter about them."

"You know what I mean."

"I do." Nadine took a sip of champagne and peered at him over the cup. "What?"

She leaned against the counter and crossed her feet. "I'm just wondering. Why did they give it up without a fight?"

Jonathan looked into his cup. "Renee did that."

"Why?"

He took a deep breath before sipping the champagne. It was cheap, but good. "Because I screwed up. I accused her of some pretty mean things. We broke up."

"I don't understand. If I were her, I would have fought out of spite."

He ran a hand over his face. Fought back the guilt that kept hovering around him whenever he thought of their last conversation. "She's not spiteful."

"Women who are in love are the most spiteful."

Regret tightened around Jonathan's chest. He'd fallen for her. Loved her and instead of showing that to her, had hurt her. "I don't think she was in love with me. Which is for the best anyway."

"God you're dumb," Nadine said.

Jonathan's head jerked up. "What?"

"The woman told me she loved you. Even though I made it pretty clear I wasn't happy finding her half-naked in your kitchen. She still confessed her love and that she wouldn't do anything to hurt you."

Jonathan's heart raced. "She said that."

"Yeah. And then you go and break up with her, and she still gives you the land back." Nadine took a sip of the champagne and shook her head. "That woman is crazy about you."

"Then why didn't she call me?"

Nadine gave him an *are you an idiot* look. "What did you say to her when you broke up?"

Jonathan grimaced. "That I couldn't trust her. I pretty much called her a puppet to her family."

Nadine whistled low. "I wouldn't call your ass either."

He glared at Nadine, but she smiled back. Leave it to little sisters to kick you when you were down.

"How do I get her back?"

"Do you really want her back?"

He'd wanted her back the second she'd walked out of his office, regretted what he'd said as soon as the words left, except he'd been too angry to call her back. The immature teenage move he promised her he wouldn't do. All in a reactionary mode to protect himself from the pain he'd felt when he thought she'd knowingly signed the papers. "Yes."

Nadine stood straight. "Good. Then be my date."

Jonathan frowned at Nadine. "Date? I'm telling you I want Renee back and you're asking me to take you somewhere?"

"I need a date."

"Then ask that lady in your yoga class you've been secretly admiring."

Nadine blushed and waved a hand. "I have not been secretly admiring her."

"Yes. You have."

"Whatever. Besides, you're going to want to come with me. It's a formal affair."

Did she think he'd suddenly grown a fondness for tuxedos? "Who says I want to go to some fancy formal affair?"

"Jonathan, shut up and listen. My boss is nominated for Woman of the Year and each nominee gets a table to fill with their guests. Well, I've been selected to go support the boss, and I'm not going alone."

Jonathan's heart pounded. "South Carolina Woman of the Year?"

Nadine's grinned and nodded. "Yep. I read the list of nominees. Should be an interesting crowd."

He'd see Renee. Talk to her. Maybe get a hint if she missed him as much as he missed her.

She hasn't called in two weeks, asshole. She's moved on.

No, she was too proud to call after the things he said. If she told Nadine she loved him, then they had a chance. He could fix this. He hoped he could fix this. He wanted her back. Interloping family and all. He wanted Renee.

He met Nadine's eyes and lifted his cup of champagne. "I'd be happy to escort you."

CHAPTER 24

Renee glared across the crowded Marriott ballroom at Ryan and Eva. When she'd told Ryan to bring a date and help her round out the eight people at her table at the Woman of the Year banquet, she hadn't expected him to bring the worst possible date. If Eva's husband beat Ryan to a pulp, he deserved it.

She sent up a quick prayer that Eva's husband *didn't* beat Ryan to a pulp. Then she turned away from the sickening display.

Renee's stomach fluttered and she gulped her champagne with the hope the bubbles would settle her. Punching Ryan at the award dinner wouldn't be prudent. Even if he was making everyone at the table uncomfortable.

She wanted the award. A part of her felt she deserved it. She needed something to show for her lifetime of putting the family before herself. The Woman of the Year designation wouldn't do much to keep her warm at night, but it would at least be a symbol of professional achievement. That's all she'd have to cling to for a while.

She caught sight of her parents glaring at Ryan as well and decided not to join them. She was still bruised from their treatment of Jonathan. Scanning the room, she saw the women from the Still Hopes book club. She'd purchased tickets for all of them to attend. She preferred their company to her family.

While she maneuvered through the crowd in their direction, she examined the room. She smiled and waved at familiar faces, accepted their good lucks with appreciation. Her eyes met a familiar pair of brown eyes in a round face and her body turned to stone. Jonathan's ex-girlfriend Karen.

Karen's smile was faker than fool's gold and just as shiny. It was as if the woman could sense that Renee was no longer with Jonathan. Jared wasn't in attendance. Maybe the shine had worn off that relationship too after the game. If it had, that meant Karen was free to pursue a reconciliation with Jonathan. Maybe that's why she'd given Renee the fake grin.

Renee mirrored Karen's expression. She would not be paranoid and make up conspiracy theories about Jonathan. The sooner she pushed him out of her mind, the sooner she could move on.

Karen glanced behind Renee, and her expression brightened with excitement. The hairs on the back of Renee's neck stood at attention. She slowly spun on her four-inch heels to face the door. Jonathan stood there with Nadine. His dark suit clung to wide shoulders and his curly hair was stylishly cut.

Her knees melted. All of the hurt and anger she'd harbored after their break up condensed and hardened into a hard rock that punched her in the gut. God, she still loved him.

Then she remembered Karen's happy expression. Had he come here for Karen? The very idea made Renee want to claw the woman's eyes out.

Emotions getting you in trouble again?

Blue-gray eyes snapped to hers. Flutters ran across her skin. She wanted to grin and wave. Rush to his side and ask how he'd been doing. Was he happy he got the house? Did he hate her? She looked away. She would not be silly for him again.

Her legs were unsteady as she walked toward the Still Hopes ladies.

Don't look. Just a few more steps, and you can sit down, and ignore him for the rest of the night.

Someone from one of her boards stepped in her way and stopped her. She couldn't be rude, so she chatted. She glanced over her shoulder. Karen was going straight toward Jonathan. Pain became a barbed wire knot around Renee's heart. She quickly looked away. No need to get an eye full of their happy reunion.

Like the crazy-for-him idiot she was, she looked again. Jonathan bypassed Karen and stalked toward Renee.

Her heart jumped into her throat. He was really coming her way. She didn't want to do the confrontation here. Not on her night. This was supposed to be a *good* night.

Renee turned back to the board member blocking her from freedom. "I really should head to my seat." She smiled but didn't wait to hear her response.

Renee moved toward her table instead of the book club members as if hellhounds were chomping at her high heels.

Almost there.

Strong fingers gripped her elbow. Electric heat shot up her arm, and her feet froze to the floor. She couldn't turn to face him.

Jonathan stepped around and blocked her way. "Hello, sugar."

The endearment snatched the barbed wire from her heart. He couldn't call her that. Not now. She lifted her chin and pulled her arm out of his grip. "Don't call me that."

His eyes were wary as they met hers. "How are you?"

"I'm well. Excuse me." She tried to step away. He blocked her.

She looked up to tell him to move. The words lodged in her throat. He looked her over from crown to toe. Fire spread through her body. His gaze lingered at the V-neckline of her cream silk blouse. Awareness tightened her skin. Shifting from one foot to the other, she waited for him to say something. Instead, they stood there staring like silly kids.

"Stop staring at me," she ordered.

"I can't help it. I miss you."

She couldn't do this. She took a step to her left. He blocked her again.

"Come out with me after this."

"Why?"

Someone tapped the microphone. "Ladies and Gentleman, if you'll take your seats we're about to start."

Her cue to keep going instead of hearing whatever excuse he came up with for why they should go out. They didn't need to go out for him to thank her for tearing up the contract before giving her the we-should-remain-friends speech.

"Excuse me." She stepped right.

He stepped left. "Tonight?"

Renee shook her head. "I can't."

She hurried around him before he could stop her.

"I love you, Renee."

Renee's pulse was a bass drum beat in her ears. She spun so fast on her heels she became off balance. Jonathan took her arm to prevent her from falling.

"What did you say?"

His hands clasped her upper arms. "I love you."

She shook her head and tried to pull way. She was elated. Surprised. Angry. "Now! You want to do this now." Her voice rose at the end. The people milling around the tables stopped and stared.

"Yes, now. When should we do this?"

"Not in the middle of the Woman of the Year banquet."

Jonathan didn't move. His legs were planted and he looked as if he had no cares to give about the people watching them. "I didn't know you needed me to tell you that I love you at an appropriate time. I saw you. I felt this…" He held a hand near his chest, and his brows drew together. "This thing in my chest and I knew, right then, that I had to say it."

"The time to tell me was when I explained what happened with the document," she said, forgetting the people or the second call from the emcee for attendees to take their seats. "When I explained that the people I trusted betrayed that trust. You should have told me you loved me then. Instead you threw what we had away."

"I broke my promise to you. I know I did. I was angry and hurt. I couldn't think straight."

"That doesn't make it right." She stepped back and he let her go.

"I know it doesn't. That's why I'm doing this." He reached into his pocket and pulled out papers. "I'm signing over the Big House and all the land to Caldwell Development. Burn the place down. Build a hundred houses. I don't care."

"You can't do that. You fought to keep it."

"I fought to respect my grandmother's wishes. I got the place. It's mine to do with as I please." He held out the papers. "I'm giving it back to you."

"I don't want it." Not like this.

"Then forget the house. The house, the land, none of that matters. All that matters is that I want you."

Her head was spinning. "We won't work…"

"That's bullshit, Renee. We both know we'll work. We were working until we let our insecurities get in the way. I wish I wasn't afraid of you breaking my heart, but I am. Because that's what happens when you love someone. You get scared out of your damned mind that they'll hurt you. I know we'll have to fight hard to figure out how to make this work. I know that everything won't be easy, but that doesn't mean I don't want to try." He took a step toward her. Determination, and love burning in his eyes. "Tell me you want to try."

She couldn't speak. Her throat closed up. Thoughts and feelings whipped around inside her head. She'd missed him. Constantly, from the moment she'd walked away. Someone moved at her side. She glanced that way and caught the eye of her dad. Philip lifted his chin, then smiled.

"That's a good man you've got there." He looked at Jonathan. "I'm not good at admitting when I'm wrong, but I was wrong about you. If she takes you back, then I'm trusting you to never break her heart again."

Jonathan looked back at Renee. "If you take me back, I'll cherish your heart always."

"Umm, excuse me." The emcee interrupted them. Renee and Jonathan turned to face the front. "This is lovely, really, but can you take your seats?"

She looked at all the people in the ballroom. People staring at her with open curiosity. She glanced back at Jonathan. "Dinner is starting."

He shook his head and took a step closer. "Forget dinner. I'm on my bike. Let's get out of here and work this out." He held out his hand.

Memories of that first night she'd seen him filled her head. When she'd gotten the nomination letter and wanted to jump on the back of his bike and ride away from all the expectations. She'd turned away from temptation and done what was right. She wasn't that Renee anymore.

Renee placed her hand in his. "Let's go."

***

He took her home. The ride had been scary and exhilarating. Jonathan had given her his jacket, and she'd clung to his muscled body like chewing gum in hair. Despite her fear of falling off, the warm, strong comfort of him made up her mind before they stopped. She didn't want to ever let go of this man.

They walked up her walkway but didn't go into the house. Renee leaned against her porch rail. The night was cool and she wrapped her arms around herself. "What made you come to the banquet tonight?"

Jonathan stood close to her. "To fight for you."

A million sparks of happiness filled her chest. As hard as they were to ignore, she had to be sure. "I wouldn't have thought you'd think we were worth fighting for." She looked away and took in the other houses on her street. "Okay, you love me. Does that mean I'm supposed to just forget that we haven't spoken in weeks?"

"Depends." He moved even closer. The warmth of his body chased away the remaining chill from the ride.

"On what?"

"Do you love me too, sugar?" He rested his hand on the small of her back.

She took a deep breath and clasped her arms in front of her. "It's not that easy. Shouldn't we talk more, or set some ground rules?"

"How about we just go with what feels right." He nudged her body closer. "I love you. I want to be with you. That's all that matters."

"That's what we said the last time." Her voice was soft. "Why is this time different?"

Jonathan's eyes were soft, apologetic, and bright with love. "Because I let you go when I should have held you close. Take the Big House, don't take it, I don't care. I just want that entire thing done so that I can focus on loving you the way you deserve to be loved. I love you, just as you are. Will always love you. I'll even try to love your family."

She laughed. "That may be too much to ask."

He grinned. "I'm willing to try, for you. Can you love me too? A country guy with cows, who eats way too much steak, has a niece that adores you, and frankly, who can't imagine his future without kissing with you at least once every day."

Her cell phone rang, vibrated and chimed. The sharp sounds broke the moment. She stepped back and jerked it out of her purse. Mostly to silence the noise. One message caught her attention.

"I'm Woman of the Year." She smiled, happy for the recognition, but at the moment, she didn't really care.

"Congratulations. I guess that means you're officially the most respected woman in the state."

Renee slid her phone back in her purse. She looked into Jonathan's eyes. There was only one person's respect, love, and admiration that she wanted.

"I love you, too. My family is always going to try to butt into our business. Maybe more so after this." He started to speak, and she placed her hand over his mouth. "But I won't let them. I love them, and they love me, but I won't blindly trust them again. I won't let them come between us."

His grin made her heart dance. "Is that a yes? Are you giving us a chance?"

Renee smiled and wrapped her arms around his neck. She didn't think. Only felt that she loved him deep in her heart. "On one condition. Will you love me? Even though I come with a high-handed family, I tend to be a bit of a control freak, and will probably drive you crazy when I clean those plaid shirts out of your closet?"

"Hey, I thought you liked my plaid shirts."

She lifted on her toes and kissed him. "Well, maybe we'll keep one or two for me to wear around the house."

A wicked grin covered his face. "I like that idea. If those are the terms, then yes. I'll happily take you, Renee Caldwell, just as you are."

Renee pulled him in closer and kissed him. "And I wouldn't have you any other way."

ACKNOWLEDGEMENTS

Getting Renee and Jonathan's story ready was a long journey. I really appreciate my readers for being patient with me while I worked to get the next book in the series out. Your emails and social media request for updates made sure I didn't forget to work on this story. Much thanks to Nancy at The Red Pen Coach. You and your editing team really challenged me to dig deeper and I think that made a much better story. Final thanks to my beta readers, Natoya and Liv, who gave much needed feedback when I was ready to throw this manuscript out the window.

ABOUT THE AUTHOR

Synithia Williams has loved romance novels since reading her first one at the age of 13. It was only natural that she would begin penning her own romances soon after. It wasn't until 2010 that she began to actively pursue her publishing dreams. When she isn't writing, Synithia is working hard on water quality issues in the Midlands of South Carolina and taking care of her supportive husband and two sons. You can learn more about Synithia by visiting her website, www.synithiawilliams.com, where you can sign up for all her latest updates and she blogs about writing, life and relationships.
Facebook: http://www.facebook.com/synithiarwilliams
Twitter: http://www.twitter.com/@SynithiaW

Books by Synithia Williams

Caldwell Family Series
Show Me How to Love
Love Me As I Am

Southern Love Series
You Can't Plan Love
Worth the Wait
A Heart to Heal

Henderson Family Series
Just My Type
Love's Replay
Making it Real
From One Night to Forever

Harlequin Kimani Titles
A New York Kind of Love
A Malibu Kind of Romance

CPSIA information can be obtained
at www.ICGtesting.com
Printed in the USA
LVHW091324050920
665161LV00004B/1461

9 780997 572919